MERELY PLAYERS

Works by Gregory Mcdonald:

RUNNING SCARED

LOVE AMONG THE MASHED POTATOES (Dear M. E.)

SAFEKEEPING

FLETCH
(in nine books)

FLYNN
(in three books)

WHO TOOK TOBY RINALDI?

Time^2

EXITS AND ENTRANCES

MERELY PLAYERS

WISE SAWS

A WORLD TOO WIDE

Non-fiction:

THE EDUCATION OF GREGORY MCDONALD

MERELY PLAYERS

GREGORY McDONALD

HILL & COMPANY, PUBLISHERS • BOSTON

Mcdonald, Gregory, 1937–
   Merely players / Gregory Mcdonald.
      p. cm.
   The third book of Mcdonald's Time^2 quartet.
   ISBN 0-940595-18-4 : $16.95
   I. Title.
PS3563.A278M4 1988   88-21386
813'.54—dc19   CIP

Designed by Milton Glaser, Inc.
Printed in the United States of America

The characters in MERELY PLAYERS
are fictitious.
Any resemblance to persons living or
dead is coincidental.

To
Charles Leo Martin, Junior,
constant friend.

All the world's a stage
And all the men and women merely players...

—*As You Like It*
William Shakespeare

MERELY
PLAYERS

1

Most of us felt the ground moving beneath our feet, of course, and some were glad of the movement, hopeful of the change the tremors might bring, but none knew or could guess the size, the dimensions, the universal nature of the coming quake.

2

"Oh, I don't know, Dan. The men are all mousey. The women are all kittens or cats. They all survive by keeping a wall between them. They seem to relate only through a rat hole chewed in the baseboard."

Dan Prescott was seeing her face and, in the mirrors behind each of them, he could see both sides of the room, the back of her head, his own face, the back of her head again, each element repeating, diminishing. If the restaurant table were straight, if they were sitting exactly opposite each other, he would have been able to see nothing of their reflections. Over her shoulders through the mirror, over his own shoulders, there was the whole high-ceilinged room, men in dark suits, women in long dresses, sitting at their tables more like people playing cards, he thought, than like people eating.

He and Janet were the youngest in the dining room by many years. In their coming in, taking a table, ordering, sitting talking quietly, everyone in the room at one point or another had looked at them long and hard, some with curiosity, some with envy, a few with love, a few with resentment.

"I want out, Dan."

"Out where?"

Janet had ordered a daiquiri but not finished it, sipped the wine, and treated the Duck Curaçao as usual fare. She had mentioned a few other places in Boston she had been taken to dine.

"My, but you're putting on a big splash for me, Dan. Where did you learn about all this?"

"All what?"

"I mean about the extra-dry manhattan you had, and whatever the wine is."

"I read a book."

"You must have been saving your money ever since I left."

"I have."

It was November. After a final summer of walks and swims and rides and movies, a long September kiss in the Jeep by the pond, a more familiar, relaxed kiss than their first, years before, but having in it something of the same passion, desperation, of the young's fear of the unknown, of tomorrow, he had gone to the Columbia Falls, Maine, railroad station with her, with her family, carrying her suitcases, acting happy. Janet had been dressed in a blue traveling suit, a hat, nylons, and she had looked unnatural to him. He had waved at the departing train, followed it to the farthermost part of the station platform, to stand separate from her family, from the train station, from Columbia Falls, hoping she would see him, see what he meant, that he was even less tied to the town than she, more free than anybody.

During the following three months there had been letters from her, usually written on Monday nights, telling him about her job, a few of the people with whom she worked, her two-room apartment on Joy Street, her clothes, her roommate. It seemed in every letter she told him she had just washed her hair. He wrote her at night, Tuesday night, Thursday night, finally only on Saturday nights, telling her about the school, his courses, a professor or two, how difficult it was to be a student (after having met death, been wounded, blanketed with snow near Hill 449 in an unsung little war), his games of squash.

"After all, Dan," she had said that summer, over and over. "You have been away."

"I have been away. Yes."

"That's all I want."

For the three months he had not visited her, telephoned her, been especially possessive in his letters. *Dear Janet, I'm sorry your job with the insurance company is proving such a bore . . .*

Hours had to be kept to the minute, she wrote; what work there was was dull, clerical, unimaginative, the only challenge day by day in remembering whether seven times nine is sixty-four or sixty-three. Her salary was enough to pay half her rent on the apartment, her food, bus fare back and forth to the office, but not to buy clothes. Being an only child she received cash presents from her parents with fair regularity.

"Dan, don't you think companies ought to pay people an awful lot for boring them so utterly?"

"Yes, I do. Being bored is the hardest job on earth."

His eyes slid from her face to the back of her head, to his own face.

"Come on. Let's have coffee somewhere else."

He put three ten-dollar bills on top of the check.

"I'll bet you're the only one staying at the Y.M.C.A. tonight spending so much on dinner."

They went in a cab to an espresso cafe on Charles Street, empty at nine-thirty, and ordered Turkish coffee.

She said, "Do you love me?"

"I always have."

"Since when. Tell me when."

"Since I first saw you."

"You don't remember that."

"Yes I do."

"Then tell me."

"You were twelve years old, a long kid, dressed in blue jeans and a dark blue sweatshirt, your hair tumbling down into the hood on your shoulders. You were stepping from the bow of your uncle's Lightning onto the dock, gracefully, so sure of yourself, but looking at me."

"That was the first time you saw me?"

"That was the first time I really saw you."

"What happened?"

"I felt my Adam's apple. I'm serious. I never knew I had one. I really felt my Adam's apple. It was all tight."

"I got you right in the Adam's apple."

"I was in love."

"That minute?"

"That instant."

"Just because I was looking at you?"

"Because you were concerned with something other than landing a boat."

"You."

"Me."

"And you said to yourself, 'There. That girl would make a good minister's wife.'"

To Dan the coffee tasted like syrup at the bottom of a drugstore coke. He had only heard of espresso before.

"Because you were beautiful."

"I will make a good minister's wife, Dan. But, like you, I need to get away for a while."

"Let's go someplace noisy," he said.

Another student had told him about a jazz club on Huntington Avenue, famous for giving the young a chance to play in the East, to experiment in front of an audience. A taxi they found parked against the curb brought them to the place.

They followed the sound of the piano through the bar to the room in back.

"Goodness, this place is dark," Janet said. "How do they read the music?"

"They don't."

Dan sat with his back to the platform. The place fell silent.

"And does the live entertainment always stop when you arrive, Reverend Prescott?"

He ordered two ales.

"They must know you're an embryonic minister," she whispered. "Preparing material for a lifetime of sermons. Despite your sophistication."

"Have you got your pen?" he asked. "Your notebook?"

"Essential equipment for every good minister's wife."

A jukebox was flicked on.

"I'm glad you love me," she said, hand on his, on the table. "It makes me feel better. You've always been there, you know, solid, very much a part of my home, my life."

"Everything you're trying to escape," he said.

A record stuck on the machine. Someone kicked it.

She withdrew her hand.

"Janet, I'm sorry. I didn't mean to tell you something. I thought you were conscious of it. Look, Janet, you'd only surprise me if you didn't want to fly a little."

Then he was there, standing over them, beside Dan, looking through the smoke at Janet.

"I'm David MacFarlane." He waved a hand toward Dan's shoulder. "Don't get up."

Dan did.

"Dan Prescott. Janet Twombly. From Maine."

In the dim light, MacFarlane's look seemed too long, intense, almost rude. Standing beside him, Dan felt the shock of seeing her through his eyes. A figure in context wherever she was: a clean, leggy, slim girl in shorts and a blouse, one of many kids on a cool summer lawn, a girl in blue jeans, sweatshirt, bright open slicker on the stern thwart of a little boat, forcefully emerging into another, a proud figure, head cocked, aware of her eyes, her nose, her mouth, the sunlit skin of her body enveloped in a cocktail dress, enveloped in smoke, shining in darkness ...

"Hello."

"Hi."

David, misreading the bottle labels, ordered a beer.

"You're a pianist," Janet said. "I saw your name on the sign outside."

"I play jazz piano."

"Are you famous?" Dan asked.

"Not very." David said to Janet, "I'm an itinerant musician. Boston this week. Rochester, Detroit, Milwaukee, Chicago in a month."

"Oh," Janet said quietly.

"I take it you two don't know much about jazz."

"No. We don't." Dan said.

"Then why are you here? This always puzzles me. The light is bad, the air stinks, the beer is expensive."

Dan said, "Oh, we had to go someplace to discuss our undying love for each other."

"Oh, Dan."

Slouched in his chair, hands in his pockets, jacket collar pressed up by the back of his chair to ridge behind his ears, David glanced away from Janet only when she grimaced at the taste of her ale. His legs were a perfect barrier between Janet and Dan.

Dan said, "You don't have to drink that."

"I ordered it."

"You could have something else. Or nothing."

She said to David, "Dan is studying to be a minister."

"You don't even like it."

David said, "You're very attractive."

"Do you think so?" Dan leaned forward, looked nearsightedly into her dark brown eyes, beyond them, at her clear, golden skin, again beyond, at her straight, more golden hair, an expanding, lightening pool of brown, from brown to gold, her eyes deep, wide-set, separated by a fine thin nose, her eyes first unsure, then smiling at Dan, thin, straight lips tightening at the corners, then rising, over a delicate chin. "I never noticed."

Smiling fully at Dan, her old friend from home, protecting her from the tiresome men in a bar, itinerant musicians, Janet excused herself and stood up to find the ladies' room.

David pulled in his legs, his knees hitting the underside of the little table, pushed himself up in his chair, nearly upsetting it, leapt up.

Her hips moving lithely, she was three tables away.

Someone turned the jukebox down.

Hands over his glass, musing, chin on his hands, then, David said, "What did you say her name is?"

"Janet."

"I mean her last name."

"Twombly. Janet Twombly. From Maine."

"Janet Twombly. From Maine. My God. She's as fresh as."

"Isn't she. We're going to get married, one day."

"Are you engaged right now?"

"Not exactly."

"How do you know you're going to get married?"

"I've always thought so."

"That's wonderful. Damn, that's wonderful."

"Wonderful?"

"Wonderful. It rounds out the picture, you know? Restores my faith in television-movie America. Damn, there is a girl somewhere, a beautiful girl, fresh-skinned, blonde, sitting under pine trees, near a waterfall. And she likes boys."

"You must be on the road a lot."

"Fresh. Wholesome. Solid. Family. Love. Small town. Nobody great or famous, going anywhere. Grow up, marry the boy next door, who just happens to look like you, a minister-to-be, a whole mess of kids. I can just see them lined up beside her in the first pew."

"Would you like another beer?"

"Not now. You know you look just like her."

"Who?"

"Janet. You could be her brother."

"I'm not her brother."

She came back then and David was smoother on his feet. He held her chair as if it were glass.

David questioned her then, gently, politely, putting aside her questions about him, his music, with simple evasions. He asked about Columbia Falls, the high school, the number of churches, the fish pier, exactly where the post office was, her parents, their hardware store, Miss Leighton's School for Girls. He even wanted to know, from her, about Dan Prescott, at what point he then was in his studies.

Someone, another musician, called David back to the platform by hitting a high sharp note five or six times.

He stood, hesitated, looked from one to the other.

"Dan, would you mind if I asked Janet for a date?"

"A date?"

"I'm only in town a few days."

She said, "Of course."

Janet and Dan remained, then, partway through the set, listening, not talking to each other.

David's music seemed oddly complicated. Dan felt he was waiting for a melody, a theme, even a rhythm to emerge that he could grasp, feel, ride a while. Everything seemed under the surface, out of reach.

At quarter to twelve, going toward Beacon Hill in a cab, Dan asked, "You going on a date with MacFarlane?"

"I think he would be interesting to know." Spotting lint against the dark blue of her coat as the beam of a streetlight raked the back seat, she brushed it off in the dark. "I want to swing a little. You do understand that, don't you, Dan?"

"Yes, I do."

Beyond the iron railings of Park Street, the flat cement around the subway kiosk darkened, widened into triangular lawn.

"But if you're going to swing," he said, "don't you really think you ought to swing from something?"

"Oh, Dan. Why do you say things like that? You always have."

"Because I'm a pompous bastard, an embryonic minister, that's why."

The cab waited for the light at Beacon Street, then turned left.

"I guess the next place for you is New York. Right?"

"Maybe," Janet said. "Something like that."

3

In that final set David would play only those things he had already played, his own piece, "Deme Lo," then "Misty," even "Tenderly," to induce the customers toward and through that door, home to bed or to someone's bed. *Ms Tuesday, where are you. Where, in this cold, Godforsaken world are you, the warmth of you, the freshness.* He had gone through the bright white kitchen of the club in Chicago, Harry's Club, nodding to the grinning sandwich man, the only person in that place that David thought listened to him, through the steel-plated door to the fire escape. *In New York now; the letter said New York, as if I could ever get there. Not while the world is full of Harrys, so many Harrys.* He was standing, smoking, listening to the after-midnight roar of the city from this place where nothing could be seen but garbage cans and red brick walls, with the streetlights shining on them in circles out toward the main streets.

A tin can somewhere in the alley hit the pavement, rattled.

Harry was known as a smart proprietor, which means in that business as it means in all business that he knew what the public wanted, especially the Chicago-conventional public—a dark place, many expensive but weak drinks, available girls, overdone steak, wall-to-wall carpeting, tiny tables, and entertainment, in that order. Harry was a killer of the golden goose; a reaper, but not a sower. For entertainment, he would rather have had a famous musician, a name burned out, beyond the point of doing anything of interest, wheedled down, than anyone young or new or exciting or fresh. Some of the young ones could play better, but the old ones sold more steak-carbon, Scotch-water. There had been no burning-out musicians available that week, so Harry had taken on David "as a favor to his agent, what's his name?" for less than Harry had ever paid before, more than David had ever earned. But with no accompaniment. "Who needs bass? You've got a left hand, so use it." Then later, he had agreed to hire Al, a tin-pan drummer, cheap, just up, barely up from the strip joints.

David was twenty-seven, experiencing the first, horrible, dry sensation of possible failure, realizing, knowing, that all the things he had hoped would happen, successes, had not happened, or if they had happened, in so small a way they had meant nothing, changed nothing, just made present work, future work, more discouraging. He had made a recording for a major company, a record he had never heard played again, never heard of again, never even saw again. He had made a record, and it had not sold. He was playing whenever he could, in whatever bar he could, seconded by a jukebox. There had been all the effort to escape, move away, go beyond the jukebox: there had been trains and planes, cold cities, sweat in lined clothes, late nights, exhausted days, the loneliness, the conspicuousness, the tiredness of the social freak, there had been bars, girls, hotels, curbstones, neon lights, suitcases, cardboard sandwiches, always carrying around intact, hopeful, reasonably operative this mind in which his work really happened, rhythms and harmonies, notes and chords, confined and protected by the thick walls of other people's most human inattention.

There was the sound of an ash barrel scraping an inch or two on the pavement.

In love with something, suddenly smitten that night in Boston a month before, either by Janet Twombly, or by what she represented, pine trees and cool streams, David had been before fiercely, exclusively in love with his piano, with what he could do with it, with himself, really, never really having been one more struggling musician, having more pride, more detachment, more ability. David had never used the tired musician's sarcasm of the moment, the insulting jest, the easy banter, the occasional display of bad temper. Even as a kid, playing in his parents' forever-empty house, he had been detached, cool, a teacher's idea of a gentleman, a coach's idea of an unapproachable, unpep-able kid, forever forgiving his parents' need to work eight hours a day in offices and then to have long dinners out together, as there was nothing for them to do at home; appreciating the hours alone, making a musical idea cooler and cooler, so cool it left the listener cold. David had seen the bleakness of isolation, its eternity. *Ms Tuesday, could you understand this, stand this? Suitcases, little bars of soap, wrapped in paper, never any large bath towels.* Her letter said she had just washed her hair. *Of course she had just washed her hair.*

Quiet, all by itself, there was the sound of the saxophone, low, muttering. It came out of the blackness of the alley.

Al came through the door and heard it.

"Who is it?"

"I don't know."

It was the slowest sound in the world.

"How long has it been going on?"

"Just now. Just before you came out."

Al's lighter flared below a thin cigarette, crooked nose, thin, white face.

The saxophone stopped and the alley again became quiet, more quiet from the absence of the noise that had been there. Then it began again, sounding even slower than before, pushing up, through the blackness, shimmering like light on the walls of the alley, near them, over the after-midnight roar of the city, but as lonely and as far away as a train whistle on a cold Dakota winter night.

"It must be someone," David said.

They went down the iron steps of the fire escape, making noise with their feet but still hearing the sound. They prowled along the alley in their dinner jackets, separated like two cops, peering among the boxes and crates.

He was lying straight on the alley pavement, ankles crossed, his shoulders, head, propped against the brick wall, saxophone held on his stomach, trash cans both sides of him. His shoes were caked with mud and cracked.

"Pal," Al said. "Old buddy."

The kid raised the saxophone from his mouth. He looked at them. Then he rolled himself onto his right side and, with apparent effort, tiredness, raised himself to his knees and one hand. The other hand clutched the saxophone to his chest. He crawled away, to his right, through the rubbish barrels.

"He's drunk," Al said. "High on something."

David put the tips of his fingers into the thick wetness where the kid had been lying.

"Blood."

There were many garbage pails and crates and boxes, all at odd angles to each other, in a jumble. The kid crawled through and under them.

"We've got to get back to the club," Al said.

"No."

The sound came again and they went directly to it. He was between two ash barrels, roofed with a crate. David heaved the crate aside.

The kid was more in the light then. There was blood clotted on his gray, incredibly dirty, cloth overcoat.

This time when he saw them he rolled over on his right side. He drew his knees up, keeping the saxophone in his mouth. He played one long, muttering note, his eyes closed.

"Hey, Axelrod," Al said. "What's the tune?" He crouched, looked at the blood on the coat. "I think they cut him with a knife."

"They cut me with the knife," the boy said. He put the horn back to his lips. It was a long moment before anything came out.

"Come on, boy," David said. "You need a doctor."

"I don't need a doctor."

"You're sick," David said.

"I'm not sick."

"You've got a bad case of blood," Al said.

Eyes still closed, the kid tried to find the horn with his mouth, his mouth with his horn. "My blood."

"Where did you get that horn?" David asked.

"My horn." He blew the same, wavering note.

"We've got to get back to the club, David."

"Not now."

David stooped to help the kid up.

The kid rolled himself up more. "Go away," he said.

"Come on."

Al took the kid's other side. A garbage pail fell over.

"My horn, my horn."

Walking, limping with him, David asked, "Who knifed you?"

The toe of the kid's left shoe was dragging behind them on the pavement.

"Someone."

Al said, "They weren't nice people, I'll bet."

"No. They weren't nice people."

"What did they want?"

"I don't know. Is my horn all right?"

"Yes, your horn is all right."

"You're all right. You take my horn for me so it won't get blood."

David carried the saxophone in his left hand.

"But give me my horn," he said.

"I will," David said. "After you see the doctor."

"I don't want to see the doctor. I can't see the doctor. I can't pay for the doctor."

"That's all right," David said.

"Give me my horn while I'm seeing the doctor."

"All right."

"Don't give the horn my doctor."

"He's really high," Al said.

Harry was looking for them in the kitchen.

"What I pay you boys for? What that?"

"He's hurt. Get a doctor, will you, Harry?"

Al said nothing.

"I'm hurt. My business is hurt. I pay you to play music, not clean out the alley."

"All right," David said. "Get a doctor."

"No. You can't bring him in here. Not in the kitchen. Against health regulation."

Ellie came through the swinging door. "David."

Harry said, "This is the busy time. I pay you good money, David. Three, four convention in town, and you bring in bloody drunk. Disappear in the alley."

Ellie was talking into the wall phone.

"He's hurt, Harry."

Al was looking at the blood on his dinner jacket.

"I'm hurt," Harry said. "My business is hurt. People want to hear you."

David said, "Shut up, Harry."

Ellie hung up. "The doctor's coming. Put him down."

They sat him on the floor. He wanted his horn so David gave it to him.

"Don't you play that," Harry said. "You heard me, kid. Don't you play that."

"All right."

"Damn. All over my floor, the blood. My kitchen, David."

The knife was chopping on the sandwich board. From the sandwich man had been a white-eyeballed glance, a white-toothed smile.

David and Al stood by the swinging door.

Harry said, "I don't mean to speak bad, David. I have a heart."

"I know."

"All these people. Blood all over the floor. The health regulation, building inspector." Harry was keeping a musician happy. "You know I am sorry for the kid."

"Yes, Harry."

The saxophone burped.

"Don't you play that thing," Harry said.

Ellie knelt beside the kid but did not touch him.

"Come on, kid. Lie down."

Chump's blonde hair was long, matted with the dirt of the entire world. The circles under his eyes were blue.

"You go play, David," said Harry. "Send the people home. My business is ruined."

4

Beneath the sound his horn was making he heard the slow rhythm of someone climbing the stairwell.

Even at that hour his room was dark. The bare-bulb light from the corridor spread across his bed as the door was pushed open. The boards of packing crates had been nailed over the one window in that room, to prevent anything being thrown from the inside, or seen from the outside.

Dave stood in the door, hand on the knob, peering in. His shoulders seemed round beneath his overcoat. "Doesn't this room have a light?"

"I don't need it."

Chump had been sending his sound through that house-hotel day and night, lying on his bed beneath covers, head propped on pillows, saxophone on his stomach. Muttering, burping, occasionally soaring.

The sound of the saxophone had oozed out of his room, down corridors, up and down stairwells, covering up, even for him, some of the other noises of that house, love-brawl noises, giggles, screams, shouts, slamming doors.

Dave switched on the shadeless light on the drawerless bureau.

"I brought you a steak. Harry's charred special. I'm afraid I forgot a knife and fork."

"That's all right."

"I thought perhaps you'd had enough of Ellie's chicken vermicelli."

The closest thing to a nurse she had ever been, or he had ever had,

Ellie had delivered hot plastic cups of chicken vermicelli to him six times a day. She had been buying it from the pizza place downstairs. She would sit on the edge of the bed and spoon it into Chump's mouth while he continued to finger the saxophone on his stomach.

Dave sat at the foot of the bed, his overcoat open. "You all right?"

"Fine."

Chump slid the plate out of the brown paper bag. The saxophone was beside him on the bed.

"Don't they usually rent these rooms by the hour?" Chump asked.

"By the hour or less."

"Hope it's not too expensive."

"Ellie knows the manager."

Chump picked the steak up in both hands, a breadless sandwich, and bit into it. On the plate were mashed potatoes and string beans.

"How do you feel?"

"Better." Chump chewed. "Foggy alley. Foggy in my eyes until I heard the good piano sound and I listened."

"Hope it isn't too cold."

"That drummer was off. But the piano was good, so I sat down to listen. That drummer was way off, I remember."

"Al."

"Then they stopped the music and I sat there, waiting. I waited and waited and when there was no more for sure I made some noises with my horn. I always have my horn with me, you know."

"I guess so. I was listening to you downstairs."

Chump's chewing sounded good to him. Holding two fingers close together he scooped mashed potatoes into his mouth.

Dave said, "I thought it might be time for you to get out of here."

"You didn't bring anything to drink, did you?"

"No. I forgot. I mean, I thought it might be time for you to come down to the club and try it with me there. The horn, I mean."

Chump chewed and swallowed. "Okay," he said.

They met Ellie on the stairs. She walked with them to the club, carrying the cup of chicken vermicelli in one hand, the naked saxophone in the other.

Chump sat on the floor against the wall. Chairs were up on tables and at first there was a man running a vacuum cleaner. The place smelled as only a bar in the morning can, whiskey-dank, as if the vomit of all the people the night before were seeping back in, from the street, their hotel bathrooms, to haunt the place, incongruously dim in the bright day.

Dave played while Chump sat, fingering his saxophone, while

Ellie pretended to be just-there, not-there. On the third piece, Dave began to tighten up a little, in annoyance, to clip notes. Ellie began to prod her hair.

To David, music was holy, a prayer, a good, complete thought, a logical progression, something that had its beginning, its middle, its end in his mind; something made possible, barely possible, only sometimes possible by the wood and the steel, the felt and the strings, the ivory, of the piano, his *prie-Dieu*, which he approached as a sacred thing itself. For years, he had worked, prayed, by himself, ignoring the fact no one was listening to him, really listening, that there was no god, audience, to hear him. He tossed in his bed at night, sweating at the recollection of any musically careless, undeserving, sloppy thing he had done; even though heard, witnessed by no one but himself. Yet it mattered a great deal to him whether people heard him, listened to him, understood him; he hadn't such conceit that he could play in a vacuum all his life. He listened to his audiences, hearing their murmuring and breathing over the sounds of his own piano, gauging what they were hearing despite themselves, what they were missing. He had played in his vacuum a long time, longer than any of his contemporaries, at least those who were ever to succeed, and therefore was far superior to them, had something newer, more advanced, more interesting to say to his audience, and was gradually, at this point, becoming more explicit in his saying.

After the release of the fourth piece Chump began to work his horn, curiously, tentatively, sputtering, chattering questions to David's statements, picking David's most obscure phrases and turning them, simply, into something clear and mellow.

It was David's own piece, "Deme Lo," they first played together.

Dave said, "Let's try that again."

Chump cut in immediately the second time through. First the vacuum cleaner went off and then a blower even Chump had not heard before went off. The vacuum man sat on one of the bar stools, a rag in his hands. Ellie stood away, staring at Chump as if she were frightened. Then the sandwich maker, whom they did not know was there, pushed open the door from the kitchen and stood against the frame, hand on his hip, listening, grinning. All the suppressed, concealed emotion implicit in David's work was pouring out of Chump's horn, shivering feeling, the warmth of a tear on a cold cheek.

"My God, David."

Dave stood at the edge of the platform a moment, shoulders slightly hunched, fists at his side, staring down at Chump.

Ellie said again, "My God."

"Again, again," Dave said.

"Coffee, coffee," Chump said. "Coffee, Ellie."

The sandwich man said, "Coffee." He whirled, flung his arm up, cowboy-yelled, slapped his thigh. "Coffee, coffee." He went to get coffee.

Ellie giggled, bumped the table edge with her hip—the cup of chicken vermicelli spilled.

Chump had already begun to play, again.

Tired of trying, needing the story, the journalist finally had asked Chump, "Mr. Hardy, how did you arrive in Chicago? By lake barge?"

"Yes."

"Had you been thrown overboard?"

"Yes."

"What were you aboard the barge, a cook?"

"Yes."

"Now, when you arrived in Chicago, what did you do for food?"

The reporter's San Francisco newspaper reported factually and in great detail how Chump came to be in that alley. He had been thrown off a lake barge by the crew for having misrepresented himself as a cook. He had been beaten up in a diner because he was unable to pay for a hamburger he had ordered. He had been knifed in a fight between two gangs, each of which thought he belonged to the other.

A magazine article reported he had been knifed by someone trying to take his saxophone away from him.

No one knew how Chump came to be in that alley, including Chump. For a few days Ellie and David asked him, bluntly, subtly. After that they began to know Chump, to know how useless asking him was.

An old man on a pier somewhere had taught him, sometime, an old tune called "Celery Stalks at Midnight." Last week, last month, last year. The more David came to know Chump the more the incident receded in his past until David had to decide it must have happened when Chump was nine, ten, eleven, maybe when he was seven or eight. This incident, this sole incident, to him, was his past, his only past.

They brought him to Ellie's studio apartment the next day and stripped him, plopped him in her bathroom, among the sponges and facecloths and soap.

"Don't come out until you're clean."

David closed the door.

On his first try, Chump just made a sodden mess of his bandages. He opened the door and tried to crawl out, dragging his broken leg.

"Get back in there."

David and Ellie pushed him back into the bathroom. He slid on his knees on the wet tile floor.

"I want my saxophone."

"Not until you're clean."

David slammed the door. Each time Chump tried to get out they inspected him briefly, pushed him back, slammed the door. Finally he was clean enough, with dripping bandages, soaked cast, for Ellie to sponge bathe him again, well.

David bought him clothes, a suit, shirts, tie, socks, shoes, underwear, overcoat, guessing at the size of everything, and a cane. Ellie cut his hair, so he would be presentable enough to go to a barber, washed it, then found it apparently as long as when she had begun, and cut it again. In the clothes Chump looked perfectly square, physically. Late in the afternoon, David took him to a barber shop.

"Here. Cut his hair, will you?" For the forty minutes Chump sat in the barber's chair he said "Beep, beep" to the rhythm of the scissors. David tipped the speechless barber enough to take the rest of the day off if he wanted to, then dragged Chump away, as respectable looking as he ever would be, to his own hotel. In the elevator David noticed Chump's collar was already looking shrunk, wrinkled, dirty.

"Up the shaft," Chump said. "I'm getting shafted."

It was weeks of nothing but practice then, building a repertoire. Then it was Detroit, New Orleans, San Francisco, two appearances on local television in Los Angeles, a long-playing record, *This Is MacFarlane, This Is Hardy*, one appearance on national television, Philadelphia, Boston in grander style, then Chicago, New York, Washington, more television, their second album, *Dos-a-Dos*, then that horrible, circular tour of the Southwest, diddling while New York burned, waiting for Chump to discover where he had been born, then London, Paris, Berlin, Rome, even Bombay.

Perpetual, strangely boring excitement, movement. In the United States they played in the clubs where the people came to pay too much for Scotch to hear them play; universally, in the espresso places where people came to pay too much for coffee to hear them play. The young people sat in the dark clubs not talking and not drinking their Scotch or coffee and not dancing, but just listening. When they played a university town the students who were being musicologists that week wrote articles in the college newspapers telling them what they were doing that was so effective and how they were doing it. QUALITY SOUNDS: BEYOND THE WHIMS OF FAD. In Bombay, India, one old man suggested to them that their sound was a bit like ancient snake charming music, in its slowness and clarity. It was the first jazz the Spanish people really liked, hearing in it what they thought of as Moorish strains, beginning to disappear from their own music.

Chump was the strange American genius, academically ignorant, more learned in what he wanted and needed to know than professors or critics. An old man on a pier somewhere had taught him something, sometime, perhaps the only human ever to pay attention to Chump Hardy, to make some small segment of life have meaning for him, a melody, a rhythm, a beginning, a middle, an end, given him an instrument with which to filter the world, communicate with it as much as he wanted. "Celery Stalks at Midnight." From a pawn shop, perhaps, or from the old man himself, Chump had laid hands on a saxophone and with that saxophone he was like some boys with a jackknife, a baseball, able to aim it anywhere, twirl it, curve it, calculate the distance it had to go, the effect of all things that might influence it, wind, angle, slope, hit the mark exactly, it being forever in his hands, sticking it into logs, walls, the ground, peppering it into his mitt, an extension of himself, really, a means of thinking, responding: he could do anything with it. Through the years of his growing up, learning, knowing nothing else, he had invented music for himself, passed through all phases of it relevant to him, played with every recording or song as he heard it, played as well with every other sound, the swells of city traffic, rumble of subways, the ripple of brooks, of conversation, worked through every melody, arrangements he heard again and again and many he had not heard. In hearing anything, now, he knew it, not the name, or the composer; he knew in the first bar where the melody would go, could go, everything conceivable that could happen to its rhythm, its harmony, and what he could do to it that would be different, exciting, fresh.

Mostly, then, it became something between them, between David and Chump, better than anything else. They went from city to city hardly speaking on the train or airplane, David reading and Chump Hardy looking out the window or sleeping. In the hotels, David arranged for the rooms and then went out to see the agent or managers or whomever had to be seen while Chump sat propped up on his bed holding his saxophone on his stomach, blowing a note, wondering what a note was. He would not really play; instead, mutter, stutter, burp, hold himself for that night. At about five, David would come in from seeing people and do the same with the piano, if there happened to be a piano in the rooms, pick at it, but not really play. Sometimes they would carry a drum set with them, as a gross luxury, and they would warm up on that, after the bellboys had helped them set it up, one playing badly and the other laughing uproariously.

In the dining rooms of the hotels they would eat only a light meal, saving themselves for the night's playing.

"Dave, who was Verdi?"

"A composer. How did you hear of him?"

"Some kid mentioned him. Was he any good?"

"Verdi good."

Later, at two or three in the morning, after whatever club had closed, they would find someplace for bratwurst sandwiches and a quart of milk each.

Sometimes, in some cities, David would have a woman, and Chump would go back to the hotel quietly while David went to meet her. David tried getting Chump a girl once or twice and Chump would go along but be sleepy and bored and everyone would be bored. Going from one place to another Chump would stop on a curbstone and stand, listening to the traffic and the noise of buses starting up and he would detect the sound of a train somewhere in the distance, a plane in the sky, the wail of a siren, quite forgetting he was with people going someplace. Chump had to stop and listen to these sounds but the girls always wanted to get to the next bar or the next restaurant or the next someplace, and they would be impatient. If they ever succeeded in getting Chump into someplace and seated at a table he would forget all about them again, have no idea what they were saying, but be listening to their speech rhythms, closely, hearing the sounds of the cups and the saucers and the tables and the chairs as they moved against each other, saying nothing.

"Spaghetti, Chump?"

The girls would giggle.

"Chump, spaghetti, spaghetti, spaghetti?"

"Phew, what a stiff."

David would tell the waiter, "Chump will have spaghetti and roast beef and beer."

"Where is the hole you put the formaldehyde in?"

David would say, "Chump is a saxophone player."

"Come on! He's deaf!"

So David would go out sometimes and Chump would go back to the hotel, hungry those nights, never trusting himself to find a bratwurst place and then the hotel, finding the hotel was tricky enough, and be asleep when David came in.

Usually when they were through for the night they would be hungry and sleepy and sometimes silly from tiredness. Eating bratwurst or rolled beef or a cheeseburger or pizza David would do something that would strike Chump as hilarious and he would begin laughing and then David would begin laughing and they would kill themselves laughing, all at nothing, or at least at nothing very much. Sometimes they would be so tired from the playing, keyed up, let down, whatever, all they needed to do was look at each other and they would be laughing. Then they would sleep as if they had had women galore.

A beautiful thing between them: they had their language, cues, and when they were playing they told each other things the audience, even those who were musicologists that week, could never hear. Within the rhythm and sound there was another rhythm and sound, for them, between them, exclusively their own, hints to each other about where each was going, what different thing he was going to do this time, comments about what the other had just done. Between them was the conversation, the compatibility, the correspondence, the copulation, impossible without them, of the piano and the saxophone themselves.

The young people would sit in the clubs, halls, watching, listening, fascinated, holding their eternal question still for a moment in their chests, witnessing this statement without apparent semantic problems, accepting its clarity, reacting more to its unreachable depth, complexity, seeing in it the power, profundity of the question itself, not expecting to answer it, really, or to comment, but appreciating, respecting, loving its being said/asked.

But before all the traveling around the world, circumstances forced Dave to attempt a formal, verbal conversation with Chump.

In a hotel room in Las Vegas, Dave finally brought himself to begin by saying, "Milton says we're going abroad. Do you have a passport?"

"No."

"That's not what I meant. What I mean is, can you get a passport?"

"Why not?"

"Where were you born?"

"In Canada?"

"Were you born in Canada?"

Chump said, "Canada, I think."

It took weeks while managers, distributors, agents fumed and tore their hair, screamed dates at each other over telephones, and while David and Chump went in circles in the American Southwest, played clubs, took quick bookings no one had ever heard of, marked time, to establish Chump had not been born in Canada.

In a hotel room in Los Angeles, hanging up the phone, David said to Chump, "At least they can't get you for illegal entry."

"That's nice."

"You weren't born in Canada."

"Oh."

"If you were born in this country, have you ever registered for the draft?"

"What's that?"

"The Selective Service System. You're supposed to register when you're eighteen."

"Did anyone ever tell me about it?"

It was discovered, after weeks of more fuming, hair-tearing, telephoning in New York while they circled the Southwest, that five years before a card had been returned to Selective Service Local Board Number 933 with, written on it, between the lines, in the little blank spaces, the following: *Deer sirs I am not a studant and dunt wont to be nor a soldure. I dunt kno what you meen in good halth, I blow my nos las week. Mosly I play with my axe. Respex, Ch. Hardy.* The card had been put in a file marked *Undesirable.*

In a hotel room in Scottsdale, Arizona, again hanging up the phone, Dave said to Chump, "Your name is Charles Thompson Hardy, you're twenty-three years old, and you were born in Jameson, Tennessee."

Chump thought a second, a fraction of a second, shook his head no and said, "I don't think so."

5

The train jerked once. At first through his window John had been able to read C I N Z A and then C I N Z A N. People were still moving along the platform: two black-skirted, sombreroed priests, without luggage, hands behind their backs, eternally strolling in their garden; a fat, top-coated daddy with a skinny, bare-legged little boy; a fashionably dressed older woman arm-in-arm with a dark-suited boy of twenty; a porter with two black suitcases and one briefcase. A fat mama, a grandmama, in a black, unrestraining dress stood outside, at the edge of John's window weeping and wringing her hands and waving at the window behind him, shouting things he could not hear.

He lit a French cigarette and returned to Marcuse's *Eros and Civilization*. He had arrived early, bought his first-class ticket before a line had formed, walked directly to the train carrying his own luggage, found his empty compartment. He had settled his two bags on the rack and sat below them, in a corner, near the window. *The "claim for happiness," if truly affirmed, aggravates the conflict with a society which allows only controlled happiness, and the exposure of the moral taboos extends this conflict to an attack on the vital layers of society.*

"May I sit in here?"

The door had been fumbled open. A girl, blonde, brown eyes.

"Let me help you with your bag."

She stepped up into the compartment directly, straight, not

sideways. Her tan skirt rose well above her knee. *She is used to shorts, absolutely used to existing in shorts.*

He pulled the bag up behind her and put it on the rack over where she was already sitting, her vanity case upright at her feet.

"Thank you. Everything I own is in that thing, almost."

John smiled and brought the book back to his lap.

The affirmative attitude toward the claim for happiness then becomes practicable only if happiness and the "productive development of the personality" are redefined so that they become compatible with the prevailing values, that is to say, if they are internalized and idealized.

There were more jerks of the train, shouts, slamming doors, sounds of people calling to each other. C I N Z A N O. The fat grandmama was walking outside, at the edge of the window, wringing the handkerchief in her hands, putting it to her eyes with both hands, waving it with one. She was overtaken by the window frame. The train passed the porter walking slowly away, head down. One priest remained standing on the platform, apparently waiting for the whole train to pass.

. . . in a repressive society, individual happiness and productive development are in contradiction to society; if they are defined as values to be realized within this society, they become themselves repressive.

"I didn't have time to get a magazine," the girl said to John.

"Oh?"

"No. I never can find the American ones anyway."

"Why do you need an American one?"

"Because I can't read anything else."

"Perhaps you could. It's a long way to Paris. You could have figured out a few words."

They were going through the trainyards, then, north of the city, each track true only to its mate, running through a maze of other tracks.

"Are you going all the way to Paris?"

"Not immediately," he said. "I'm changing in Genoa for Antibes."

"Oh, that's nice. That's on the Riviera, isn't it? The French Riviera."

"Yes. I have an old uncle there."

"How did you know I was going to Paris?"

"Where else would you go?"

. . . the question is only how much resignation the individual

can bear without breaking up. In this sense, therapy is a course in resignation. . . .

"Why are you snubbing me?"

"Am I? I'm sorry. I didn't mean to be."

"Yes, you do mean to be. But why?"

"I don't know." He put his index finger between pages 246 and 247. "You open a door to a compartment and immediately speak English, assuming whoever is in the compartment has the courtesy and the good sense to speak your language."

"Oh, dear. I'm sorry. But I get so tired of the question, Do you speak English? Don't you? I mean, don't you get tired of the question?"

"Awfully."

"That and the American way of saying *tout de suite, tout de suite*. Over and over. *Tout de suite*."

"Terrible."

"Isn't it?"

"Awful."

"Even in Rome: *tout de suite*. Even *chop-chop*. Maybe I was just assuming whoever was in the compartment was beautiful enough to speak every language, including my own. Can you speak Italian?"

"Yes."

"French?"

"Yes."

"That's beautiful. I can't speak anything. Maybe I just assumed you're American because you're black."

"That, I think, is more like it."

"But you are from the North, aren't you?"

"Yes. I'm from North America."

"Here I go again. I mean, you're from the northern half of the United States."

"In fact, I'm from the northern eighth of the United States. My ancestors didn't quite make it over the border."

"Oh, listen. I'm sorry. I know I'm just a dumb American. I don't mean to be."

"I'm sorry, too. I'm not really very sensitive. I'm just playing with you."

"My name is Janet Twombly."

"Twombly? John Bart Nelson, Ma'm. At your service."

"I wish you really were." Her eyes, her grin played with him.

"Were what?"

"At my service. You're the largest man I've ever seen in my life."

"As a matter of fact, I'm not."

"How tall are you?"

"Maybe it's the American propensity to be personal. I'm six foot five."

"Your head is enormous. How much do you weigh?"

"Two hundred and forty pounds."

"You don't look fat."

"I'm not fat."

"Are you a basketball player or something?"

"No."

"No, with those shoulders you'd be a boxer. You'd have to be."

"I would not have to be. And I'm not."

"What are you?"

"I'm John Bart Nelson."

"No, I mean. What are you?"

"I'm an apprentice railway porter. I'm a taxi driver. I'm a garbage man."

"Come on. Be serious."

"I'm a poet. A serious poet."

"You're frightening."

"I'm a rapist. I get lynched on Saturdays."

"My God."

"No, Ma'm: John Bart Nelson."

The train was crawling through the backyards of northern Rome, past square houses set at odd angles to each other, strung, festooned with laundry.

"I'm trying to be a poet," he said. "I work at it, when I can."

She was looking through the window, too.

"How did you like Rome, John?"

"Very much."

"Is there much you could do there?"

There was a triangular cement park, with a cafe on one side.

"I'm sorry," she said. "Dumb American."

The light from the window made the skin over her cheekbones, nose, forehead whiter than that of her throat.

"Have you ever been in Paris?" she asked.

"I think I live there."

"More dumb questions. How do you say I'm sorry in Spanish?"

"*Lo siento.*"

"*Lo siento.* Will you forgive me?"

"You bet."

They talked. Green fields blurred by their windows. Hills in the distance revolved slowly. A country road ran along the tracks, bending toward them and then away again. They went through groves, saw vineyards in the distance.

They discovered they had been brought up in towns near each other. Gilmore High had played Columbia Falls High annually, and Janet remembered in particular one run John had made, a miraculous run, through the length of the line, sideways, and then up the length of the field.

"Ninety yards," she said.

"Seventy-eight."

He had been in Rome the last four months tutoring the young son of a Brazilian industrialist there on business. John had been recommended by the Academy in Paris. In four months he had taught the boy the rudiments of Italian, something of English poetry, stimulated an interest in mathematics, introduced him to the painting of Michelangelo, and to the mechanics, the art, the character of Leonardo, as well as taught him how to center a ball and receive a lateral pass. The father had asked John to return to Rio with them. In an envelope in John's pocket was the equivalent of twelve hundred dollars in cash, enough to pay for a year in Paris, writing.

He described things in Paris that were precious to him and asked her to see them. The late afternoon shadows of short trees, squat houses reached toward the railroad train.

"Where should I look for a room, John?"

"That all depends."

"Depends on what? Oh, yes. I'm sorry, I don't care about that. I want to be on the Left Bank. I want to see something."

"See what?"

"I don't know. Something. Where should I start?"

He said, "There are many tourists on the Left Bank."

"No, I mean to live there. To get into it. Don't you think I'd be accepted on the Left Bank?"

"Get into what?"

"I don't know. You know what I mean."

"I guess so."

They both laughed at her. Smoking his last French cigarette he wrote the name of a friend who would help her find rooms.

They said goodbye a thousand times. He gave her *Eros and Civilization.*

From Genoa he went along the coast in a wonderfully modern train, looking down the green slopes, over the roofs and pastel garden walls into the Mediterranean blue, in and out of tunnels, along curves leaning into the hillsides.

The blue Rolls Royce was parked beside the first station beyond Nice. In a white jacket, his uncle stood on the platform, looking at the wrong coach.

"Is that my very own Uncle Sam?"

The man's eyes grew wide at the sight of his nephew.

"My God, Jay. How did you get so big?"

"You really fetch a body in style, don't you, Sam?"

John put down his bag to shake hands. The balding man picked the bag up.

"You're the biggest body we ever had in this family. Your mother said you were big, now."

"That is your Rolls, isn't it?"

"Well, I timed picking you up with a trip downtown for Bourbon. Nobody ever questions a trip downtown if Bourbon is brought back. How are you, you orangutan?"

John slid his hand under the bag handle and lifted it above his uncle's elbow, taking it from him.

"Fine, Sam, fine. You look fit to wrassle."

"Not with you, you monster."

There were puffy areas under his eyes.

From behind the steering wheel he looked at John, at the top of his head against the roof.

"God, Jay. You should have gone to the ring."

The engine started but then John could not hear it. He was surprised when they rolled forward.

"I'll never get you on my knee again, I guess."

"Do I still look like my mother?"

"Except for the moustache."

"I don't have a moustache."

"She has."

They rolled farther west along the coast, sunlight gleaming from the car stabbing John in the eye.

"How's the job, Sam?"

"I don't know. I guess we'll be in Europe a while longer. They don't drink too much."

John was given an empty servant's room at the back of the house, down the corridor from his uncle's. The Herseys were nice to him, both making a point of coming into the kitchen the first night, before a dinner party, to meet him.

"You may not realize this, but Sam is our dearest friend."

John realized it.

He found himself dusting the Rolls, the Alfa Romeo, the Ford station wagon every morning for his uncle, taking out the garbage for the cook, sawing broken limbs off orange trees. From the pantry one night he heard the Herseys at dinner mention this enormous Negro boy in the kitchen who could speak French, Italian, Spanish, and English.

"He's a nephew of our Sam. I think he's a teacher, or something, of American children in Paris. It's wonderful what these people can do nowadays. You know, Sam is our dearest friend. We'd do anything for Sam."

John walked along the roads over the sea at night, smelling the wonderful scents of Riviera gardens, of orange trees, and lilac, and of many things he did not know, one by one in the gentle night breeze, and hearing, in infinite, subtle combinations, only the whispering of fat tires on the road beside him, the occasional roar of a sports car or motor scooter on the Upper Cheyenne. He sunbathed on a blanket behind the garage, listening to the million different songs of Riviera birds.

"Sam, I've got to go tomorrow." They were eating supper in the kitchen. The French cook was at the sink, washing up. "A friend who might need help has just gotten to Paris."

"You were good to come see your old uncle, at last. Have you checked the trains?"

"I thought I'd fly. Can you take me into Cannes?"

"Of course."

"Trop gentil."

"What?"

Sam drove him to Cannes in the station wagon. On the back seat were clothes to be dropped off at the cleaner's.

"You don't seem happy, Jay."

"I don't?"

"You smile like an educated man, now, all with the mouth as if everything was ironic, not really funny. There is no light in your face when you laugh."

"I've had a terrible sunburn."

"You know what I mean."

"Yes, I do."

"You know what I mean. I haven't had education and I have never tried to write poetry, and I miss all that. But I am a rich man, and I am a happy man."

"I'm glad to hear it, Sam."

"I may have spent my life a servant, but I am retiring a rich man. I have saved four hundred thousand dollars."

At the airport they waited near John's gate for the flight to be called. They both admired the fashions of the stewardesses.

"This friend of yours in Paris, Jay. The one you think might get lost. Is she a girl?"

"No," John said. "No."

6

They were in Paris again, straggling down the airplane steps, facing a cold winter dawn over the gray cement runways and buildings. They exchanged courtesies with the customs people again and found a taxi to take them into the city, bumping along the roads of the outskirts, looking through the back windows at the houses not yet awakened, seeing the one or two civil servants starting out from their houses with pasty faces and lunch boxes. There was the hotel desk clerk again who was expecting them because their names were in the book of people to be expected, and there were the bellhops looking at them shrewdly from shoes to collar, measuring the amount of gratuity they might expect. There was the senselessness of going to bed at eight o'clock in the morning and waking at four-thirty in the afternoon, lying for a moment on the bed looking at the wallpaper and window curtains, remembering where one was.

The airplane ride from Amsterdam and then Munich, bumpy over the Alps in the snow, had confused David's ears. He got up heavily, tiredly, and went to the window and looked down at the street below. It was a winter dusk and the people were going along the streets in ones and twos without looking at each other. The sidewalk cafe below his window and across the street had all its chairs and tables in, making the sidewalk look broad and the corners of the building clean.

He thought about going back to sleep but looked at his watch and saw it was quarter to five. Chump's horn was muttering in the other bedroom.

David pulled on his shoes and went into the living room.

The door was open to Chump's room and when he saw David he took the saxophone out of his mouth. David found his overcoat where he had thrown it over the luggage when they came in.

"I'm going out for a while," he said to Chump.

"Okay."

"I'll see you at the club. Do you remember how to get there?"

"What club is it?"

"Club Solo," David said. "The one with the green walls."

"Oh, yeah. I remember."

"Do you remember how to get there?"

A-flat, held a moment. "Oh, yeah. I remember."

"Okay." David opened the door. "I'll see you there. Nine o'clock."

He knew Chump would leave for the club within an hour and arrive there one way or the other by nine o'clock, having been lost, cheated, laughed at, insulted, helped, probably loved. He would never be able to explain how he got there.

Once in Detroit, when David had left Chump with instructions that he promptly forgot, Chump had hired a taxi and gone to nearly every club in the city introducing himself to the bartenders and asking if he were playing there that night. One told Chump he was playing there that night and Chump brought his saxophone in and let the taxi go. When David did not show up Chump got into another taxi and started all over again. He was only a few minutes late.

David went down in the elevator and across the lobby and into the street. The wind was from the north, what there was of it, and the air was cold and clear. David thought he could smell the dry, powder snow of the mountains. He walked along the broad sidewalk, dodging the homeward-pouring foot traffic, seeing the pigeons picking along the cracks in the sidewalks where the cafe tables and chairs usually were. The lights were on by now, and the cafes inside looked warm and mellow. Some of them still had their metal tables and chairs outside, the chairs tipped forward to lean upon the tables, and there were more pigeons around these. He heard a cooing and looked up and saw a pigeon looking down at him from the ledge of the building, pop-eyed and demanding, like a schoolmaster. He smiled at the bird and the bird seemed satisfied and walked stiff-legged a few feet along the ledge. At a corner, a boy sold David a French newspaper that David could not read. On the front page were the charred, twisted, gray metal, the broken trees and plowed earth of an air crash. The flight number was 84. David put the newspaper into a litter basket.

He found the cafe he was looking for and went in.

There was a bar running along the back wall and high ceilings and booths with tall brown partitions between them. David sat in one of the booths, his back to the street door, facing the bar. There were three workmen wrapped in dark overcoats standing at the bar drinking quietly, one separated from the other two and drinking alone. Horses at a feeding trough.

David did not recognize the waiter.

"Hot toddy," he said. "Hot toddy?"

"Hot coffee? Cafe?"

"Whiskey," David said. "Whiskey, whiskey. *Tout de suite.*"

He watched the waiter go toward the bar. *She smiles at you as if she were about to beat you in tennis, straight lips a little chiding, eyes challenging.* Somewhere, there was a green valley floor, yellow-green fields fitting against each other like large puzzle pieces, dark green pine trees clumped in the center of the town, a white church steeple sticking through them, its bell tolling slowly, ever so slowly, on Sunday morning ...

The waiter brought him a glass with ice in it and a bottle of whiskey and soda syphon and mixed the drink in front of David. It had taken him a moment to find the ice.

"Have you any cold milk?" David asked.

"No. Whiskey."

"Milk? Cold milk?"

"No, no. Whiskey."

David sipped his whiskey.

In a few moments the door behind David opened and a group of people came in, talking loudly as if they were still in the street. David did not turn around but examined them as they passed him. Only one skirt was with them, the tan skirt, and the brown suede jacket. They went directly to the bar and began demanding service raucously, playfully, pounding their fists on the solid bar, repeating their orders over and over.

They were Americans, theater people, little-theater, would-be big-theater, television, movie people. Even inside they projected their voices, declaimed lines, gestured expansively. They went to the right end of the bar, forcing the three workmen further to the left, ordered gin, each one calling the barkeep Prometheus, thanking him at length, stylistically, for bringing fire to Man. One was authoritative, fat, wore glasses: the Director. One had flowing blonde hair, a big nose. The third was short and lithe, dressed and built like a seven-year-old boy, with a deep voice. They would address a loud remark to Ms Tuesday, ask a question, then exclude her somehow, address a remark across her, away from her.

She slipped away, through a door at the right end of the bar that David knew was the ladies' room.

It was a moment before the deep-voiced one said, "Where is she?"

"Where's who?" the director asked.

"She, of course. The Mother of Us All."

"Don't be stupid," the director said. "Where you'd like to be."

"Oh."

In a moment, while they were screaming about how the bartender would look standing naked in a stream, Ms Tuesday came out, saw David. She stole quickly to him, slid into the booth, her back to the bar.

"Have you been here?"

"I always know where to find you."

"Hi," she said.

"Hi."

She took David's hand away from the whiskey glass and held it on the table, looking at him.

"You look tired."

"I'm twenty-nine," he said. "Going on ninety."

"I espy gray among the hair. I'm glad you're back."

"Are you?"

"Yes. Very glad."

She held his hand a moment, and then he took it to handle the whiskey. She had been looking into his eyes and David wondered what she had seen.

"Why didn't you tell me when you were coming?" she asked.

"I didn't hear from you."

"I didn't write. There was too much to say."

"I know."

"Are you disappointed I didn't write?"

"No," David said. "There was nothing to say."

From the bar they heard the deep-voiced one say, "Where is she?"

Ms Tuesday ducked her head.

"I told you, stupid."

"But that was minutes ago."

He wandered over to the closed door.

"Miss Twombly? Miss Twombly?"

David was watching, but Ms. Tuesday was trying to stay hidden. She said to David, "Don't give me away. Please."

She was grinning.

"What are you doing with them?"

"They want me to act in a play."

"Are you going to?"

"They don't have the play yet."

The small, deep-voiced one was still standing at the door with a glass in his hand.

"Miss Twombly? Miss Twombly? On stage please, Miss Twombly."

He looked at David over the back of the booth and grinned at him. He kicked against the door, sloshing his drink, and said loudly, "Come out in the name of the Law!" and then grinned at David again. The other two were paying him no attention.

Prometheus scowled at him from behind the bar.

He went back to the bar, shrugging and grinning at David.

"At least you're safe with them," David said. "Do you want something to drink?"

Her first drink was standing on the bar.

"Not now."

They sat. She was looking at him, into his eyes again, curiously, uncertain.

"Did you come here to find me?" she asked.

"To Paris? No, I came to play the piano."

"I mean here. This cafe."

"Yes."

"That's nice."

She smiled then, and covered both his hands with hers.

David heard the door behind him open. Looking over his shoulder Ms Tuesday showed surprise, recognition. He turned his head to see who it was.

The guy was enormous; he loomed like a mountain beside the table. His was the biggest head David had ever seen. He blocked out the wall, the ceiling, more than half the side of the room. He was grinning and putting out his hand, half a ham, to Ms Tuesday.

She said, "Hello there."

She looked from one to the other.

"Hello, Miss Twombly."

"Not Twombly," David said, helping. "Tuesday."

He looked at David. "What?"

"On the train from Rome," Ms Tuesday said. "I met you on the train from Rome. John somebody or other. You gave me that book and sent me to that nice man."

Her cheeks had colored.

"John Bart Nelson," he said.

"Yes, that was the name of the man. He was a great help. This is the man who sent me to that nice Mister Nelson, David."

David stood, his legs bent forward at the knee by the bench. "Hello."

His hand felt as if it were in a baseball mitt.

"Sit down," Ms Tuesday rattled on. "Oh, yes. This is David MacFarlane. I'm afraid I don't remember your name."

"John Bart Nelson." He took off his hat. "My name is John Bart Nelson."

"David MacFarlane," David repeated.

"Not Friday? January, March?"

"What? Oh, no. David Massasoit."

John sat down on David's side of the bench, leaning forward on one elbow, keeping his hat under the table. His overcoat was open.

"I hate introductions," John said, grinning.

"If they're all like that, you should."

David looked at Ms Tuesday.

"What do you mean?" she asked. "I remembered his name, didn't I?"

Grinning widely, John said, "No. You didn't."

"Anyway, that was months ago. And anyway, David, John is terribly anti-American."

"Is he?"

"Terribly. He railed at me all the way up from Rome about how he hates Americans. Didn't you, John?"

"No."

"He did so. About how he hates Americans saying *tout de suite* all over the map. Didn't you?"

He said to David, "I refuse to answer."

David said, "I would, too."

7

"By any chance, Mister MacFarlane, are you related to the composer by the same name?"

Three Americans, youngmen, were chattering noisily at the bar.

"Slightly."

"He is David MacFarlane."

"He's the son of the woman my father married. We're related."

David's head was down. He was looking at his drink, at his hands on the table, at the thick, cracked varnish of the table surface.

John said, "Yours is one of the few permanent names in the contemporary music world."

"Nothing is permanent in the music world."

"Oh, I forgot to ask." Miss Twombly asked, "How's Chump? Is he in one piece this week?"

"He's fine."

"I like your work," John said. "I have one of your recordings, the third one, I believe, 'Sorry.'"

"Don't become a nuisance," David said.

"All right, then. I don't like your work."

"That's better."

"I wouldn't have one of your recordings if you gave it to me."

"Now, John, don't talk that way."

"He's right. He's not going to get a recording anyway," David said.

"I think he's lovely." Miss Twombly brought David's hands together between hers. "Don't say anything about my David."

One of the few, very few permanent names in contemporary music: John thought how young he looked, really was, for such a known name, talent. David was only a few years older than himself, not quite thirty, yet he could walk through city streets anywhere and hear snatches of his own songs, from passing car radios, through apartment windows, maybe from the lips of kids walking behind him. He would know that the girl, woman, walking toward him had already heard his thoughts, listened to him, carried in that part of her being, wherever music is carried, a melody he had made. Not yet thirty, but David MacFarlane looked tired, life-tired, like a man in his forties who had worked constantly, thought constantly, been constantly in motion, who was beginning to measure things not in relation to his own accomplishment, his own youth, but rather in long-range strain, in the weight of personal and public pressure he felt now, leading to that ultimate exhaustion, even that inevitable heart attack. His were bright, restless, nervous, young blue eyes in a white, puffy, creased, sagging, anxious face.

The permanence of his fame rested mostly on his being a composer, a good one. It had been only two or three years before that John had first heard of him, and then he had heard of him again and again. There had been "Deme Lo," "Greasy Pig," and then a song called "Both of Us: The Absolute We." Then "Sorry," "Don't," "Red, White and You," "Sunday," "Number 95," "Lech," "Lunch Counter," "Too Long," others: perfectly formed poems in music; songs by David MacFarlane originally played by David MacFarlane, Chump Hardy, then played by practically everybody else, songs given words by singers, deeper rhythms by dance bands, lush arrangements by full orchestras. The melody of "Lech," with variations, had been used as the sound track of a short film that had won the Cannes Film Festival.

"Is there really a girl named Sorry?"

"An old flame of David's," Miss Twombly said. "One of many."

"Her name is Sarah," David answered. "The wife of a friend. A beautiful girl. They have a plantation in the West Indies."

"Another girl," Miss Twombly said slowly, so slowly, "with whom David has never made love."

She squeezed his hands.

"There aren't many," she said. "But those are the ones he truly loves."

Quickly, very quickly, John said, "I admit I've been looking all over Paris for you."

"That's good," she said. "Isn't that nice."

"I have some letters for you."

"Letters?"

Letters, letters. Immediately after arriving in Paris he had gone to the friend he had asked to arrange rooms for Miss Twombly, an old friend, a good friend. Nothing was left unsaid between them: a girl, a beautiful girl, fresh, wholesome, so innocent. John had written, "She could find a neighborhood that would charm her and please her, by daylight; horrify, frighten, and endanger her at night." A girl, an American girl, brave, adventuresome, a tourist. Marcel wrote back, "She would be lost, miserable, without her hot and cold running water, her shower, her central heat." Marcel had put her in rooms in a clean, restored house across the street from a Catholic school.

When John arrived in Paris, he took an attic room on the same street, around the corner from the Café Jérome. He ordered his stuff out of storage and unpacked. Then he walked down and rang the bell at Miss Twombly's house.

The concierge said the American girl had moved out after two days. She must have written letters from that address because there was mail waiting for her. The concierge had no idea where the American girl had gone. Maybe she had left Paris. The concierge had been reluctant to return the letters to the sender for fear they would cause consternation, worry. If John was a friend of the young American lady, would he not take the letters with him to give to her when he found her?

He agreed. Surely she would have returned, sent a forwarding address by now, if she intended to. They were all from the same address: Saint Bartholomew's Parish House, Columbia Falls, Maine. He left his own name and address with the concierge.

He looked wherever he was in Paris, wherever Americans were likely to be, in their being tourists, in their being not tourists. He followed an American girl into the modern American Express building only to discover when she turned that she was terribly broken out with pimples. He thought he caught glimpses of her in one or two cafes, but was always disappointed. He sat through a film twice one night because a girl took a seat in front of him who he thought distinctly resembled Janet Twombly, and he wanted to see her when the light went on. Once he thought he saw her entering a German restaurant with an older, well-dressed man. He stopped carrying the letters, finally leaving them at home on top of his own correspondence box. Then one dusk he had been walking around Paris and had become cold and stopped in at an improbable cafe for a cognac.

"What letters could you have?"

The three youngmen at the bar were starting to sing "I'll take you home again, Kathleen," trying harmony.

"They arrived at the rooms Marcel arranged for you," he said. "After you left."

"Oh."

"If you let me know where you're staying, I can get them to you." He said, "For some reason I don't seem to have them on me at the moment."

She said, "Oh."

The short American with the deep voice saw Miss Twombly's head over the brown partition. Singing, "Onward, Christian Soldiers," he marched to the booth triumphantly, holding his glass in front of him like a baton.

The barkeep, washing glasses, shook his head tiredly.

"Hello, Mommy! I found her, the Mother of Us All. Hiding behind a big, brown fence!"

The other two came after him, bringing their drinks. The three crawled into the booths on either side, knelt on the benches. They leaned over the partitions, breathing down on everybody, shouting, giggling at each other.

David MacFarlane shrugged.

Miss Twombly said, in a fluster, with embarrassment, "This is Meeny, Myny, and Mo."

"Who's Meeny?" said one of them, the short one. "Am I Meeny?"

"Yes, you're terribly Meeny."

"Who's this boy?" asked the second one, the blonde, the Myny, nodding to David.

"George Washington O'Hara," said David.

"You have unusual hands, George," said Myny. "I notice things like that."

"I'm Charles Thompson Hardy," John said.

"This fellow, Charles Thompson Hardy, writes," said Miss Twombly. "Maybe he could make a play for us."

"Oh, do you write?" asked Mo.

Courteously, John said, "Not plays."

"But you could write a play?"

"I'm a poet."

"You could make us a poetic play."

They laughed: "Very good, Francis."

"But you could write us a good play, couldn't you?"

"I doubt it," courteously. "Anyway, I'm working on something else."

"Is it a play?"

"It's a play of voices," John answered. "A perspective mobile. Nothing for you."

"How do you know? If it's good, we'll put it on."

"You won't put it on."

David said, "You've got to get along in the theater, John."

"No, I don't. I don't have to have anything to do with the theater."

David turned sideways to John and leaned his head back on the brown partition. "Why do you write poetry that is not understandable?"

"I didn't say it wasn't understandable. I said you, they wouldn't understand it."

"Why write it if I don't understand it?"

"You will understand it, in a way. If you will only take it as a sound, at first, you will understand it. Then as a playing with perspective."

"Then let us put it on," Mo said. "We understand everything there is to know about sound."

David's head came away from the partition. He stared at Mo. He buttoned his overcoat.

"Let's go," he said to Miss Twombly.

"Do we have to? I haven't had a drink yet."

"Yes. I have to play tonight."

"Oh, do you play?" asked Myny.

"What do you play?" asked Mo.

David was moving faster than anyone else, standing up, trying to get out of the crowded booth. "Merely players," David said. "We're all merely players."

The barkeep looked up. Everyone in the booth, out of the booth, was moving, scrambling, scurrying. He smiled.

David and Miss Twombly stood just inside the door. He was settling his scarf and she was buttoning her suede coat.

John handed David his hat.

"Mister MacFarlane," he asked, "where are you playing tonight?"

"At the Club Solo. Want to come?"

"Is it all right if I do come?"

"Of course it's all right. Why wouldn't it be?" David turned his head away.

"I'll come in later. I've got to meet some friends."

"All right. See you later."

David was through the door, on the sidewalk, breathing air.

"Goodbye," said Miss Twombly. "See you later."

"See you later."

John fussed with his coat, waiting for them to be completely gone. The three American youngmen were still in the booth the others had vacated, shouting orders at the bartender, who was reacting slowly, drying his hands on his apron. He smiled at John.

John waved at him and went out.

8

"If you hate taxis so much, why do you take them?"

"Goddamn it, can't you shut up once?"

David had said the name of the restaurant, *Chez Michèle*, simply that, using French pronunciation as he understood it, even slurring it, and then had kept absolutely quiet.

"Oh, David. I can't say nothing in a taxi. I feel positively weird."

"Damn it. Shut up. It costs too much money to speak English in a taxi."

"What do you care? You could have your own car in every city. And driver."

"You be quiet in a taxi. They waltz you all over the city, to run up the meter."

"You and your taxis."

"I want you to be quiet in a taxi. Rome, Paris, even in London."

"Now be nice. You're helping him send his children to school."

"Yeah. In Switzerland. Swiss schools are full of the kids of European taxi drivers."

"You hate them all. Did you ever think some of them might be honest?"

"No."

He could find his way around Berlin, Munich, Amsterdam, Paris, Toulon, Nice, Genoa, Rome, London, Sydney—even in Bombay he could pedal around to Malabar Point without a road map. Still he was a foreigner, obviously a foreigner, everywhere. His clothes never looked exactly like the clothes in that region, wherever—too light, too heavy, too foreign, too American—and taxi drivers were the first to notice. He never knew much of the language, a few words, the same few words; I want, Where is, Yes, No, Please, I'm sorry, Beer, Steak, Eggs, How much, never the recent history of the weather or of the politics. Frequently he was carrying a suitcase, directing the driver to hotels that were unabashedly tourist. Too often they took him around unnecessary blocks, assumed he did not know the currency, tried to demand more than was on the meter.

"Oh, well," he said. "I guess we're going to go for a ride tonight. We might as well enjoy it. What a pretty neon sign. Did you see the pretty neon sign?"

"Aren't your hands cold?"

"No."

"Mine are freezing. Here, take my hands. Yours are nice and warm. Yours are never cold."

"Beautiful Paris. Lots of pretty neon signs."

"You do have nice hands."

"I'm sorry," he said.

He moved almost on top of her, trying to embrace her and kiss her. His overcoat bunched between them.

"Hello," David said.

"Hello."

"How have you been?"

"Terrible. I missed you. Do you know I missed you?"

"I missed you, too," David said.

"Did you bring me a trinket?"

"No."

"Did you bring me a teddy bear, to sleep with?"

"No. I didn't bring you anything."

"What a mean old fellow you are."

"I wasn't sure you'd be here."

"Of course I'd be here. Where do you think I might go?"

"I don't know."

The streetlights they were passing were sending lights and shadows down her face with an exact rhythm. Going around a corner the taxi swayed, throwing more of his weight on her.

She turned her head on the cushion and looked out the window.

"Isn't it odd," she said. "You and I go away from each other and we don't know if we will ever see each other again and we don't even write."

David sat back in his seat, facing front. The taxi was going up a broad, straight boulevard, between trees.

"I guess we're too busy," he said. "Too much travel and too fast."

"It's not that. I don't know what it is." She asked, "Can you tell me what it is?"

"I don't know."

She took his hand again, bringing it to her lap. "It's all right now. We're together."

"Yes."

"I didn't hear you."

"Yes. I said it's okay."

In the restaurant they sat in a corner. The waiter had taken their coats. The table tops and counters were black and white marble and the chairs black wrought iron. The place was flooded with light.

"It's cold out," she said.

"Are we going to have supper?"

Her chair was against the back wall.

"Don't you want supper?" he asked.

Unbeautiful, unwarm Chez Michèle had good food.

"You never eat supper."

"You do." David said to the waiter, "Bring us the menu."

They were sitting across from each other, looking at each other over the marble top of the table.

"Do you still like Paris?" he asked.

"Yes. Nobody does anything."

"What do you do?"

"Nothing."

The waiter brought them the menus and waited.

"What are you going to have?" she asked.

David said to the waiter, "Do you have any milk? Cold milk?"

"Yes," he answered.

"I mean refrigerated milk."

She closed her menu. "I'll have milk, too," she said. "Only make it Scotch for me."

When the waiter gave his order the barman looked over at them.

"I'm sorry I didn't bring you anything from Amsterdam."

"It would be much too conventional. I'm glad you didn't."

"Do you mind my not bringing anything?"

"I would have thrown it away if you had. You were probably mad at me anyway. Were you?"

"I don't know. No, I don't think so."

"Don't ever be angry with me."

"I don't think I could be."

"Because when you're away I sit and listen to your recordings over and over again. You know I love you."

"We aren't going to say that, remember?"

"I forgot. I don't love you, then."

"We weren't going to say that either."

The waiter brought one milk and one Scotch and water on a tray.

"Don't you want any supper?"

"Not really."

"All right. You can have a sandwich later at the club."

"That will be nice."

"You are coming to the club, aren't you?"

"Of course. Don't you want me?"

"Yes. I want you very much. You know that."

"Yes. I do."

She was touching his hands again.

"How's the milk?"

"Warm."

"Poor David. Poor, poor David."

The skin around Ms Tuesday's mouth was beginning to draw in, toward her mouth, draw down, toward her chin. Gray had gotten into the skin under her eyes, darker than the gray around the brown of her eyes. The bone of her nose was just beginning to be visible.

"Oh," she said. "I don't want those letters."

"You made that pretty obvious."

"I'm afraid they're from Dan Prescott. Oh, David, may I have another Scotch?"

He waved his hand at the waiter and pointed to her glass.

"How does John what's-his-name come to have any letters of yours?"

"You remember when you put me on the train in Rome, to come up here? I met John on the train. At first he snubbed me, so I made him talk to me all the way up Italy."

"Why did he snub you?"

"He was perfectly polite and all that. I guess he came to Europe to get away from Americans, and here was one, plunk in his lap."

"Maybe he just didn't want to be attracted to you."

"Do you think so? David, really, you're so understanding. I never thought of that."

"He is attracted to you. And I don't think he likes it much."

"For heaven's sake, why not?"

"Pride."

"Pride? Thank you." She put her empty glass on the tray. "I don't care about that. I don't care about the letters, either. I don't want to read them. I bet there are stacks of them."

"So how did John come to have them?"

"He sent me to this friend of his in Paris, a real estate dealer, in fact, whose name I absolutely forget. I went to see him after I was here a week. The man called a woman in French, even escorted me to the rooms himself, carried my bag, everything. What could I do? The rooms were terrible. Awful. I said, 'Oh, how lovely.' I didn't feel I could walk out immediately. He'd been so nice. So I hedged on the week's rent and walked out in two days."

"So what was wrong with the rooms?"

"They were right across the street from a Catholic school. Think of it. A Catholic school. I came to Paris to live in a Catholic school-yard. The bells would ring in the morning and the children would sing their prayers in their little smocks by the windows and more bells would ring and they'd go out into the play yard and play sweet games with the nuns watching from the windows to make sure nothing nasty or evil came into the games."

"Sounds great."

"That's not what I came to Paris for. I've had all that before, believe me, at Miss Leighton's School for Girls."

"What did you come to Paris for?"

"I don't know. Oh, David, do help me."

"I can't help you. I want to marry you."

"Help me with your love."

"All right."

"Do you still want to marry me and settle down in New England and burn leaves in the autumn?"

"Yes. I do."

"Oh, David. I don't know how you can help me."

The ice cubes were perfectly solid at the bottom of her empty glass.

"I don't either."

The waiter said, "Would you like to order now?"

"David, please may I have a drink?"

"No."

"A Scotch," she said to the waiter. "Things just aren't that way, David. Things aren't that nice."

"Why not? Maybe they can be. That's the way I would like things."

"You wouldn't really. Not really."

"Yes, I would. Believe me."

"It's all so conventional. I had such a crappy conventional up-bringing."

"Well, I didn't. I wish I had. I wish I had gone to school in a small town deep in the country, married the girl next door, taken over my father's hardware business and gone to church every Sunday."

"And made love in the Standard Number One Position every Friday, Sunday, and Wednesday."

"Something like that."

"Not you, David."

"Me."

"Would you trade your music for it?"

"Absolutely," he answered. "Without a moment's hesitation."

This time she left the empty glass on the table. The waiter replaced it.

"Maybe *you* should marry Dan Prescott."

David said, "He's going to be better looking than you are, very soon."

She drained the glass, ice cubes against her lips, head tipped back, her throat swallowing one-two-three-four-five times.

She said, "His father is a minister and he is a minister and everything, David, is very girl-scouty and picnicy on Sunday."

"Come on," he said. "I've got to go to work."

"Will you come with me later, back to my rooms?"

He stood, slid his chair under, against the table.

"You've never seen them," she said.

"No. I haven't."

"Why haven't you, ever?"

He stood near her, waiting for her to rise. "For some unknown reason, I've been thinking I shouldn't."

"You will come. Tonight."

She was still in her chair. He reached for her elbow.

He said, "We'll see."

9

The music, the music was real, absolute, there, always there, moving, swinging, jumping, leaping, sliding, soaring.

Dave, surprising Chump, stated the theme of "Greasy Pig," briskly, alone, ready to go ahead with or without him, introducing the secondary rhythm almost immediately, insinuating it in the third bar, including it completely in the fifth. Somewhere between his two hands was a third rhythm then, clear but unexpected to Chump, one that only the best drummer could have picked up fast enough, without sounding late, lost, confused, one that the audience would not consciously hear at all. Chump brushed the harmony, barely outlined it, tried to wake up, catch up with this one o'clock playing at 9:03. He lurched into the first variation of the theme a little more loudly than usual, glad to dominate, lead, put Dave behind him, get on top of, with, the motion, stretching it a little further than usual, leaving in it more threads than usual to be picked up later, pulled, used. The piano came up behind him and the two dovetailed beautifully, Chump finishing what he was doing with an unlikely, simple repeat, immediately falling behind the piano sound, to mutter, to outline again by hitting the harmony sequentially that third rhythm Dave had buried, somewhere. Dave pushed the theme, bringing out the secondary rhythm more, keeping the primary rhythm consistent in the left hand, then viscerally at least, inconsistent, just reminding the audience of it again and again, rhythmically, keeping it in their minds. Then suddenly, loudly, perfectly, Chump rose, giving the third rhythm complete, absolute, from the horn, Dave retreating to just the two on the piano, neatly, then all three, behind Chump with two, absolutely with Chump with one. The theme again, growing, a note, two notes, the phrase: Dave and Chump hit the theme of "Greasy Pig" together in the third rhythm, now absolute, total, there had never been a first, a second; cut to a simple line, worked it again, then hit only that phrase, finally that note, harmony, in upbeat.

Through the streams of platform light piercing the smoke Chump saw the audience surprised, obviously awakened early from their cocktail-dinner-after-dinner-drinks and liking it, being roused, being happy. Their applause was rapid, their feet were moving, there was a lot of chatter. Unusual for this time of the evening, for the first set, the first piece, the chairs were not facing each other over the tables; most had been turned, facing the platform.

Immediately Dave began the old "Deme Lo," ignoring the applause, Chump more with him, it, this time. In the first bar Chump turned to the piano, to hear it, send his own sound into its body, mix it with Dave's. Under the lid, with a perfectly serious face, trying to concentrate, Dave winked at Chump. Expecting, knowing this defection would throw Dave off, Chump turned, swung the barrel of his horn out to the audience, raised it over their heads, gave them the phrase upside down, distracted them. He could hear the audience, its breath, react more to his noise than to Dave's slight stammer. This was one piece everyone knew, one thing they came to hear, waited for, greeted like an old friend, with smiles, interest, a high critical sense, demanding it be played, especially by these two, at least as well as it was on their records at home, on their radios. Tonight Dave and Chump not only played it, they played with it, with themselves, their fame, their own recording: after the first release they began understating themselves, leaving holes the audience could, would, did fill in. Sometimes either Dave or Chump hit only a single note of an outstanding phrase, the other continuing anyway, keeping going, loyally. In the final release Dave imitated the arrangement of another pianist, equally popular, playing too with him and his fame now, exaggerating wildly, humorously, a trick or two of the man's style, for a phrase falling a beat behind Chump, then a beat ahead, then emerging, perfectly, scurrying into the theme finally with Chump, as Dave MacFarlane.

The audience roared, cheered, yelled, called, stomped their feet uselessly on the carpet at the end of the second piece. Along the wall by the kitchen door were the white-coated waiters, lined up, not moving.

Again not waiting, this time purposely flat, falsetto, Chump went "Wang, Wang Blues." From behind him, the piano strident, marching muffled through the muddy windows of a church basement came "Glory, glory, hallelujah." Then, together, rapidly, breathlessly, like a speeded-up Chaplin, they played the melody of "Red, White and You," Chump hitting, holding the last note, C, for sixteen bars while Dave smoothly, ever so smoothly established all the character of that song, all its peculiar northern-southern prairie national-personal loneliness. Chump fell off, burping his C, then came in behind Dave smooth himself, letting Dave push forward with it. With Dave again, then behind his sound, then together again, camp style, Chump finally broke to the "Battle Hymn" again, high up, out of key, hitting only the last note in perfect harmony with the piano, holding it, the piano going, diddling, then returning to that harmony again.

The white coats along the walls rushed then, the waiters grabbing up their trays, going from table to table, snatching up glasses, trying to get orders. Many of the men were standing.

Ms Tuesday gave a little wave. The three men at her table were not standing. Her lips said, "Hi, Chump."

Two were shouting "727" and one shouted in strange, sideways English, "No Mo' Money."

They played "Trainman's Dust," continuing their pace, their excitement. Then more quietly, sweetly, "Both of Us: The Absolute We." But to finish that set they raised everything again, themselves, the audience, with a new one, a just-out one, "727."

"We're going to be hard to follow," Dave said.

No one, nothing, was playing at that club but themselves.

Chump followed Dave to Ms Tuesday's table.

"You're playing especially well tonight, boys. Nat Hentoff must be here."

She kissed each of them on the cheek.

He sat down and she turned to him.

"You still have it, haven't you, Chump?"

He said nothing.

"You'll always have it."

Dave was still standing.

"Oh, let me introduce you to these other gentlemen."

Her voice hung in midair, a question, to someone. Everyone was standing.

"John?"

Chump stood up, too.

Basso profundo, rumbling, kind, with the rhythm of the current at the bottom of a deep, broad river, John said who the other two men where.

Chump listened. The sentences were short, hesitant, questioning, afraid, each one willing to be pushed aside, discounted, swept out by the next. One man, heavy, about forty, turned toward Dave, his forearm flat on the table. He had a voice as dry as chalk. The other, almost as old, lean, paused several beats before he spoke each time, apparently thinking, as if what he was going to say were too important to blurt out, and when he spoke his voice had a slight catch to it, a quake, most noticeable in the second and third words.

John was silent, using his eyes, his smile, his short, deep laughs to bring speech from others. He was interested not in what they were saying, contrary to his gestures and laughter, but that they were saying. His noises, nervous too, were urging, encouraging, gently pushing.

The oldest of the three said, "I enjoyed your playing very much. I'm black, but I must confess I know very little about jazz."

"You probably know more than I do," said Dave.

"Simply speaking," the man said, "what is jazz? I mean, at this point in history."

"I don't know, sir," said Dave. "What is jazz, Chump?"

All but Ms Tuesday's head swiveled to Chump.

"It's play," said Dave. "Everything is play."

"I was expecting something loud and stomping," the man said. "Not light, and intricate."

"Not from Mister MacFarlane," John said.

"I wish you'd call me David, or something. What's all this use of the word Mister?"

"All right. David."

"Or something," said Ms Tuesday.

"I was expecting loud and stomping stuff, what we used to call washboard music." The man's voice went up a quarter tone. "It's really quite nice."

"This is the way the young are," the other said. "They sit and chew their cuds and say nothing."

The oldest said, "I have some nice recordings. But they are of the classics. Bach, in particular."

"You can buy recordings of David and Chump," John said.

"Oh, can I buy your recordings?" The voice went down the quarter tone again. "I didn't know that."

"I'll give some to you. I'll send them over."

"That would be very kind. I enjoy my high fidelity very much."

"You're all being very erudite," said Ms Tuesday. "Let's talk about sex."

Her voice was louder, harsher, more direct. Chump counted sixteen beats in the following silence.

"Whose?" Dave asked.

Loud, purposeful, but slurring, she said, "How's your sex life, John?"

Forward, backward: John's voice continue to encourage, but not happily, not even with that degree of sincere insincerity. "Fine."

"Is it very difficult for you here in Paris?"

"Have a sandwich," Dave said to her.

"Nothing is very difficult here in Paris," said the eldest. His voice was up a half tone.

"Have a sandwich. You haven't eaten yet."

"It's all right," John said.

"I'll order a sandwich for you."

"They don't serve Scotch sandwiches."

"You don't need a Scotch sandwich."

"But, darling, I really don't want a sandwich. I want to find out about John's sex life."

"I don't care."

"It's all right," John said.

"I'll have a glass of milk instead. Milk will make you happy."

"I'm afraid we've got to be leaving," the eldest said, standing up. "I promised John I would give him a copy of the new book tonight."

Everyone stood up, leaving Ms Tuesday to blink at the tablecloth. They were all shaking hands, talking, saying good night. Dave promised to send over a recording the next day. They were glad to have met Dave, and Chump, too.

Chump started back to the platform ahead of Dave.

Dave was saying to Ms Tuesday, "You just sit there. Don't drink anything."

"All right. I won't."

"Just sit there."

" 'Lech'! 'Lech'!"

" 'Too Long'!"

"Lunch Counter," "Lech," "Number 95," "Sorry," "727," again, "Don't." Then another set, and another, another.

Chump faced the broad, two-o'clock-in-the-morning street. There was no wind. Across the street under a tree was a taxi. Its headlights and motor were off.

Chump took his free hand out of his topcoat pocket and waved at the taxi. The motor did not start, the headlights did not go on. He crossed, opened the street-side door, and sat in the backseat.

"The hotel of Michael Mass," he said.

The driver was slumped forward. His forehead was against the top of the wheel. His jaw was forward, toward the horn button. Beneath a heavy woolen shirt his shoulders were rounded, relaxed.

Chump got out the sidewalk-side, stood for a moment, looking both ways, then headed in the direction from which there seemed to be more sound, of traffic.

Walking, naked saxophone under his arm, both hands in his pockets, he said to himself, "The hotel of Michael Mass, the hotel of Michael Mass."

10

The night suddenly had warmed. John walked the long way home, new book in his overcoat pocket, past the Club Solo, closed, dark now, past a taxi parked under a tree, its driver apparently asleep, along the broad still boulevard. He turned right at the Café Jérome, past the house where Miss Twombly did not live, the schoolyard, up the narrow street to where he did live.

The closet door was open a crack, as he had left it, enough for the ceiling light to stripe the darkness. He hung his overcoat before removing the book from its outside pocket.

Reaching from the Morris chair he pulled the chain on the reading light.

To Johnny Nelson, the Bart, with fondest regards. There had been the music, the conversation, the cognac anyway. In his own room now was absolute silence.

His was a big attic room with one huge window running the length of one inside wall of the roof. Along the window he had built a shelf that he used as a desk. On one part of the shelf he had the long poem he was working on, "Pentecost," pencils and notebooks and scrap paper all neatly arranged. There was a typewriter with a little easel in front of it he used for holding papers he was copying, lines he wanted to sit back and think about, walk around the room and glance at. Between two piles of manuscript, the original and the copy, was an apple. To the left was an area where he did occasional work, scribbled notes to himself; to the right was a place for his correspondence. At the left end of the shelf, in the corner, was a red leather book, with "RECORD, Harvard Cooperative Society," on the binding in gold. There was a light chair he moved back and forth from one place along the shelf to another.

Against the inside wall of the room was a cot he had built himself, six feet seven inches long, not very wide, a bright Indian blanket taut on top. Over the cot he had built bookshelves, filled neatly but to their capacity, Flaubert beside Saroyan, Eliot and Frost a few volumes away from each other, Grenier, David Grayson, Camus in between. Among several volumes of Oriental poetry was Milton's *Paradise Lost*. John would reach up from his cot, pull down two or three before sleeping, listen to them, have them converse through his mind, read a line from this, a paragraph from that. All the voices, of the *Bhagavad-Gita*, of *Aquinas*, of Nietzsche, Thoreau, and Paul Tillich would speak to him quietly in the stillness of his room.

A new book he would read facing away from the window in his Morris chair, his legs stretched out, shoes off, feet resting on the bottom of the cot. Beside the chair was a small, square table, a pipe stand, canister, ashtray, and pile of new books crowding the shaded reading light.

Another table was against the peaked, outside wall of that room. There was a record player on it, a few albums. In its exact center was a hot plate, a coffeepot on one burner, a saucepan he sometimes used for making soup or tea on the other. He rinsed these things in the bathroom, between the foot of his bed and the closet. On the floor was a circular, bright Indian rug he had had in his bedroom as a boy. The opposite inside wall was, except for the door, floor-to-ceiling bookcase, the books arranged alphabetically by author, *Life Against Death*, Brown, after *Jane Eyre*, Brontë.

In his closet were clothes he had had made for himself in Spain, all dark, conservatively cut, freshly brushed and pressed, with white shirts and dark ties. He had no other clothes, no workpants, no sweaters.

Even reading in his chair, alone in the room in the middle of the night, his suit coat was on, his necktie was tight.

> When the Am is Swingin' Low:
> Hear me my song?
> When the Am is swingin' low
> And the Do is swingin' high,
> What man, Man, is safe
> From cryin', O, why?
> The world is sure, o little God,

While work is bein' done;
And baby-safe
While out there doin' fun.
But standin' lone, in the
Bottom of a coffee cup,
The world is awful still, an'
Them sneakin' why's come up.
Help me keep this prayer, o little God,
And keep me on workin' and on tryin'.
Keep the Am a swingin' low
An' the Do a swingin' high, Man . . .

He flipped *Hear Me My Song*, Candler Press, onto the cot. He filled a pipe from the canister. Without lighting the pipe, he moved the light chair to the left end of the shelf. He sharpened two pencils with his pocket knife, thinking, dropping the shavings onto a piece of paper. He crumpled the paper, threw it into the wastebasket.

Lighting his pipe, he looked at what was on the easel, his own work.

(Looking to a point before the moon,
The voices behind him, in the room.)

The Drunk saying:
Christ, I'm not intoxicated.
Of course not, the whiskey said. Did you think
whiskey was intoxicated?
Christ, he said. I thought whiskey was intoxication
itself. I never knew, but I thought I did.
Disappointing, whiskey said. Bitterly disappointing.

The Priest saying:
O, god Satyr, answer my plea!
I humbly pray you take your eyes
Off Thebes Land, once casting them
To the realm of the gods.
Not up you look, but moreso down;
Olympus high is petted still.

He sat facing the window, the few lights of the black city in front of, below him. He uncapped his fountain pen, a green and black Pelican 120, and opened the leather-bound book to page 342.

I do not like the black tone of voice, when it is contrived, forced—especially when it is wheedling, needling, when it assumes, makes a policy out of ignorance, no matter what it is saying. Jive is not my tone of voice. It never has been. I doubt it has ever been Clay's tone of voice, either. Reading his work just now, privately printed, I wanted to sharpen pencils, fill up rough paper, work out his own ideas in a tone of voice closer to his own, to mine. But I do not trust the after-midnight inspiration.

I do not like cartoons. I know I am foolish. I overcompensate, but I do not smoke my pipe in public, although I prefer it, and I do not wear a beard or a beret. I don't carry an attaché case or wear strange tokens in my lapel, either. Cartoon evidences of what a man is, to me, detract from his being: unsure of his reality, he presents an appearance; nothing, he is glad to be taken as anything. I believe in the universality, the multiplicity of Man. At the risk of being his own cartoon, being, in reality, many things, I prefer his attempt to appear as nothing.

What I am trying to do in "Pentecost" is to attain, or at least indicate, this multiplicity: set a dominant, sympathetic perspective, the main string of a mobile, then break it down into a few, empathic perspectives, fairly balanced strings, dependent upon, part of, the dominant. If it is clear that on paper one never attains the reality of the viewed, except as an idea, but only of the viewer, it is essential to present multiple aspects of the viewer, or at least to indicate there are multiple aspects, viewer-components. To suggest otherwise, that the mature perspective is inflexible, absolute, without a past, a coming together, is wrong, is to present only a cartoon of Man. Rather his perspective is of indefinite aspects, channeled through, individualized, controlled by the unified perspective of maturity.

In "Pentecost" there are many voices of men, or of a man, the voices of greed, lust, piety, fear, tranquility, hate, love—even the empty voice, the no-voice of the inarticulate—the censorial voice of the priest that is in all of us and the excuse-making voice of the penitent that is in all of us, brave but humble and cringing. These are the natural, universal voices of Man, not the superficial racial, ethnic, social voices. I want to make clear by contrast some of the voices, that there are voices, and put down something of the range of these voices from hope to exaltation to disgust, and to make from the sound itself the play, a meaning. Not the meaning always of the word, although that is important, too, if not in its unattainable self then in its very important approach to that single mean-

ing. More than that, I want the meaning of all the words, aspects, together, in play, in their sound and rhythm, in their simple progression in tone toward an ecstasy or a disgust—anyway, toward an exhaustion that the single profound meanings of the word do justify.

I want all the turmoil and inexact stress of the creation of Man that is spontaneous, a marvelous thing, in "Pentecost," which happens not when a man is born but sometime before he dies, which is not really Creation, but Pentecost, that moment when all the perspectives come together in voices and pressure him to a good exhaustion, horrible dryness, the unified perspective that is maturity.

Later, if there is much left to this year, this financial freedom, I would like to commence a mature play in earnest. From that single, unified perspective has come only horrid sympathy, the righteous, the superior, the absolute, the inflexible, of which we have seen enough, religiously, politically, spiritually, journalistically, artistically. One can escape such existential dryness by using that mature, unified perspective only as control, detachment, then one must break it down again, fragment it, channel through it, empathically, using all those perspectives that are genuinely one's own, multiple aspects on the more profound human relations, with oneself, one's world, one's idea of God.

Someday, when I am done, I will write a precept to "Pentecost" that will say none of this. I will take my chances with the public, risk being read as a bad realist, one whose perspective is not unified, or omniscient, whose tone of voice is not set, that is, not read at all, a sow's ear. I may not have the ability to carry it off, artistically, technically. I trust I will never find myself agreeing to buy five thousand copies from Candler Press, autographing each with fondest regards, to pay the bill, unload the stock. But in the new world, assaulted by two comprehensive, terrifying elements, technology and leisure, I believe a more inabsolute view of Man must become politically, artistically operative, even as viewer and reporter, as sexual subject and object, a more essential, variable, multiple, universal view. Society now makes a Man a child, wondering, dependent. To remain an entity, an operative man, he must have the maturity to be a child, to play, as the world bids him do. I write such nonsense in this journal to avoid writing it other places, to avoid writing other things, post-midnight-inspired.

I may find someday, if I succeed, that the black voice is partly mine. If I do, I will use it.

*   *   *

Through the window he watched the light rise in Paris, over the roofs, into the streets. Somewhere, in a museum, he had seen Boglioni's *City Awakening*. Still writing in his mind, without pen or paper, standing at his window to see: *that is New York, where a day is a surge of power, must be to contest with the machines, to rein them in, to hurry to push the right buttons at the right time, to be dressed properly in the great grinding noise of all the machines. It is not Paris, where the time passes like a good cognac going down the throat, noticeable but usually running smoothly, watching the sun slide across the street from one cafe on the sidewalk to another.*

A figure crossed the street below him wandering Paris in the dawn, head down, hands in overcoat pockets. *David? It is you, David. So you have loved the world twice tonight, once through your piano, once through Janet Twombly. I wonder, which of these moving, changing instruments, variously dependent upon you to make them swing, returned your love the better?*

11

David had slammed the door of the cab.

"Drunk."

"We can walk. It's much warmer now."

"The only cab in sight and the driver is passed out drunk."

They walked along the three-o'clock-in-the-morning street.

"Surprising how it warmed up in the middle of the night. The wind must have changed to the southwest or something." She put her arm through David's. "I feel much better now. I really do."

"It's going to rain," David said. "Later today. I can smell it."

Walking beside him she was the cheerleader who had waited for the halfback after the game. She had had a steak sandwich, french fries, a beer for supper in the Club Solo kitchen at two-thirty in the morning.

"I'm really much better."

"I'm glad."

She held his hand and skipped sideways beside him.

"David, I'd like a kitten. Can I have a kitten?"

"You can't have a kitten when you're traveling."

"I'm not traveling. I'll settle down here in Paris. I'll live all my life here in Paris so I can have a kitten."

They recrossed the road, turned left into a dark, crowded, twisting street. A woman in a figured, flared coat and brimmed hat waited in a doorway. She looked at David with exaggerated eyes.

Ms Tuesday put her hand in front of her mouth. "What do you say, old man: do you want her? Only twenty million francs for twenty minutes: a million a minute, if you can move that fast."

"Shut up."

"Will you sneak back to her, David, after you leave me, like you usually do?"

He followed Ms Tuesday up three flights. Her rooms were at the top of a short building. The foyer, steps, were well lit, scrubbed, but the smell of cooking oil hung in the halls from yesterday and a hundred years before.

He stood inside the door, lifting the scarf from his neck. He had seen apartments like this everywhere, in London, Rome, New York, Boston, Des Moines. Two rooms, a living room, a bedroom, a kitchenette—refrigerator, sink, stove—inset in the wall and hidden incompletely behind a folding screen, a bath installed in a closet long after the invention of indoor plumbing, but with original equipment. The fireplace had rubbish thrown into it. The furniture was wicker, light and stringy, with lumpy cushions. There were no real windows, only one narrow French door covered with gauze leading to a section of the roof. On the walls were posters, *Riviera, Côte D'Azur, La Rade De Villefranche-Sur-Mer, FRANCE, Minister des Travaux, des Transportes et du Tourisme—Direction Générale du Tourisme—Printed in France—Published by and for the French Government—Kodak-Extrachrome*; a blow-up of Humphrey Bogart; an anti-word, barely legible psychedelic swirl advertising a Human Be-In in Washington Square. He knew from experience there would be a copy of Van Gogh's *Sunflowers* in the bedroom. He dropped his coat over the back of the wicker divan.

He said, "Airy."

"Do you like it?"

"No."

"You make the fire," she said. "And I'll make some cocoa."

"All right."

On his knees he removed some of the charred cans, the smokey bottle, to the lip of the fireplace.

She came back with two glasses of Scotch.

"Here, I'll light the fire," she said.

David sat back on the floor and watched her.

In a moment she sat back with him and said, "Kiss me."

Then she got up to turn out the lights and came back.

"I really am sorry if I was rude to John," she said. "I guess I was a little drunk. Those damn letters. I don't want to open them."

"Don't be afraid of them."

"How's the cocoa?" she asked.

David picked up his glass of Scotch. "You're a fine cook." She had not had a drink of hard liquor since ten o'clock.

"David, what do you really want?"

"You."

"No, I mean seriously. For all time."

"You. Burning those autumn leaves you mentioned."

"And milk to drink with your lunch and cold beer on Saturday afternoon and frankfurts and beans for Saturday night supper. Meat-loaf once a week."

"Yes. I guess so."

"That sounds terrible."

"Not to me."

"But you can't have that, can you? You can't ever live that way. Not with the piano."

"No, I guess not. Not for a while, anyway."

"I'm glad you can't," she said. "That sounds terrible."

Humphrey Bogart was smiling paternally in the flickering light of the wall.

"I want something good, Ms Tuesday. Something solid and fine: a marriage that is real, and lasting; an old automobile that will run just great."

"And you want to grow fat gracefully, make love on Fridays, Sundays, and Wednesdays."

"Maybe I do."

"That's not what I want."

"What do you want?"

"I don't know. Please, David. I want a kitten. Will you get me a kitten?"

Her tears glistened in the firelight, in the corner of her eyes, on her cheeks, suddenly, inexplicably there.

"Of course you can have a kitten. I'll get you a hundred kittens."

"I don't want a hundred kittens. You can't love a hundred kittens. I only want one."

David said, "We could have a dog, if we lived in New England."

"You want a dog?"

"Very much."

"We'll have a dog and a cat and live in New England."

"No, we won't," David said. "You know we won't."

With her index finger she drew a line in the dust on the floor.

"David, you know that New England doesn't exist anymore. Your dream has turned to cement and plate glass windows. The village green has been plowed under for a six-lane highway and white-steepled churches are gray with exhaust. The few areas that have been preserved, by vigorous battles with the auto-politicians, are terribly phony. Even as a suburb, New England is inferior: the roads are so bad."

The fire was not doing well.

"That's quite a pretty speech."

"I've thought about it. David, there is no such America. There are no pretty snowstorms. Instead there is the sound of glass and steel smashing into each other, the unavoidable sight of blood on filthy cement."

"There might be places left."

"Not for long."

"There are a lot of places outside the megalopolises."

"Filled with interbred half-wits."

"That's not true."

"Go see how many share your concern for B-flat in Podunk, Alabama. Blues?" She put on a drawl. "We ain't heard none of that nigger music 'round here in years. Good guitar music, country and western: people in this country know what they want."

"Well, someone is buying a hell of a lot of records."

In the dark behind the screen she was dropping three ice cubes into her empty glass. A bottle poured for a long moment; the tap went on for an instant.

"David?"

He did not look around.

"Can we make love now?"

"No."

"Why not?"

He turned, his side to the low fire, knees drawn up, arms around his legs.

"You know why."

"You know I don't? I never really have known why."

She was standing at the edge of the screen, her hair most blonde in that light, waiting, hesitating, expecting, a full glass in her right hand.

"I guess I'm crazy," he said.

"You have other women. All the time."

Slowly, listening to himself as if he were working something out on the piano, he said, "I have the crazy idea I'd like to keep this one thing good. I'd like to marry you. I'd like to think I met you one

Sunday after church and I asked you to the country club dance the following Saturday. And you said I had to meet your parents, which was easy because they were right there and had always known my parents. And they liked me, maybe remembered me from the Boy Scout parades. And we're both thinking that one day we'd like to get married and live in a house a half-mile between the houses of our parents. Let's pretend, just with each other, that there is something sacred and holy about ourselves, and that people love us, and care what we do."

The edge of the thin carpet near the fireplace had brown holes burned in it.

She said, "David, could you possibly be thinking I'm a virgin?"

He crossed his legs, then rested his forearms on his thighs.

"Because I'm not, David."

"Of course not."

She sat on the floor again, her back to the edge of the divan seat, her drink beside her. "I have a friend who says anyone who is a virgin beyond the age of twenty-one is vaguely suspicious."

"Who is that?"

"A German doctor I know. A gynecologist. I've never told him I was a virgin at twenty-one. I'm not vaguely suspicious. I'm just a half-wit from Columbia Falls, Maine."

David felt the smoke of the fire in his eyes. The fire was not bright enough to see how thick the smoke in the room was. He looked at the gauze-covered French door.

"I've got to go."

"No, you haven't," she said.

He stood up, saw the bulk of his overcoat on the back of the divan.

"Honestly, David. This is the last time."

"The last time for what?"

"The last time you leave me." Her voice was breaking through tightness, sincerely complaining. "This has been going on almost three years now. I went to New York thinking you'd be there. You came to Europe, and I followed you here. I've been in city after city with you, London, Rome, Paris, meeting you like a stranger, an acquaintance, in each one. I've played with every other three-legged animal in my path, but not you. Not precious David MacFarlane."

Reaching around her, he pulled the coat toward him.

She grabbed it, jerked it out of his hand.

"No. If you leave now, David, you can stay gone. I'm sick of this."

"I know, Ms Tuesday, you're right, you're right. But just at this moment, I don't feel like it. I'm tired. I got off an airplane yesterday morning, I worked all night, all the night before. I don't even remember what country I was in this morning."

"You're also angry."

She let go of his coat.

"I'm also angry."

He put on his coat, the scarf around his neck.

She stood, smoothed the scarf under his lapels. "Do you understand why you're angry?"

"What I don't need is phony psychoanalysis from an escaped alien."

Going around the divan, toward the door, leaving, he stopped. "Do you know what I want?"

She stood like a lady at a tea, waiting to be told how Jason's broken elbow is feeling. "No. I don't."

"I want a son. Is that hard to understand? I want a woman-wife-mother who can have and take care of a son, with grace and wit. God, is that hard to understand? Dickie-dunking I can get anywhere. Better lays, I dare say, than you—despite your considerable, post-twenty-one experience."

Saying nothing, slowly she took the few steps toward him in the almost-dark, grinning, and slapped his face. Both hands pulling down on the lapels of his overcoat, she kissed him on the mouth.

He said, "And turn the lights on. If you're going to drink by yourself, you won't get so drunk if the lights are on."

12

"Reverend, we noticed you are traveling Tourist. I'm sure if we spoke to the Captain you could join us at table in First. Your conversation would be so much better than that of those people we have. People named Baldwin, from Philadelphia."

Two little women, side by side at the ship rail, small eyes in small faces under big hats.

"We've noticed you every day standing by this rail, looking at the water. But you're not traveling First Class."

They were in the glass-enclosed A-Deck promenade.

"I've never seen the water from so high up. I mean from a ship."

From his little sailboat the water had slid by beside him, bubbled behind him. On the troop ship on that long ride to that war to defend his heritage in a nation whose name his schoolbooks had missed he did not remember ever having seen the water, just having felt the giant, slow movement beginning in the bow, quivering, cracking, rolling to the stern, just having seen the green faces of his unit everywhere, the mess nearly empty meal after meal.

"I'm Mrs Parkhurst. This is Mrs Webb."

"Daniel Prescott," he said.

"Are you going to London, Reverend?"

"No, Ma'm. Paris. I'm being sent to our International Seminary there for three months, then to school in Provence for nine."

He had received a letter from Rome but only a postcard from Paris. *Wish you were here and all that glop. Love and good cookies, Janet.* His letters had not been answered or returned.

"We have a new young minister," said Mrs Parkhurst. "He's so intelligent we don't understand a word he says. I suppose all the young ones are alike."

He was carrying Feuerback's *The Essence of Christianity*. From Waterville to New York, through Boston by train, in three days at sea he had read twenty-five pages.

"Should we be calling you Doctor Prescott?" asked Mrs Webb.

"No, Ma'm."

"You look no older than the boys I used to teach," said Mrs Parkhurst. "I doubt you can convert our crusty ship captain!"

He believed in taking his rifle and his old dog over the ridge in the early morning to see what the animals were doing. He loved talking to his father. He believed in getting as sweaty and grimy as possible on the football field, cleaning up in a hot shower conscious she was waiting for him, finishing with a cold shower, dressing in clean good clothes, and walking Janet Twombly home in the crisp autumn air, brown loafers, white socks kicking fallen leaves in step.

"I've never converted anybody," Dan said. "At the moment I'm not sure I ever will."

According to their families he had nearly broken Janet's nose with his fist when they were seven. At ten he was protecting her from friendly bullies. When she was twelve years old she had looked at him quietly one day stepping from a Lightning onto a dock and he had felt the look, seen her, the sensation from his eyes tightening his throat, going to his arms, his legs. Laughing, panting, they tussled when they were thirteen. At fourteen he allowed her to teach him a few silly dances. At fifteen she astonished him with the full complication of a kiss. In most uncomfortable positions, deliriously, they necked in the Jeep on summer nights in the moonlight by the pond when they were sixteen.

"I'm afraid our new curate has a tendency to be rather high church," said Mrs Webb. "Intellectually formal."

She would sit on the football bench hour after hour, day after day, her light brown jacket wrapped around her, waiting for him to be through practice, to shower, dress. He waited for her letters in army training camp, and read them over and over sitting on the edge of his bunk.

"What do you think, Reverend, of those people who bring that dreadful music into the church service? I mean, guitars, if you can believe it."

After his short war, wounded badly, healing completely in his first two years of college, they would each return to Columbia Falls for the weekends, to see the football game, for movie dates, to attend his father's service. Dan loved the Westerns, seeing in them the parables of good and evil upon which American religious understanding is truly based. Before and after the snows he and Janet would trek the woods together with their rifles, sit on fallen trees, share the chocolate she had always carried, listen to the sounds. The boots he had bought her from L. L. Bean fitted her perfectly; always the exact amount of red sock lay over their tops; her red hunting cap was always at the same angle, off her forehead. Frowning, she would watch from the hill the new highway being pushed through in the valley, bright yellow bull-dozers working up and down mounds of rich brown earth, red trucks in a line waiting patiently to be filled.

Dan quoted *Bambi*: " 'Man.' "

She said, "Houses will be all through there soon. Cheap little houses without trees between them."

The late autumn or early spring air always put a red in her cheeks, complementing the shade of her brown eyes.

"I hate to be uncharitable, Reverend Prescott, but these people at our table, the Baldwins, are downright show-offs. You should have seen them dancing at the formal last night. And they're at least thirty-five."

Then one night, coming home from the movies, she had said, "This is boring."

He said, "Would you rather play cards?"

The home economics teacher at Miss Leighton's School for Girls had given her money and keys to the school station wagon, and sent her to the store in mid-morning to buy material for the class. She saw a hat, high, with flowers and ribbons, and bought it. She re-turned before lunch and said she had lost the fifty dollars. The extreme hat was noticed in her room while she was at study hall. *I'm sure it's not a matter of fifty dollars, or of this particularly silly-looking hat, a milliner's dream,* the letter to her parents, ask-ing for the fifty dollars back, said, *but more a matter of her wanting to do something impulsive, wild, a little rebellious, express her femininity, as it were.* The following weekend at home she blasted the hat with her father's twelve-gauge shotgun. She said she would never again wear a hat.

"I'm sorry I said that about the card playing," Dan said. "We'll do whatever you think will be fun."

"Fun? I think it would be fun to realize we're two healthy young animals with the whole damned world in front of us. Why are we waiting?"

"You are waiting," he said. "You're waiting for me."

"And then we are married and we wait for a child, for some parish to allot you one in the penny box. And then we wait for it to grow up. And then we wait to die. Dan, this isn't good enough."

"What do you want?" he asked.

"You. I want the world to go a little faster."

"You mean you and I should cohabitate."

"Cohabitate? Copulate, fornicate, screw; the word, Dan, is fuck."

"I'm sorry. I'm sorry I'm such a fuddy-duddy."

"No, I don't mean it, Dan. I mean I'd like there to be enough experience, frankness between us so you will not use the word cohabitate."

"I know."

She said, "I'm going to Boston, to get a job. Then God knows where."

"Why?"

"Why not? You went halfway around the world to play international football, shoot a lot of little, starving savages. Why shouldn't I have some fun?"

"Janet, you don't know what you're talking about."

"I mean, you got out once, away from the path of that damned, creeping bulldozer. At least you got to drive it once. Dan, I've got to get out, too, or I won't know what to do."

"The war was no fun, friend."

"I know it wasn't, Dan. Maybe I'll get wounded, too. But you learned something."

"Yes. I did."

"Please don't make it difficult for me," she said.

During that year he spent one weekend in Boston, visiting her, one in New York.

"Reverend, I don't know what you mean by Projection Theory, and I used to teach school." Mrs Parkhurst's little eyes in her little face under her big hat were dubious. "What do you mean we project our own wishes onto a cloud and call it heaven?"

"Actually, I haven't read much of the book yet," Dan said. "I had it in a course once, and never got a chance to read it."

Janet wrote him all about the interesting things the Harvard boys she knew were doing, and he scratched his head trying to make himself, Maine, interesting, exciting. She would ignore what he had written, writing back, *Doug got out of that Argentinian thing.* From New York she wrote *Have you heard that record David MacFarlane made? It's called* This Is MacFarlane, This is Hardy. *You re-*

member, we met him that night you took me out in Boston. Abraham is going to Greece this summer to do some research for his junior thesis at Princeton.

Mrs Webb said, "Don't you love these old Cunarders? They're so seaworthy."

"I hope so."

In New York her apartment was east of First Avenue, in the 60s. On the phone Janet had said she and her roommate were giving a party.

The place was crowded. Record music blared from a stereo against one wall through the open door.

"Hi, whoever you are. Come in."

"My name is Jones," Dan said.

Janet was in the middle of a mob, dressed in a pants suit, talking to three or four men.

On the bookshelf were Kafka, Kant, Kerouac, *A Handbook on How to Think*, next to it a book called *Think*.

The girl who owned the flat was fat. She sat in Dan's lap.

"We have some old Tom Lehrer recordings," she said. "Shall we play them later?"

"Sure."

Someone else said, "You want a drink, Jones?"

"Sure," he said. "This is Mrs Jones."

She was twisting and turning in his lap, one arm around his shoulders, to talk to people who passed.

The music was electric guitars, a bass violin, tambourine, drum. The bass of the stereo was set too high and the rhythm of the bass violin thumped in the room like a heartbeat. The singing was nasal and sad. *Just last night I saw you all alone. Tonight you wouldn't answer the phone.* Chatter, laughter, exclamations, collegiate vulgarities drifted through the room above and beneath the music. The noise made a few shout, insanely. Janet was drinking. Across the way from Dan were four young people on a divan, all beer-drunk, necking laboriously.

"What are you thinking about, handsome?" Mrs Jones asked.

"I'm wondering where my drink went to," he said.

"It's in the kitchen. You'll have to go into the kitchen and get it for yourself. But not now."

"You like sitting on my lap?"

"Very much. So far. Don't you like it?"

"I'm afraid you're ruining my fly."

In the kitchen there was a young lawyer trying to figure out the bottles. He told Dan how powerful he was, being a lawyer. He could tell a cop or a sergeant to go to hell. He knew his rights. He asked Dan what Dan was studying to be.

"An architect," he said. "I'm going to specialize in whorehouses."

"You're going to need me," the lawyer said.

"Not in a whorehouse."

He went outside again, holding his drink and watching Janet.

In a while he went over and kissed her, said good night.

"Oh, Dan, I never got to see you. Where are you staying?"

Aboard the ship, Mrs Parkhurst was saying, "If it's a matter of expense, I'm sure we could make it up. Heavens, you couldn't have anybody to talk to in Tourist."

13

Chump had just gotten up for the day when Dave came in from the evening.

Dave asked, "Had breakfast?"

He ordered through the phone and in a few moments a cart was wheeled into their living room with sausage and coffee and eggs and toast. While they were waiting Chump had dressed for the day and Dave had dressed in pajamas.

Dave smoked a Chesterfield while they finished the pot of coffee together.

He said, "Did you ever know all the churches are locked at night?"

He was later than usual and his voice sounded tired.

"Why did you go there?"

"I don't know. I wanted to hear the silence." His spoon hit the lip of his coffee cup. "There's a special kind of silence in churches. I guess they're the only buildings around today with thick enough walls." He stirred his coffee slowly.

"I think all these airplanes are really beginning to bother my ears."

Dave had said that before.

Then Dave went into his bedroom, closing the door, to sleep, and Chump went into his bedroom, closing his door, to wonder why he had gotten up.

Chump sat propped on his bed, fingering, mouthing his saxophone. He was trying to be quiet so Dave could sleep but every once in a while a few notes would come out.

He could not be entirely quiet. A year before he had been arrested in Boston for playing his saxophone in a subway station, bouncing his sound off the tile walls, sending it in curves up the vaulted ceilings, in straight, echoing lines out through the tunnels, using the rumble of the trains for bass, at eight-twenty in the morning. The people had looked at him with hatred: an ear-vibrating intrusion, hardness into their soft morning stupor. The judge might have acquitted him, he said, except that Chump also played his saxophone in court while evidence against him was being given. He spent the rest of the day and the night playing his saxophone in jail, where the cement walls and tunnels were almost as good as in the subway station, the other inmates protesting more noisily but able to do less about it. The police in the jail liked his playing.

At about eleven-thirty the telephone in the sitting room rang and Chump went in and picked it up, held it to his ear, saying nothing into it.

"Chump?"

It was Ms Tuesday.

"Asleep."

"Will you wake him up?"

"Sure."

Dave came to the phone scratching his jaw and Chump sat on the divan waiting for the conversation to be over so he could make some real noise with his horn.

"I didn't realize you had the letters," Dave said.

He said, "You mean he's already here? Well, he's only come here to study, hasn't he? Of course he'll want to see you. Hometown and all that. Why are you so upset?

"Look, don't worry."

He said, "Yes, I know. I agree, this is a bad idea; I don't know what I'm doing, I'm being unrealistic. I guess I'm a romantic, despite everything. I spent a long time walking, this morning, thinking, before coming back to the Michaelmas.

"That's the trouble with us," he said. "We can't do anything natural without thinking about it."

"I say to hell with all that, too. I've been pretty stupid. I'll be over. Will that be all right?

He said, "Don't worry about him. You'll be glad to see him. I'll put my things in a taxi and come over."

Dave put the receiver down and lit a Chesterfield.

Chump understood that Dave wanted to say something, all at once, in a word, and he knew there was no such word.

Chump said, "All right."

Finally, Dave said, "What do you think of marriage?"

"Whose?"

"Mine. I've been thinking of marrying Ms Tuesday since the night I met her. Which is why, I guess, I've been acting so stupidly toward her. I have a lot to make up to her."

His slippers moving toward the window made a horrid, dry sound on the carpet.

"I've thought of marriage as a house where there are children, toys in the hall. I've even considered it as an apartment in the city with paintings on the wall. I've thought of it like a church, maybe, a place that is always in a place, where there are people you know and recognize and can pretend to be certain about and where you do things together, like sing."

He had to come back to grind his cigarette in a metal ashtray that had an uneven bottom. It rattled on the table top.

"Our thinking of marriage and churches doesn't make sense. We live at night, not because we're robbers but because that's where our life is. Churches are locked at night."

Chump stood in the door, watching Dave pack. Usually they packed together, at the same time, each in his own room.

"The hotel bill still goes on the joint expense sheet," Dave said.

"It's not as if we were married," Chump said. "My god. We're just business associates."

Dave snapped his suitcase closed and put on his shirt and coat.

"I'll see you at the Club Solo tonight," he said. "Usual time."

"Sure," Chump said. "You're going to live with Ms Tuesday."

"Yes, that's right."

Then Dave was at the door with his raincoat on and his suitcase in his hand.

"I thought you'd be the first one off," Dave said. "It usually works that way."

Chump still had his horn in his hands.

"You come have supper with us sometime."

"Sure," Chump said.

They never ate supper.

"See you at the Club Solo," Dave said.

"See you."

Chump sat on the divan, his legs drawn up, heels jammed into the cushion, saxophone between his legs. He found the valve, found G, and held it for sixteen bars.

14

Dan found himself a taxi and sat in the back seat, his luggage at his feet, and looked out the window as he rode through Paris in the rain. It was late afternoon. He was stiff from having sat so long, dried out from the steam heat of the train, and weary from the seasickness he had felt, for the first time in his life, crossing the English Channel.

The driver rode the taxi as he would a mule, pulling up with effort at every crossroad, making its horn bray, his thumb on the horn button, through every intersection. Once or twice he chortled back at his passenger—obviously a man of the cloth—apparently accrediting his survival, his success as a driver in Paris to divine benevolence. Going down some boulevard the driver pointed to a curb, and said something about a cabbie having been shot there, killed, the night before by a hold-up man, who had then turned off the lights and the motor.

The avenues were broad and did project an impression of space, but being a New Englander Dan did not believe there was such a thing as an engaging view that merely lay flat upon the ground. He saw what he thought was an oil derrick in the middle of the city and marveled at it and began to think sad thoughts about crass commercialism, materialism in the modern age. After being driven as much as thirty degrees around it he recognized it, blushing in the back seat, not willing to laugh at himself. He had read that the Eiffel Tower existed mainly as an engineering achievement from another age, but having always seen it on postcards, in news photographs, on the walls of too many restaurants, he had also thought it would appear an object of art, a thing of beauty.

The Crillon was the only name of a hotel in Paris he knew, as he had read Benjamin Franklin had stayed there and that the place was still standing, and although this caused him some concern about the plumbing, he thought he would chance it for a night or two until he found rooms of his own, through the school. It was much too expensive for him, but he did not know that and the hotel clerk did, so he was given a perfectly adequate small room on the third floor, in back, just two dozen steps beyond the end of the corridor carpet.

While waiting for the bellman, Dan made some comment to the hotel clerk about the small, cheery fireplace in the lobby.

Then he asked if there were any messages for him.

"No, M'sieu. None for you."

In fact, Dan had looked for her after going through customs at Calais, and again at the station in Paris. The only reason he had made reservations at the Crillon was so he could tell her someplace he would be.

He unpacked and took a long warm shower, trying to loosen his muscles, trying not to think of Janet, to think of steak and eggs instead, not to think of searching for an address after dark in a foreign city, instead, of a short walk, early bed.

Over chateaubriand in the Club Room he was aware of a woman alone eyeing him from another table. She was purple-haired, beyond middle-aged. Her rings flashed at him in just the right way, to show substance on every finger, and yet there was a lack of flamboyance in the use of her hands. He silently recited to himself the conversation they would have, of how high, how low was her own curate, how brilliant, how stupid, with every uncharitable remark pointed out as such, but made anyway. Somewhere in the conversation there would be a financial hook cast, an innocent offer such as the use of a car, a season's ticket, a hotel bill taken care of, in return for companionship, handholding, more conversation, the street-and-restaurant services of a gigolo, made respectable, and cheaper. He finished his tea quickly and signed the check. Passing her he nodded to her briskly. He followed his glance toward her with a hurried check of his wristwatch. Dan had already learned pastoral evasiveness.

He sauntered through the pleasant lobby, stopping for a moment to admire the fireplace, noticing at the same time that his friend, the clerk, had gone off duty. He put himself through the revolving door, barely getting out of the way of a dinner party coming in from a

Rolls Royce. They all looked awfully large in their evening clothes. He stood under the portico of the hotel noticing the enormity of the Rolls Royce, the largest car he had ever seen, as it moved away from the curb, turned in a big circle, and slid into traffic.

Facing him was the broad, flat Champs Elysées, running away from him, stately buildings and wide sidewalks and small trees on each side. At the end of the Champs Elysées was the Arc de Triomphe, bathed in light. Over the winter trees to the right were the lights at the top of the Eiffel Tower. And running away from him to the left was the Place de la Concorde.

He turned left, passing the Louvre without knowing what it was, not seeing Maxim's, and strolled down the Place de la Concorde without his overcoat, not knowing where he was going. Dickens had said sewers and intrigue; Dumas had said sewers and injustice: he had understood it as a place for artists, those who must milk a place, a time, a person, life, for what they create, must destroy something as they create from it, as pioneers destroy land, but live off it, as they push the frontier forward. We shall use Paris this year, London next: moving in and out, leaving paint on the floor, bricks chipped from the chimney; to sculpt you, to paint you, I must love you, take from you, know your form in my hands, your flesh against mine.

Shivering, he sat on a damp bench watching the girls walk up and down, no two together, mesh stockings and mini skirts, short veils, tight pants and pony tails. He wanted to love, all of them. They noticed Dan's collar and smiled at him. *What would I do if solicited? Would you like me, would you like to love me? I would lie, or I could say yes, then walk away tight in the grip of my own life-negation, of my having evaded, once more, my own nature, the nature of others, made of yes a no.* Around him were searchlights and facade lights and streetlights in the still-raw air, glistening on the still-wet stone and cement. *I am twenty-four years old, a college graduate and a veteran, and I have never made love.* He remained on the park bench a long time.

The fire in the lobby was so perfectly set it had neither grown nor diminished since he had left.

"Are there any messages for Prescott; Daniel Prescott?"

"No, M'sieu."

"I thought perhaps, telephone messages."

"No, M'sieu. Sleep well."

15

David waited a long moment before pushing the button again.

"Oh, I'm sorry, M'sieu." Her eyes were openly surprised, apologetic. "I thought it was the old German who rang, whom I always let wait."

"Old German?"

"Herr Schatz, a friend of Madame Twombly."

"Madame Twombly?"

Eyes still wide, surprised, alert to change, news, perhaps slightly afraid, slightly amused, noticing the suitcase, the kitten peeking out of his raincoat pocket, she said, "So you have come to stay?"

"Yes, I, too, am a friend of the Mademoiselle."

He let her lead him up the stairs, chattering irrelevantly, her broad beam swaying slowly from stair to stair as would normally that of a person much older than herself. "Ah, this weather, M'sieu. Cold last night, and now it will rain this afternoon, I am sure." She used the turn in the stair to glance at him. "Do you ask what Paris is? Paris is going out on a spring day to buy flowers, to bring them back to the house and place them on a table and make the sun fall on them properly."

On the second landing, after a glance, she said, "And what is love? Love is the joy a young man and a young woman can have in seeing the sunlight on the flowers on the table, together."

Now that it was indoors, the kitten was mewing fretfully and trying to climb out of David's pocket.

On the second staircase, after another glance, she said, "Paris, my friend, is understanding eyes."

On the landing of the third floor she knocked and called loudly, "Madame? Madame?"

It was only a minute before Ms Tuesday opened the door.

"Oh, David! You brought me a kitten!"

Standing aside, judicious, satisfied, the concierge said, "So. For you I will put one more pillow on the bed."

Ms Tuesday danced the kitten around the living room, cupped in her hands, swung it in circles. The kitten clawed at her hands, eyes bulging at the floor.

"I shall call her Madame Sudar. David, have you met Madame Sudar?"

He hung his damp raincoat over a wicker chair to dry.

"How do you do."

The concierge smiled, pleased to meet him, pleased to share her name with a cat.

"There's not a drop of milk in the house," said Ms Tuesday. "And Madame, nothing for a sandbox!"

"Newspapers," Madame Sudar said. "Once the politicians have used them, why should not the cats, for the same purpose on the bathroom floor?"

David brought his suitcase into the bedroom and investigated the closet space. He pushed Ms Tuesday's things to the left, making room for his own suits and overcoat on the right. From the bathroom he could hear Ms Tuesday asking Madame Sudar's advice on the cat, not waiting for answers, and Madame Sudar's voice apparently talking to the cat. As there were no hats in Ms Tuesday's closet there was space for his empty suitcase on the shelf. Together, they were lecturing the kitten on matters of cleanliness, health and aim, telling it with mock sternness to direct its excretion towards the newspapers. "Like a Social Democrat," said Madame Sudar.

Instead of *Sunflowers* on the bedroom wall was an enlarged photograph of Michelangelo's *David*, shot from the front, from a height just above the knees, giving his cleanliness, grace, a bigger-than-life aspect. The bed was unmade and strewn with letters. He emptied the third, bottom drawer of the bureau into the second, for his shirts, underwear, and socks.

The kitten dashed into the bedroom in an African-veld lope, stopped a few feet from David, examined him.

"No, Madame Sudar, we can get the milk ourselves, later. I'm sure David will want to go out."

The kitten mewed at David and sat down to taste its paws.

Ms Tuesday walked with Madame Sudar to the door, full of talk.

David went in to say goodbye. Madame told David it had been nice meeting him and that she liked the kitten.

Her steps were fading through the door. Ms Tuesday was sitting in the chair, holding the kitten to her breast with both hands.

"Who is Herr Schatz?"

"Schatz? Schatzy. He's the man who has been paying the rent on this apartment."

Her chin was stroking the back of the kitten's neck.

"Well, don't look so surprised, David." She had not looked at him. "It doesn't need pointing out that you haven't been."

"There's been no reason for me to."

"Precisely."

"I will from now on," he said.

"You have a big blonde somewhere in Paris, haven't you, David? Don't deny it. I know you have."

David said, "Where is he now?"

"Gone to Spain. For a short holiday. Alone. He's probably organizing a motorcycle brigade of American leather-boys to take over Valencia."

"Why do you say that?"

"Oh, David. He spent six years in a Russian prison camp. He's a gynecologist. He kept himself out of the army and earned his way through school performing certain operations for the Nazis."

David said, "Shit."

"A long time ago, David. Actually, he's a very generous, sweet man."

"I don't care. I'm warning you right now. Don't ever let me see him."

"Will I ever see your big blonde?"

"Do you understand me?"

She said, "Yes."

The kitten was being rubbed against her cheek, purring.

In the bedroom, he arranged his neckties on a wire hanger. Then he stood at the window, looking out at the rain, gleaming on the gray roofs.

Ms Tuesday was on the bed, reading a letter. Her legs looked long in the tight white slacks, knees bent at two different angles, feet bare.

"I thought you had read them," David said.

Madame Sudar, the kitten, was browsing through some laundry on the floor.

"I only read that he was arriving today and then I called you.

Listen to this: 'You know you are precious to me, like my ministry, and to have you taken from me would be to have taken from me the specific reason for my life.' "

"Let's have a fire," David said.

" 'I am sorry,' " he says, " 'that we seem to be growing apart.' Rather slow to get the point, wouldn't you say?"

"No, I wouldn't."

"Honestly, it's been more than three years. The kid's a riot."

"No, he's not a riot."

"What's the matter with you, David?"

"You don't have to laugh at his letters. You don't have to laugh at his love."

"I'm not doing that."

"All right."

"He says there are children in heaven that are already ours."

"Let's have a fire."

David went into the other room. The charred tin cans, the smokey bottle were back in the fireplace.

"Well, make one," she said from the bedroom.

"Are you sure I can?"

"For God's sake, David. What do you have up your nose?"

"You shouldn't read love letters out loud."

She came out to him, the letters crumpled in her hands.

"But I don't love him, David. I love you."

"Then don't read his letters to me."

David was on his knees, making a fire.

"I'm sorry," she said. She tossed the letters over her shoulder, onto the logs to be burned. "I guess it's a cheap way to be brave."

"Why are you putting the letters in the fireplace?"

"Because I don't want them. Why should I want them?"

"Well, you want to know when the kid's arriving, and where he's staying."

"He's arriving at this instant and he's staying at the Hotel Crillon." David put a match to the paper under the kindling. "He'll have supper with some old dowager who sees him as the beautiful, sexy boy he is." Elbows cupped in her hands, she stood close to the gauze curtain, looking through the French door. "It's really raining, now."

David brushed the dust from his pants.

"That's a lovely fire," she said. "Let's have a drink."

"All right."

"You sit here and I'll get your pipe, slippers, and a highball."

"That would be nice."

He was sitting in the armchair before the fire.

Leaning to kiss him, she said, "Of course it's nice, darling. We're going to play house together."

She was bending from the hips, hands on knees, looking into the refrigerator.

"Would you rather have milk?"

"You don't have any milk."

"I can go out and get some."

"It's raining out."

They drank their highballs in the chair. Ms Tuesday sat across David's lap.

There was no light in the room but the firelight. He was listening to the rain on the roof.

"Think of Dan Prescott in Paris," she said. "Out looking for me in the rain."

"Why don't you call him," David said. "Save him some trouble."

"Don't ask me to do that. I wish John had never told me about the letters, never brought them to me last night at the club. So considerate. I wish I didn't know he was here."

"He is here, you know. And you'll have to see him."

"I know."

"Ms Tuesday, you really loved him."

She was gazing into the fire from David's lap, rubbing her lips with the glass.

"Who wouldn't love him? He's a wonderful boy. Very fine looking. Very clean, tall, and he stands very straight. He accepts himself beautifully. I do love him. Do you mind that I love him?"

"Yes."

"He was the football hero in high school. The quarterback, very bright, very fast. He exuded happiness when he played. You could see it from the stands. He exuded happiness all the time, even sitting on an old log in the woods, soaked to his knees and freezing. I had a good pair of hunting boots, but he never had the money for a good pair for himself. He was the fine son of our minister and the handsomest kid you ever saw. I'm sure he still is. He was very much a boy. He went away to war and got wounded. He loves his parents, his country, his God, and the girl next door. I happened to be the girl next door."

"That all sounds very fine."

"It is, I suppose."

For a few minutes she sat looking into the fire, curiously not blinking, saying nothing. Madame Sudar stretched before the fire and then stalked into the other room.

"David," she asked. "Do you believe in God?"

"I don't know. I would like to."

"You would like to do and be a lot of things you aren't."

"I guess that's right."

"What do you believe in, David?"

In his left hand his glass was almost empty. In her right hand her glass was half full.

"I don't know what, Ms Tuesday. I know that playing the piano, composing, working a piece out, whatever you call it, you get into a groove, or on a path. You know it is there only after you've started. Then once you have started you know where you're going because you know where you've been. There is a force, and a direction, and it takes every cell and fiber of your being to follow it. You have got to concentrate on it. Once you fall off the path, disturb the rhythm or hit a clinker, you have to try very hard to get back to it. Maybe the whole thing is ruined. Am I making any sense?"

"No."

"I guess I mean that there is a meaning in music. Something makes things go together, and it is not harmony, and all the other things they teach in school. Chump is a holy man, a saint. He knows more about it than any man in the world. There is a totality in music you can reach. It's a type of meaning."

"So what."

"So what?" He finished his drink. "I don't know so what. So I guess I believe one can create a meaning in life, a reachable totality. Does that make any sense?"

"Not much. I don't know."

He wondered a moment about getting another drink, about disturbing her. The rain was pelting the roof and every minute or so it would spray in a gust against the French door. He did not want to disturb her and he did not want to get her another drink.

"David," she asked. "Are you sad about life?"

"No. Why should I be?"

"Because some people think they are more precious than others. Want another highball?"

"No."

"I could go out and get some milk."

"No. It's raining."

She said, "The letters are all burned up."

"Don't worry about the letters."

He moved his right foot and heard the clink of the bottle on the hearth as it hit the tin cans. He wondered if he could get Madame Sudar—the human—to clean for them, every few days.

She said, "David? You have known many women, haven't you."

"One or two."

"A great many?"

"Three or four."

"That's good," she said. "Some people think they are more precious than others."

He lowered his empty glass to the floor.

She asked, "What shall we talk about?"

"Marriage. That's another thing I believe in. I want you to marry me."

She put her fingertips under his chin, turned his face up to her. "Do you really think you have to propose to me before we fuck?" Her eyes were black with the light of the fire behind them, round, laughing.

He said, "I rather thought we might get married."

"You don't believe in it, and you know it." Her voice was low, chiding.

"I would like to believe in it," he said.

She smiled. "Come off it, David." She saw her glass was empty and put it on the floor. "We can smash a bottle, tear a tin can, and call us married."

"All right. Let's do that. Let's break a jug and call us married."

She picked up his left hand, pressed it to her cheek, caressed herself. Then she put his two fingers into her mouth and bit down on them.

"Jesus Christ!"

Standing up quickly he dumped her off his lap onto the floor. She knelt in white pants before him, her face upturned.

He cuffed her with the back of his hand, sprawling her toward the fireplace, toward the bottles.

"If you want to screw up somebody's hands, marry a taxi driver."

Her brown eyes appeared completely calm, steady. He put his fingers into his own mouth, feeling her teeth marks with his tongue. Her eyes turned to the jagged edge of the smokey bottle, back to him.

Picking up only his own glass he went to the bottle on the counter next to the sink and poured himself a half.

She went into the bedroom.

Sitting alone in the chair he heard her move on the bed.

"David?"

He drank a mouthful of the straight Scotch and watched the fire flickering on the wicker base of the divan and listened to the rain pushing against the door, steady on the roof.

"David?"

A melody came to him on top of the rhythm, of an old American song, a work song, sung by a large male chorus. There was space in it and breath and listening to it he saw a flat prairie from a train window, golden yellow with wheat, tall trees in the distance and, beyond them, gray mountains, jagged, their tops smooth with snow. The melody was simple; the voices were lusty, and they brought to the simplicity, the grandeur, a happiness.

"David? I want you."

In a second mouthful he finished the drink.

Then, hurt, angry, disappointed, he loved Ms Tuesday.

16

From where the corridor carpet began there were one or two pairs of shoes outside every door, freshly shined. Where there was no carpet, near his own door, there were no shoes. He had shined his own shoes the night before.

His friend the hotel clerk was on duty so Dan asked him for a map of the city and went over it with him, his black raincoat at his elbow on the desk. The clerk showed him with a long fingernail about where Janet's address was.

"You're not a priest, are you?"

"No. Why?"

"There is a Catholic school near there."

In the breakfast room of the hotel Dan had toast, eggs, a little glass of orange juice, coffee. The other tables had nothing on them but white linen.

A taxi was found for him immediately outside the hotel and Dan gave the driver the address. It was a bright Citroen, remarkably clean, considering the weather. Trying his French, Dan mentioned the taxi driver who had been shot two nights before, but the driver had not heard of the incident.

A gray, damp day, due to rain again at any moment: the car went across a bridge and began to navigate a series of small, twisting, sloping streets. *So there are hills in Paris. I thought so.* The houses were old, and for the most part small. Some of the shops were still completely shuttered.

The taxi stopped and Dan looked for the school. The driver

pointed to a side street across the road and tried to say through his cigar that the house the Reverend was looking for was just down the street.

He opened the sidewalk door of the cab and saw *merde* written on the sidewalk in chalk. On the wall was a sign that said, in English, EQUALITY AND FRATERNITY. There were no trees, and it was noisy, vendors shouting at women, women shouting at children, children shouting at each other. Down the road a man in a beret was sweeping the sidewalk.

Dan crossed and entered the little street. There was a cafe on the corner with a woodcut of an old monk with a quill for a sign. The houses had painted window boxes, with nothing in them, painted window frames and doors, polished brass doorknobs. The schoolyard was to his right. He took the number out of his pocket and looked for the house.

The concierge appeared almost immediately.

Au nom du Père

"Yes, M'sieu? Good day."

"Good day, Madame. I am looking for Miss Janet Twombly, an American miss who makes her home here."

et du Fils

"No longer, M'sieu. She has not had her home here for a long time, and this house was her home only shortly."

et du Saint-Esprit.

"Ah, I see. You see I am a minister of God and I am her friend. Would you tell me where she makes her home now?"

Ainsi soit-il.

"Yes, M'sieu, and it is a good thing she has friends who are ministers of God, yet I do not know the place of her new home. I asked her the morning she left to give me her new address, but I never did hear of it. The miss does not speak French too well."

Ainsi soit-il.

"She left your house some time ago?"

"Yes, M'sieu. Yet I had no place to send her mail."

"And you do not know where she is now? Pardon me, my French is not too good as well."

"Your French is very good, M'sieu. No, I do not know her address. Yet there is her friend, who lives quite close by, another American gentleman, whose address I do know. He gave it me one time when he was looking for her and thought I might see her before him."

"I do not understand you."

"One moment, M'sieu, and I will give you the address."

She came out the gate again in a minute, with a slip of paper.

"You are American?" she asked.

"Yes. From the United States."

"And you are a minister of God."

"Yes."

"Mostly it is soldiers we see from your country, disguised as tourists. And tourists disguised as artists. Here is the address of her friend, Father. Perhaps he will tell you where she lives. He may have found her by now."

"Thank you, Madame. And where is this address?"

"This same street. It must be some house on the left."

"I understand. Thank you. Tell me, Madame, does the American miss owe you money for her lodging?"

"No, my Father. She is a very nice girl. She said she did not like the school."

Across the street children were playing in the schoolyard, nuns in their veils standing up straight among them.

"My plumbing is quite good," the concierge said.

"Thank you, Madame. Until later."

"Until later, my Father."

Going up the street, looking from the paper, *John Bart Nelson* on it in small, neat handwriting, to the numbers of the doors, Dan felt a rubber ball bounce against his right ankle. It rolled forward, toward the gutter. Two small boys had run to the gate of the schoolyard and stopped, their eyes round and solemn on the ball. A slim nun, young, waved at him, white hand at the end of a long black sleeve against the sky. Dan picked the ball up and threw it over the fence at her, in a slow, gentle arc. She caught it in the air, before it had bounced once.

Dan grinned at her and waved. The two boys had dashed to her. She handed the ball to them, waved back, grinning.

Dan stepped around the woman who was scrubbing the hall floor. She looked up at him and answered Dan's question about finding the right apartment. He climbed the stone steps to the top story and knocked on the only door off that landing.

An enormous black man in white pajamas stood in the door, daylight from the room behind him a sharp white.

"Good day, Monsieur," Dan said.

"Good day, Monsieur. What do you want?"

"I wonder if you could tell me the address—"

"You're an American," he said in English. "Come in."

Of course he's an American. What else could he be?

"I'm sorry," Dan said.

A window along the length of one wall was filled with gray sky. On the shelf below the window were stacks of papers, pads, a typewriter, rows of pens, pencils, all square, parallel to each other, evenly spaced, neat.

"Would you like some coffee, Reverend Prescott?"

"How do you know me?"

His back to him, the man was plugging a hot plate into the wall.

"I'm John Bart Nelson," he said.

He took the coffeepot into the bathroom. Dan heard the water running. Coming out the man had the full white light of the room on him.

"Ninety-seven. I'll be damned. You're Jack Nelson! What are you doing here? You were the best man I ever played against."

"You were no poke yourself, Reverend." Jack was pushing the plug more tightly into the hot plate socket, wriggling it. "We were both great football players in high school in Maine. Now you are a minister and I am trying to write poetry in Paris. What will happen to us next?"

"Poetry is not quite what I thought you'd turn to next. You were the scourge of our locker-room pep talks."

"Was I? That's nice to know. I remember I had to pin you fast or I'd lose you altogether. Man, you were a rabbit on your feet."

"And every time I thought I was clear of the line this damned tank would hit me."

"Favored position of the halfback. What's been happening to you since?" Jack swung the easy chair around, to face the hot plate, the window, the shelf.

"School and some war."

"Were you in it long? The war?"

"No. I got pinned pretty fast then, too."

"Lucky boy."

"What have you been doing since then?"

"School and some war. I was assigned to jumping out of planes in Germany. Just war games, really. Actually they only made us jump when they thought we were all drinking too much beer, having too much of a good time."

Jack had put two cups on saucers, instant coffee powder into each. He was pouring the hot water into the cups.

"Sit down, Reverend. We'll have some coffee."

"I'll sit down, but don't call me Reverend. You remember my name is Dan. Someone just called me Father."

"Mon Père."

Dan sat in the green reading chair. Jack sat in the light desk chair without turning it around. He straddled it, a leg either side of the back.

"I'm sorry I woke you up."

Jack's chest, shoulders, head were in silhouette against the window. He could still have been in football uniform, helmet.

"That's all right. I was up quite late working."

"Are you publishing, Jack?"

"No. I'm not up late working because there is a demand for my work." He said, "You're looking for Miss Twombly."

"Yes."

"She's from Columbia Falls, too, isn't she? Are you in love with her?"

"Yes. Always have been."

"How long has it been since you've seen her?"

The light from the window behind Jack was too bright.

"It's been a while."

"A lot can happen, Dan."

"What has happened? I haven't been hearing from her."

"You haven't been hearing from her, that's all. Of course you haven't been hearing from her. Do you like being a minister?"

"Yes."

"Then I suggest you go back to Columbia Falls and be a minister."

"What does that mean?"

"She'll never make a minister's wife, Danny boy. She's flown a little too high, a little too free for that." He put his coffee cup and saucer on the shelf behind him. "Do you like music?"

Jack went to the table, unplugged the hot plate, and plugged in the record player. "Luckily enough, the hot plate never emanates enough heat to damage the records." He took a record from the stack, slid it out of its jacket, and placed it carefully on the turntable.

"Has she gotten my letters?"

"I was only able to give them to her the night before last."

"Then why didn't she call me at the hotel last night and let me know where she was?"

"She might have been otherwise occupied."

"Doing what?"

"Listen," Jack said.

"Sorry": Dan had understood from somewhere, a record jacket, a disc jockey, it was the name of a girl.

"That's MacFarlane on piano and Hardy on saxophone, isn't it?"

"Yes. You like music?"

"I met MacFarlane once, years ago."

"Was Miss Twombly with you when you met him?"

"As a matter of fact, she was."

They listened to the whole record, "Sorry," "Theme from Carnaby Street," "727," two the titles of which Dan did not know, until finally the arm raised, swung over. The machine clicked itself off.

"You like that?" Jack asked.

"Sure."

"Quite a man, that David MacFarlane. You know, he's probably one of the most important composers writing today. His music is infinitely adaptable. And he's only thirty."

"Jack, believe it or not I didn't come here to get a lecture on contemporary jazz."

"Miss Twombly is in love with David MacFarlane," Jack said. "In fact, I suspect they're sort of living together. Would you like some more coffee?"

He took his own cup, and Dan's, to the table, spooned more instant powder into each. He poured the water into the cups without reheating it.

Dan said, "It's beginning to rain out."

Drops were spattering the big window.

"Sure it is."

Jack handed Dan his cup and then put some sugar into it. Dan had not tasted it.

"You ought to be a doctor," Dan said. "You have a nice bedside manner."

Jack said, "Don't be annoyed with me." He put the sugar bowl on the desk-shelf. "I'm sorry, Dan. You were probably in love with her in high school."

"Yes. What about yourself?"

"One black boy in a white town." He was looking through the window, his back to Dan. "I've been in love lots of times, only nobody has ever known it. Except me."

"And sometimes you haven't known it."

"That's right. Not many times."

Dan's coffee was almost cold.

"What's this MacFarlane like?" he asked.

"I've only met him a couple of times, briefly. A very decent sort, I guess. I hope he is."

"So do I." Dan finished his cup quickly, looking into its bottom. "Are we going to sit here all day like a couple of veterans feeling sorry for ourselves?"

"If you want to."

Jack put his coffee cup and saucer on the desk-shelf again and sat in the light chair again, backwards.

"Dan," he said, "Paris is a very real place. Maybe it is like every other place. Anyway, here, this place, caters to many lies and therefore it takes a greater truth. Do you see?"

"No. What are you saying?"

"I suppose I am lying by saying Paris. Poets wear beards and priests wear collars here, too. I believe we are all better off without these things."

"I still don't see."

"What am I saying? I am saying you woke me up to say Good day, Monsieur, to show me your collar, to drink my coffee and to have a polite little conversation, bringing the right things up at the right time. Then we sit and tell each other we hope MacFarlane is a decent sort."

"I guess you're saying I'm a fuddy-duddy," Dan said. "I've been told that before. Tell me something new."

"All right. Here's something new: I asked you questions you shouldn't let me ask, and you gave me the answers to them."

"Maybe that's because I feel as though I've known you always, at least as a football player."

"Still, I'm a stranger. We're not in some nice, tight little community. You're not my minister, and I don't want you to be my minister. And I don't want to be your minister, either."

"I've changed my mind. Your bedside manner stinks."

"When was the last time you got drunk?"

"It's been a while."

"I suggest you do so again, very soon."

"Oh, go to hell."

"That's better," Jack said.

"What do you want me to do, go poke this goddamned bastard in the nose?"

Jack said, quietly, "No. But that would be better than breaking in on them, flashing your collar, laying some claim on them."

"Oh, screw you. I am Janet's minister. And you're not mine."

"That's the boy."

Even with the light behind him, Jack's grin was white and wide. "Bug off, Nelson."

"That's better. Much better. Now, would you like another cup of coffee?"

"No. All I want from you is Janet's address."

Dan stood up, to leave.

Jack said, "It's raining pretty hard out."

"I don't care. Give me Janet's address."

Jack wrote on a pad on the desk-shelf, then tore off the piece and handed it to Dan.

"Here. Go out the door and turn right, back down to the boulevard. Then go left. After you walk about half a mile show this to someone and he will tell you where it is."

"I can speak French."

"I forgot."

"You've been a big help."

Dan put the slip of paper in his pocket. Then he buttoned his raincoat to the collar.

Jack said, "And think twice about going right now. Remember, they are shacking up together, and you have no real claims on either one of them."

"I ought to punch you in the mouth."

Jack was standing close to him.

He said, "I'm bigger than you are, son."

Dan belted him square in the mouth.

Jack's head jerked back. He threw out his arms, uselessly, to steady himself, grab something, but he fell across the room, his legs not keeping up with his body, his head, shoulders, going down, cracking his head on the lower frame of the table, his shoulders, head finally hitting the floor under the table. The coffeepot fell off the hot plate, its water spilling on the table surface.

Jack sat up slowly, lowering his head under the table frame. He wiped the blood from his mouth with his thumb.

"You got any more to say?" Dan asked.

"Yeah," Jack said quietly. "Go away."

"Would you like my flashy collar stuffed down your throat, too?"

"Go away," Jack said. "Just go away."

The scrubwoman was standing in the foyer, hands on her hips, looking up the stairs to see what the noise was about.

"Good day, *mon père*."

Dan passed her.

"Good day."

17

He sat in the back seat a moment, staring through the windshield, trying to remember the name of the place he was going, half hoping the car would go there by itself without having to be told.

The driver turned around and asked him in French.

Chump said, "Noerdaime."

"*Comment?*"

"It's a church. Noerdain, I think."

"Noher Dymie?"

"It's here in Paris. Noher Dain."

"Ah, *Notre-Dame! Notre-Dame?*"

"I guess so. I don't know. It's a church."

The car swung in a half-circle away from the curb in the quiet Sunday morning traffic. Chump sat on the back seat in his hat, soap still crackling in one ear looking out the window at the bridges as they went along the river.

He had listened from his bed to the Sunday morning silence of the city, the world, the silence of the suite, to the lack of noises from Dave's room, putting his hand over to touch the saxophone which always spent the night with him on the covers of his bed, and then finished the bottle of Coca-Cola he always left half empty beside his bed at night. For a while he had blown little noises into the silence, making the silence worse, more resounding. Then he had thought of getting up, entering the silence physically, doing something about it, disturbing it, with footsteps, running water, the sound of the bathroom glass against the sink. Ellie had taught him what to do, and he had always tried to do it, every morning, this one set of things, stripping, showering, shaving, combing his hair, dressing in fresh clothes, no matter how long it took him, how many distractions he had to resist, so he could play in front of people at night. He let an hour and a half go by between his first waking up and his beginning to get up.

He had to begin by undressing from the night before, in his own way, Chump's way, first standing beside the bed and removing his belt, then sitting down to remove one shoe, up to slip off his necktie, down to grab off one sock, the other shoe, up to unbutton his shirt, down to remove his other sock. His pants were only half off when he thought of a noise he could make and took his saxophone from his bed and played it for a moment, losing himself in that noise so completely he forgot about his pants. When he was through with that noise, believing himself naked, he started for the bathroom and sprawled on the floor.

In the shower he turned on both faucets at once, full force, taking whatever came, openly, on his chest, shoulders, head, then tried to adjust them, temper them, at first freezing, then scalding himself, then freezing again. When he had the taps adjusted right he turned them both off and soaped himself thoroughly, from his feet to his hair, as Ellie had done for him, then began with the taps all over again. Standing in front of the steamed mirror, a soaked towel around his waist, he lathered his left cheek first, shaved it, then lathered his chin, shaved it, then lathered his right cheek, shaved it. To get the shaving cream out of his hair, off his chest, shoulders, and arms, he had to shower again, leaving only a little in his ear he did not hear until it began to dry.

He used more than half of a small tube of toothpaste in brushing his teeth, leaning over the sink, so none of the foam would spill on him, on anything but his chin, and then played the saxophone softly for a half hour, to get the taste out of his mouth. Before going back to bed and sleeping for another two hours he spent time in front of the mirror combing his hair, starting at the crown again and again, trying to find a part which had never been there.

Being alone, finally dressed, he had breakfast in the dining room downstairs, of steak and eggs, a side order of spinach, which took time to prepare, more Coca-Cola, ice cream with chocolate nut sauce, and black coffee. The waiters said nothing to him but yes, sir, right away, sir.

*   *   *

"I'm from Chicago," he said to the driver. "Chicago, you know? Near Canada."

"*Notre-Dame*," the driver said. He put his thumb and forefinger together like a conductor urging a certain sound, a tone, from a full orchestra. "*Notre-Dame.*"

"Oh," said Chump, sure he was being taken to the wrong place.

Rubbering over one of the bridges he saw a church standing to the left. He jumped forward in his seat. "Here!"

"*Voilà!*" the driver said. "*Notre-Dame.*"

"Yes," Chump said. "*Si.*"

He gave the driver fifteen American dollars, hoping it was enough.

Chump stood at the door, just inside the line of sunlight. From inside the church there were the sounds of clothes rustling, the creaking of dry wood, but no sound of the human voice, except for an occasional cough.

A man came over and said to him, softly, "*Chapeau?*"

"Yes," Chump said, softly. "Chapel. Church."

"Hat," the man said.

Chump grabbed off his hat and held it out to the man.

"Seat?"

"*Si.* I would like to."

He followed the man down the aisle and entered the pew to which the man pointed.

"Wait a minute," Chump said.

He gave the man some change out of his pocket.

"*Merci bien, M'sieu.*" The man was smiling, glancing at others, in pews behind them. "For the poor, I take it."

In the pew with Chump was a French family, kneeling; next to him, staring, a small boy with brown, round eyes. Chump knelt too, and said, "Be bop de nop."

Everyone stood and he stood too. A bell had rung and three men and two boys in long gowns had entered the front section of the church and arranged themselves on the steps. They knelt and everyone knelt.

The man in the middle would say something, almost sing it. The others dressed in gowns would begin to murmur something and then the whole church would begin to buzz, everyone talking softly, at once. They were saying something about Angie Wattell, which surprised Chump, because the last he had heard Angie had gone to jail for dope; Chump could not understand how these people in Paris knew about the misfortune of a drummer in Detroit. But he understood they were praying for Angie, and he was glad he had come; he would listen closely and the next time they said Angie Wattell he would try to say it too, loudly, with them, as he had known Angie, and was personally sorry about his trouble.

Right cheek against his hand on the back of the bench in front of him, the little boy's eyes pulsated as he watched Chump.

Chump said, "Angie Wattell!"

There was no singing.

One night in Harlem Chump had heard singing from a church, the strong, deep, rich voice of a male working out a phrase, repeated by a full, loose chorus, the voices of men and women together, with the sound of one high, clear, female voice soaring above them all, working the phrase upside down. Handclapping, which sounded happy, open, free, kept the sounds going, playing with each other. He sat on the steps in front of the building and listened. The people in the church worked the same simple melodic line, the same rhythm up and up for an hour. Then the doors behind him burst open, suddenly, the instant the music stopped, and several almost stumbled over him in the dark.

And once when their rented car broke down in a small town in Ohio Chump had heard singing from a church again, a glistening white church, with a steeple, and again Chump sat down, in the sun, to the right on the steps, behind a rattling stanchion, to listen. He sat looking at a store sign, DONUTS, across the street, smelling the coffee from inside. It was a long time between songs and although they were all different melodies they all had the same rhythm and they all seemed the same. For a long time a man's voice droned in monotone, while seats creaked and people sneezed. When Chump returned they were singing again; he ate all eleven donuts from the bag before the singing stopped completely and the doors opened. Then the people stood in the door, at the top of the steps, in bunches, talking to each other. Only a few came directly down the stairs, and even these seemed to be moving slowly, tiredly.

Chump said, "Angie Wattell!"

Then he saw the window, the great blue window, over the boy's brown eyes, his white face, over the heads of the people, to his right: huge, circular, glass in little frames, each frame a different blue, more shades of blue than Chump had ever known existed, fantastically fragmented, complete, the total essence of blue, broken down like a melody into every note on the scale, recombined, built up again in harmonies of blue, the white-yellow morning sun behind it, through it, giving it power, full exposition, yet contrast. For the first time in his life Chump, who knew the world through its sound and its silence, who knew a cat on the floor from the sound of its feet, nails on the wood, its gentle purring, rather than by its actual, physical presence or sight, was seeing something, really seeing it, not just looking, aware of something, but seeing, knowing the full presence of something through his eyes. Above the center of the window, to the left, sunlight shimmered most whitely, breaking down immediately outside its own center into all the different frames of blue, almost being lost completely in the lower right curve.

"Angie Wattell."

The boy snickered, turned his face away, toward his family.

Kneeling, sitting, standing, Chump moved with the French family, only a little behind them, seeing the window.

Ite, missa est.

"Angie Wattell."

He sat back on the bench to let them out. The aisle was crowded with people shuffling toward the door.

Chump left his pew and walked around inside the empty church. He kept his eyes on the window, playing with it, first walking slowly toward the front, then backward along the rail, away from it. He went down the outside aisle, watching the white-yellow shaft of sunlight shift slightly from pane of blue to pane, to one side, the other, up, down. He walked up the aisle nearest to the window, seeing it flat, almost in two dimensions. Then he went around the back of the altar and came out the other side, having the huge, flat, circular blue window reveal itself to him bit by bit.

The white-yellow shaft of sunlight became long, fell the whole length of the window as noon passed, was still to the left of center, then faded. During the afternoon Chump sat on a bench the far side of the church, opposite the window. As if modulated, gradually, all the blues of the window darkened together, in relation to each other. Surprisingly then, late in the afternoon, it lightened; curious horizontal stripes of yellow, orange, red in the sky perceptible through the window but still affecting the blues only by increasing their blueness, making of them nothing but what they were, realizing, exposing them fully, blues capable of enfolding whites and yellows and oranges and reds, still being blue.

The window darkened, then, rapidly, seemed to draw together toward its center, to become smaller as the light left it, drew down from the ceiling, up from the floor. Even darkness brought to the window only blue, dark blues in relation to each other, no real black.

In a coffee shop a block to the west Chump sat with his back to the fire, drinking hot chocolate, looking through the plate glass window at his big blue window in the wall of the church. It was now a round, dark orb, darker than the sky above it, behind it, a wonderful, performing piece of sky, which had been fully exposed, explored, experienced in a single day.

That night at the Club Solo, he said to Dave, "I went to church today. I prayed for Angie Wattell."

Dave said, "Oh? Look, Chump," he said. "Try to pick up the first release of 'Greasy Pig' a little harder, will you? If we don't hit the audience right then, we never will."

There was gray in Dave's hair, just a little, at the temples.

Chump said, "Okay."

18

She was in a robe, furry slippers. Her hair was stringy and darker than he had ever seen it. Her eyes were bloodshot, and there was a welt high on her right cheekbone. A kitten rubbed against her pajama cuffs.

"Why, Dan," she said.

She did not look surprised.

"Hello, Janet."

"Come in."

An old dead movie actor grinned at him from the wall. There was not enough light in the room from a French door to bring out the tropical blues and greens of a travel poster farther along the same wall. Dishes on a counter, a kitchen faucet, refrigerator, and oven doors were not covered by a screen, which had been pushed aside, folded, near the bathroom door. The place smelled of cat.

Janet moved some clothes, a man's shirt, a slip, some slacks, off a chair for him to sit.

"It's nice to see you, Dan."

"Is it?"

She sat on the small divan, across from him.

"Yes, it really is. I didn't think it would be, but truly, it is." She was not wearing make-up. She had never needed it before. "But really, you mustn't act like a minister."

Legs in white pajama pants were crossed under her bathrobe. Her foot bobbed up and down.

"You're here for school," she said. "Have you found someplace to live?"

"Yes. I found a place a week ago."

"How did you ever do that? Good, cheap places are hard to find in Paris, unless you know someone."

Ashes and soot from the fireplace spotted the hearth, the rug.

"Doctor Murdock gave me a list of student rooms along with the reading lists. I took the first room I saw."

"Doctor Murdock?"

"Advisor for American students. He's from Philadelphia."

"You always have an advisor somewhere, haven't you, Dan? Either your father or some little priest in Montparnasse."

Her fingers were long, and white, strangely boney, with too much skin over the joints. He could not see these hands around a gunstock now or unwrapping a bar of chocolate.

She said, "You know, this is the first time I've ever seen you actually in a collar." She was not looking at him, but into the cold fireplace. "You had to be a minister, didn't you. And now you are."

She brushed her hair back with her hands.

"I look quite a slut, don't I?" she said. "I've been sleeping late these mornings. With David's work, I get to sleep quite late."

"David MacFarlane."

"Yes. How did you know?"

"Jack Nelson mentioned you are living with him."

"Do you know John? You mean the Negro."

"He used to play against us, for Gilmore High. You remember number ninety-seven, don't you? The only player I used to dread."

"Was that his number? But I didn't know you knew him, I mean actually know him. When did you see him?"

"My first day in Paris. Your old landlady sent me to him, for your address."

Finally looking at him, eyes narrowed with anger, annoyance, she said, "Your spy system is quite complete, isn't it?"

"I'm not spying, Janet."

"It seems like it."

The kitten stood in front of her on its hind legs, trying to catch the bobbing slipper in its paws.

"Would you like some tea, Dan? Coffee?"

"I want you to tell me if you love him."

Absently, eyes running over the walls, the ceilings, she said, "David? I think so."

"Who belted you?"

"David did." She did not put her hand to it, touch the welt with her fingertips, but gazed at him round-eyed, with openness, honesty, letting him see. "I got thrown against a bedpost."

She leaned forward, brushed the cat away, then folded her hands around her knee, as if to keep the leg still.

He said, "You live with him and you don't know whether or not you love him?"

"Yes, I live with him, Dan. We are cohabiting."

Her foot was still, toes a few inches from the floor, pointing to it. Her robe, belted but not buttoned, was open to her waist.

"Have you lived with many men?"

"Lots," she said. "Lots."

With no energy, speed, grace, poise, or bounce, but instead as if performing a task, a ritual, with heaviness, she half filled the teakettle from the faucet, put it on a burner.

Dan said, "Janet, you are not married."

"Should I be? Lots of people are."

"You are living with a man and you are not married to him."

She took cups out of the cupboard, cleared a place for them on the counter by brushing things aside with her wrist. She put a tea bag in each, and poured the hot water into them.

"No one needs a minister, Dan. The world is a little beyond that."

She brought the tea across to him, a cup and saucer in each hand, not trying hard to hold her robe together with her elbows.

Dan said, "I don't drink with sluts."

Changing direction just slightly, leaning to her right, she put his cup on the reading table beside his chair. She returned to the divan.

"You'll be thirsty, Dan."

She sipped her tea, once, before putting it on the floor at her feet. She crossed her legs and lit a cigarette, waving the match out with a loose wrist.

"Any idea what happened?" he asked.

"What do you mean what happened?"

"What caused all this." He waved his hand generally, to mean her, the room, the world.

She made a face, picked a piece of tobacco from her tongue.

"Evil companions in my youth."

In the light, summer chair, cushioned, Dan crossed his arms, bent one knee, looked down his other leg, running straight to the floor, foot resting on the heel.

There was an explosion of smoke from her mouth, as she tried to inhale and swear at once. Pushing, hitting hard, she swept the kitten away from the teacup with the back of her hand.

"Oh, Prescott, come off it," she said. "Have you lived in a vacuum all your life? Haven't you ever seen anything to make you think you might be wrong?"

"Janet, you look sick and beat up. What do you expect me to say? Atta girl, Janet, old flame of my youth—whatever you're doin', keep it up?"

"You're not a medical doctor, and I feel fine. Except for a slight hangover."

"I don't care about your hangover."

"I know, it's my soul. Well there's nothing wrong with my soul a Bloody Mary wouldn't cure, either."

Elbows on his knees, trying to catch her eyes, enter them, go into her as he never had before, Dan said, "Look, Janet. To hell with my collar. I love you. Or have.... " Her face, taut, raised, was turned away, eyes closed. "Someday, you're going to need a depth you haven't got. You're going to reach for it and you're going to find it's not there. And you're going to get hurt."

Between his fingers, between his palms, was sweat.

"You'll realize that sometime or other you denied yourself this depth, refused to do something you should do, be something you should be, deprived yourself of the opportunity to grow, even in love. You'll get hurt, Janet."

The smile came, finally, Janet's smile, challenging, chin cocked, her wonderful brown eyes steady on his face, as always acknowledging that distance between them, admitting, finally, as always, she had leapt beyond him, over him, in understanding, not always of her, but of himself: "And what about you, junior? Of what opportunities to grow have you deprived yourself?"

He drew the palms of his hands along his trousers, felt the back of the chair against his shoulder blades.

"How much does it hurt, Dan?"

The door opened with a key and MacFarlane came in.

"Hi," he said. "So you finally made it."

Dan stood up.

MacFarlane stood behind Janet, behind the divan, overcoat over his arm.

Janet said, pettishly, whimpering, in the tone of a spoiled wife, "This gentleman has been calling me a slut, David."

MacFarlane dropped his coat over the divan back. Evenly, easily, he leaned over and kissed her just below the welt.

"You are a slut," he said. "A dirty little slut. What shall we do with her, Reverend?"

Not offering to shake hands, he crossed to the cupboard and took out a bottle of Scotch, three glasses, putting them on the counter where the teacups had been.

"Would you like a drink, Reverend?"

"No. I was just leaving."

"He doesn't drink with sluts," Janet said.

To the gurgle of drinks being poured, the bottle hitting the lip of one glass, then the other, Dan walked across the room, conscious in his knees of his walking, opened the door, the knob surprisingly cold in his hand, and left, not saying goodbye.

19

David put the third glass back into the cupboard and took down a pitcher.

"He could almost be your brother," he said. From habit he filled the pitcher with water, poured from it into the glasses, not bothering with ice. "He looks so much like you," he continued.

She took one of the drinks from him absently, not looking at him, not tasting it.

From where he sat on the divan, next to her, her face was in profile, her jawline pointing to the fire poker.

"Guess what," he said lightly. "I bought a car."

In her lap the middle finger of her free hand picked the skin of her thumb.

There was a cup of tea on the floor in front of her, apparently untouched, another on the reading table beside the chair.

"Your friend left in quite a hurry," David said. Then, more gently, "Don't feel badly, Ms Tuesday."

Suddenly he saw her face in full view, surprised, prepared to smile, laugh, apparently wondering if he were serious.

"Feel badly? I feel wonderful. David, don't you understand? I had to do that." She held her glass unevenly, the liquid leaning toward the lip on one side. "That was a scene I had to play. For the first time in my life I feel truly free."

His shirt, Ms Tuesday's slip, a pair of slacks were on the floor in a pile between the screen and the bathroom door.

"You do know what I mean, don't you?"

"No," he answered. "I don't."

"Why don't you?"

"I should think you'd feel badly. He gave you quite a sermon, didn't he?"

"That's what I mean. He looked so intense and silly. All those things he said. He sounded silly. And before he left, he knew it."

David had arranged with Madame Sudar to come up and clean, later, in the afternoon.

Ms Tuesday said, "People can't see the world through any one thing, David, not anymore. You can't see everything through a church, or a profession."

"It helps," he said. "To have something. To have a way of looking at things."

"No, it doesn't," she said. "Any one way is a lie. Simply because there are so many things a person could be."

"Screw philosophy," David said. "He's an old friend, and he's disappointed. I should think you'd feel sorry for him."

"Why should I feel sorry for him?" Finally, she took a swallow from her drink, a big swallow for first in the day. "And one day I shall understand you, too."

"And what will you do then?" he asked. "Chew me up and spit me out too?"

She smoothed the ridge of his ear with her thumb and index finger. "Maybe."

He said, "I bought a car. I always thought I'd buy a car, when I got married. Whether I was settled down or not."

She put her arms around his neck, her head against his chest.

"It's a very nice car," he said. "A yellow Mercedes-Benz convertible, with red leather seats."

"That's nice," she said. "Can I see it?"

"It won't be delivered for a few days. My check for cash so surprised them they decided they needed a few days to prepare it for the road."

"Oh."

David lifted his glass over her head and drank from it.

"David, where will we go in our new car?"

"To London." He rested his glass, his hand, on her back, between her shoulder blades. "I have to go to London soon to play at the Someplace. I'm going to take a week off, sometime. Then we have to go to New York to make a new recording and see some people, and I believe there is a concert in there, somewhere; I don't remember where, maybe London. Then in the spring we are due down in Cannes for a while. Will you come with me?"

Against his chest, relaxed, drowsy, she said, "Of course, darling."

He lifted his glass again, took another drink.

"You know what I was thinking, Ms Tuesday?"

"What were you thinking? Tell me."

"I was thinking that as long as I'll be taking some time off we might get married and use that for our honeymoon. We might go to Nassau."

Her body tightened perceptibly, stopped moving, froze; her eyes opened against his shirt.

"Let's not get complicated," she said. Her voice was no longer drowsy but strong, deprecating. "Things are complicated enough."

He finished his drink. "Never mind."

"Don't get angry." She sat up abruptly, swinging her legs to the floor, staring at it for the length of a thought, a connection.

"You're almost as bad as Dan Prescott."

"What did I say?"

"Everybody is trying to get me committed to some goddamned thing or another."

She picked her glass up from the floor and drained it as she walked across the room to the kitchenette. David watched her from the divan. She took a plastic bag of ice from the refrigerator, threw two cubes into her glass, covered them with Scotch. Ignoring the pitcher of water, she held her glass under the tap for a fraction of a second.

He said, "Why are you pouring yourself another drink when you haven't even gotten dressed?"

With a wonderfully feminine gesture, an underhand toss, she hurled the contents of the glass at him. Scotch-water and ice came across the room at him in a stream, widening into separate brown and silvery globules that splattered his face, his hair, his shirt.

He said, "That was very philosophical of you."

Immediately, then, she came over, solicitously, apologetically, yet as if forgiving him. "I'm sorry."

She knelt before him, lifted his necktie, dabbed his chin, his cheek, forehead, nose with it.

"I'm so sorry. Did I hurt you?"

He ran his tongue over his upper lip. "It's a little stronger than I usually like it."

"Oh, my poor darling. I got you all wet. Really, I'm terribly sorry."

"It was a bitchy thing to do," David said.

"I know it was. I don't mean to be a bitch."

He put his glass on the cushion beside him, against the back, and with both hands spread the lapels of her bathrobe. The top button of her pajamas was already undone.

"Come up here."

She lay on her back across his lap, her legs in pajama pants extending the length of the divan. She flipped her furry slippers off, over the divan arm.

He pulled the ends of the robe belt apart, spread the robe, the pajama jacket, then lay his hands on her, one on the breast farther from him, the other on the flat of her stomach, and moved them.

"You really feel through your hands, don't you," she said.

He lowered his head, stretching the back of his neck and pressing his chin into his own collarbone, raised her body with his legs. He kissed the breast nearer him.

She put her hands behind his head and held him.

"You're a fool," she said. "You're all fools. You all take yourselves so seriously."

20

Dan was walking along the sidewalk the other side of the street, head down, jacket collar up, hands in pockets. Without looking he crossed the street.

John leaned sideways from his chair and tapped on the window of the cafe.

Dan looked through the window, at John, at the glass of *vin blanc* on the little table, shook his head *no*, and walked on.

John went out to the sidewalk to catch him.

"Where are you going, Dan?"

Dan stopped, turned, looked at him without saying anything.

"Come in and have a drink with me," John said.

Dan's eyes ran over the signs pasted on the inside of the window. "That's a bar, isn't it?"

"Yes, that's a bar. Why can't you come in?"

"Because, whether anybody likes it or not, I'm a minister, and ministers aren't supposed to be seen in bars."

"Nonsense," John said. "This is France. The French have never confused liquor and sex with morality." A man in a kelly green turban passed them. "A cafe here is like a drugstore back home. A soda shop. I'm not going to argue with you. I'm offering to buy you a drink. If you don't want to drink with me, it's all right. I've had that happen to me before."

Dan said, "Always putting things in black and white, is that it?"

John put his arms around Dan's shoulders, hugged him. "You're beautiful."

"Anyway," Dan said, "Last time I saw you I belted you."

"Maybe I'll belt you before this night is over."

"How's your mouth?"

"It hurts something awful, you bastard."

"I guess I'm sorry," Dan said.

"Never mind that. Come have a drink."

The glass of *vin blanc* had been removed while John was on the sidewalk. He ordered two cognacs.

"Does it ever snow in Paris?" Dan asked.

"Of course."

Dan was not wearing a topcoat. His jacket collar was up. His light brown hair was damp on his forehead. Through perfectly clear skin his temples pulsed. His eyes were brilliant, feverish. He was shivering.

"I would like to see snow."

Dan Prescott's neck had the kind of muscle in it that meant a perfectly trim body, perpetually conditioned, kept in shape, every day, week, month, season of his life to date, motivated by something, expecting something.

Dan said, "I didn't go the other day. I saw her just this morning."

"So."

"So she's living with MacFarlane."

"So."

"So I'm in love with her. I always have been. I always will be. She's living with someone else and I'm as mad as hell."

The waiter swooped his tray at them, stopped it, lifted the two little glasses of cognac onto the table. John paid him.

"You're a nice boy, Dan."

"I'm a jerk."

"You're innocent, healthy, and good. You have the instinct to love, respect everybody. And when you find you can't, you're hurt."

"I guess so."

"You're riding in the clouds with a lot of mother-loving ideals."

"Do I have to belt you again?"

"Isn't it true?"

"Yes. I suppose so." Dan put his thumb against the side of the little glass, as if measuring its content. "What you said last week was true, too."

"Drink up, Reverend," John said. "Have you ever been drunk?"

"Yes. Once. Quite drunk."

"When was that?"

"When I was in the service."

"Tell me about it."

"No. I can't. Getting drunk stinks."

Dan took his hand away from the glass, put his hands in his lap or somewhere below the surface of the table, perhaps one inside each knee, and slouched his shoulders forward. He turned his head away, down to the side, as if reacting quietly to physical pain, an old wound, a new wound, a blow to his stomach. But his shoulders moved only slightly, with breathing, slower-than-normal breathing.

"Drink your drink," John said. "Or I will belt you."

Dan tasted his cognac, took so little none seemed to be missing from the glass when he returned it to the table. He coughed, his face screwed with distaste.

"Damn, Jack, what are we going to do? Janet is an old parishioner, a friend of my parents, her parents are friends of mine. I've got to marry them."

John said, "Your business, Reverend."

Dan sat forward, back straight, leaning on his elbows.

"What is it with Janet? What's she doing?"

"Forget about Janet," John said. "She's just a bright, beautiful girl who doesn't know what to do with herself."

"What do you mean?"

"She has an idea of freedom, but she hasn't any idea what to do with it. Freedom without a purpose is terrifying."

Listening, engrossed, willing to understand, be told, perhaps even to grasp at straws, but wanting to think, Dan looked at him. He ducked his brown eyes, put half his cognac in his mouth, then looked at him again.

"You mean she's scared."

"I mean she's terrified." His pipe: having it in his hand, the bowl between his fingers, filling it, tapping it, putting the stem in his mouth, lighting it, the first drag, an inhale, then puffing on it as the tobacco cooled in its own ash—John would love to be smoking his pipe. He lit a cigarette. "Whatever you may think of her at the moment, she's really quite nice, you know. Attractive, spirited, amusing, with a strange, hesitant perception of and reaction to people. In light of everything she's got, her fear really makes her quite lovable."

Dan's eyes, bright, desperate, went over John's face. Without looking, Dan finished his cognac.

John signaled for another.

"What will become of her, do you think?"

And a pipe can sometimes conceal an inadvertent smile.

"I think, finally, she will free herself from something from which she does not want to be free, if she hasn't already done so. Freedom has to have a purpose, even a stupid one, like poetry."

Dan said, "You ought to be a writer."

John said, "I ought to be."

On the sidewalk, two hours later, in the dark, John lit a cigarette, waiting for Dan to catch up to him. Dan insisted he wanted one too: his first one ever, he said. Then he insisted on lighting his cigarette from the streetlight, shinnying up the lamppost, finally falling. He sat on the sidewalk, laughing. John lit the cigarette for him. Dan took one breath of it, suddenly looked frightened, as if a horrid idea had occurred to him, horrid in its conception, frightening in its implication, waited a moment, got onto his hands and knees and decently, urgently, crawled to the curbstone. He vomited into the gutter. John held Dan's forehead. Then Dan sat on the sidewalk and laughed some more.

"Jack, I'm acting positively antisocial." He knelt on the curbstone again. Gently he laid his pocket handkerchief over the mess.

"Leave it," John said. "Let's go get a drink."

"Let's go get a drink," Dan said.

He got up fast, as if he had been knocked down on the football field, had the ball, had to run, dodge, dart with it. He straight-armed two garbage pails, one either side of the street, making loud clatters, swerved around a woman pedestrian, startling her, gained the corner, touched the non-existent football to the sidewalk and tossed it up in the air.

Making what appeared to be a beautiful pass, he called, "Pardon me, Madame."

He waited for John.

In Café Jérome's he sat forward in his chair again, forearms on the table, back straight, eyes bright, face hot, eager to talk this time, rather than listen. He spoke fast, everything wanting to come out at once, in a rush, a confession, before he was interrupted, before he died.

"You ask why I became a minister."

"No, I didn't," John said.

"All right. I'll tell you. You won't believe it."

"Yes, I will."

"No you won't. You may have gone to Harvard, Nelson, but you don't know everything."

"All right. So tell me why you became a minister."

"You live in a world that must deny certainties in order to survive, but what you don't know, is that so do I. Dan Prescott is not trying to sell the people any absolute bill of goods, which they must purchase or go to hell. It's because things are not certain that I became a minister. If things were certain then there would be no justification for a certain number of people putting on collars and trying to act as if there were certainties. It is because life is so damned terrifying, Jack, so rife with horrible and frightening possibilities that I have purposely adopted an essentially unpopular, but needed, necessary perspective of human existence, offering it with my hands and the strength of my arms to those who are desperate and who need it. It is only because there is genuine doubt, real doubt, true doubt that I propose the use of a religious system which, by its nature and act of faith, rules out doubt, excludes it because it is important, and too, too devastating."

There was an American couple, about thirty-five, standing at the bar, watching Dan. They seemed to know him, be interested in what he was doing, saying. They had recognized him. But they did not come over, or speak to him.

"You're an anachronism," John said.

Later on, in another bar, at another table, with the same intensity, the same damp, strained face, Dan said, "But for all that, I am the enemy of the people. I stand for something they must ignore, especially in their youth, their masculinity, their femininity, so they can see existence as it is, in all its horror and wonder, and run smack into every possibility. They must reject the act of faith, or they will never know what faith is. But in doing it, they reject me, too; they say, Don't act like a minister, attribute innocence, blindness, naivete to me. Not all that justified, they ask me, doubting it, Have you ever seen anything that might make you think you are wrong? All I have seen, Jack, indicates to me that I am wrong, terribly wrong; that people could be so much better off without faith, if they could find their own strength and courage to face existence, without having to borrow the faith of the minister in their community. Religion is the sedative, Jack, it's the great big pill. But life is the pain. It's a great big toothache. The pain is there, and it is real, intense. By itself, it can drive men mad. Because the pain can be so bad, there has to be the sedative. If everyone had his own courage, there would be no need for ministers."

"My life isn't a toothache," John said. "It's more of an electronic hum."

"What?"

"An electronic hum. There's no pain from a hum. Sometimes I get tired of listening to it but when I do I go to bed and sleep."

Without supper, at about eleven o'clock, in an unknown bar on an unknown street, Dan said, "Do you think I want to shove the Christian story down people's throats?"

"No, I don't," John said.

"I love the Christian story. I could weep over it. I love the tender baby, who is Christ, being born in the manger, and the strange dignity of youth, which is not arrogance, but which lectures wise men in a temple, and I love the fellow who sympathizes with the human need to have a party, provides people with wine at a wedding feast, when they've already had some. I love the annual sorrow of the crucifixion, the man, in the fullness of his strength, painfully destroyed, because he wasn't understood, the sip of vinegar, the sweet forgiveness, the resurrection, and the life."

"Everlasting."

"But at the same time, I don't care about it. I'm not a storyteller, Jack, or a singer of legendary songs."

"No. You're not."

"I'm a guy who wanted to take Janet to bed with me when I was fourteen, and still do. I love her and I've been horny for her since I first scratched my pubic hair."

"Why didn't you?"

"Why didn't I what?"

"Take her to bed with you?"

"Because I'm a Christian."

"You're an anachronism."

There was a girl, a sweet young girl, with a small round face cupped in dark hair, at a table with two other girls. She had been glancing at John, watching him, smiling at him. Her short skirt was bright and happy, a narrow towel, really, as if for the beach, striped in red and green and white, covering only from low on her hips to high on her thighs. Her round legs came out from under the table, and were crossed, one arced over the other's knee.

Dan said, "What I'm saying is that it means too much. Things have to be put in order and done right, or chaos prevails. Existence can overwhelm you. You have to hold if off, doing things in order and with restraint. A few must succeed in holding things off totally, doing everything perfectly right and in order. Because the rest come to these people, with desperation in their eyes, despair in their souls, terror in their hearts. And then they must have someone. They

must have their ministers, who can speak to them of taking existence in order, of doing things right, of not letting life get ahead of
them. Life can so easily, you know."

Dan put his head down, finally, on his forearms crossed on the
table. His shoulders relaxed, collapsed.

"You're an anachronism," John said.

"Jack."

"What."

"She never said, 'Goodbye, Dan.' She never said it was over. She
never told me we weren't going to be married." His voice was slow,
thick, coming up from the table surface, through his sleeves. "Why
didn't she, Jack?"

"I don't know."

The girl smiled, nodded her head at Dan.

"Why didn't she tell me?"

"Listen, Dan." He leaned over and held Dan's arm. "Listen."

"What."

John took his hand back. "I don't know."

"What, Jack."

John said, "You're an anachronism."

"You're a poet."

"You're an anachronism and I'm a poet."

Perhaps trying to get up, in a hurry again, to go somewhere
quickly, do something that needed doing decently, Dan fell sideways
out of his chair. Trying to grab the table, steady himself, he pulled it
after him, on top of him, to the floor.

Finding himself sitting alone in the middle of the room without a
table, John stood up.

Dan was lying on his back, straight, arms not far from his sides.
One leg was bent at the knee only slightly. The edge of the small,
round table top rested on his stomach. There was broken glass,
spilled brandy on the tile around his shoulders. His face was relaxed. Eyes closed, unconscious, asleep, he swallowed, with difficulty. His cheeks were wet in streams, from tears.

The three girls came over, being careful not to step on the glass.

"Is he a priest?"

"No."

A girl lifted the table off Dan, slowly, gently, as if pulling back bed
covers, looking at his face.

"He's beautiful."

"He's an actor," said John. "On his way home."

"He must be an actor," said the second girl.

The first unbuttoned Dan's jacket.

"May I see him?" asked the second.

"Sure," John said. "He's playing in *The Deputy*."

"Look at his shoulders, his hips, his legs," said the second.

"Look at his skin," said the first. Kneeling in the glass, she dried his cheeks with her fingertips. "This must be the first drink he has ever had."

"He's pretty white just now," John said.

"He's beautiful," said the second.

The first pushed his damp hair with her fingers, made a straight line of it across his forehead.

"Would he ever make love to me?" she asked John.

"Of course. Just ask him. When he's feeling better."

"I should like to have him in bed," said the second.

The third took John's hand.

Her short, bright skirt seemed far below him.

"What's your name?" he asked.

"Marianne."

"Why are you so fascinated by me?"

"Because I have never made love to a black person."

"Would you like to?"

"Of course."

His hand was wet around hers.

"I'm not feeling terribly well at the moment," he said. "Myself."

"I know that."

"I'll come back."

"All right."

"Tomorrow night."

The first girl had pulled Dan's shirt out of his trousers. She put her palm against the skin of his stomach.

"Will you bring back your friend? Tomorrow night?"

"I don't know. He has to play tomorrow night," John said. "In *The Deputy*."

The second girl was simply standing, staring.

John let go of Marianne's hand.

Dan groaned. Annoyance flickered in his face. He said, "Shit," when John picked him up, fireman-fashion, bracing Dan's feet on the floor with his own, pulling up on his arms, ducking, letting him fall over his shoulder.

"He's beautiful," said the second.

Going through the door, John heard something behind him crack against the frame. Dan said nothing.

Marianne came to the sidewalk.

"Tomorrow night," she said. "You will remember?"

John said, "I'll be back."

He had taken only a few steps, when Dan vomited down John's back.

21

There was a yellow Mercedes convertible straight against the curb, its windows rolled up, both lock buttons down. It looked terribly out of place in this neighborhood, a shining, glorious, metal, rubber, and canvas object amid slimy cobblestones, rotten wood. A beam of sunlight reflecting from the chrome at the top of the windshield stabbed Dan in the eyes. It pierced to the back of his head.

Opening the door to her apartment, Janet popped her eyes at him.

"Why, Dan. You looked absolutely dissipated."

"I have a headache."

"Were you drunk last night?"

"The night before. Yesterday I was nothing."

MacFarlane stood up from the single chair, a copy of *Time* magazine folded in his hand.

"Hello there, Reverend Dan. Been nipping the altar wine, have you?"

Sunlight gleamed on the polished floor. The gauze over the French door had been removed. The little panes of glass shone.

Dan sat on the divan.

MacFarlane said, "Would you like some coffee?"

Dan rubbed his face, his eyes, with his hands, trying to rub out all of the sunlight.

"I've come to ask you two if you won't get married."

"Why, Dan," Janet said, from somewhere to his side, somewhere near Humphrey Bogart. "How sweet of you."

"I'm not being sweet," Dan said. "In fact, I'm being a fool. But I feel some responsibility to my father's parish, of which you are a member, however absentee."

"Isn't that sweet, David?"

MacFarlane had moved to the back of the chair and was looking at Dan with steady eyes, surprised, respectful, a little amused, somehow grateful. His white shirt collar was open. "We were just about to have some coffee," MacFarlane said.

"I drank an awful lot of that stuff yesterday."

"Have tea instead," Janet said.

"All right."

She got a third cup and saucer down from the cupboard. There was nothing else on the counter but a small bottle of instant coffee. The screen had been folded to the other side of the kitchenette, against the wall.

MacFarlane put his magazine on the mantelpiece.

"I'm sorry, Dan," he said. "Ms Tuesday and I have talked this over and decided against it. We're not going to get married."

The kitten came around the side of MacFarlane's chair.

"Ms Tuesday?" It was the first Dan had heard either the description or the name.

"Janet." MacFarlane's upper arms lay straight against the chair back, sleeves rolled halfway up the forearms. Each wrist, forearm, was a remarkable cable of veins and muscles, intertwined, in strings. "It's my decision, really. My responsibility."

The kitten leapt onto Dan's lap.

"Oh, David." Janet said from the stove. "Why be so harsh?" She was pouring hot water into the three cups. "I mean, if that's what Dan wants, that's what Dan wants." She brought them each a cup. "He's an old friend, isn't he?"

She got her own cup and saucer and sat in a chair, knee under her chin. She sipped her coffee.

"You will marry me, won't you, David?"

"Ms Tuesday, what on earth are you saying?"

"I'm asking you to marry me," she said into her coffee cup.

"Are you serious?"

"Of course I'm serious. Why wouldn't I be?" The kitten left Dan's lap and wandered up the divan. "Here this nice gentleman comes to the door, asking us to get married, and the least we can do is oblige. You will marry me, won't you, David?"

His fingers were gripping the cushion either side of her head. His knuckles were white.

He said, "Of course."

"And Dan will marry us," she said. "Won't you, Dan?"

He said, "Of course."

"Great."

She lowered her foot and the coffee cup to the floor, sat forward, her fingers reaching to her chin, her eyes and mouth flashing with eagerness, happiness, anticipation.

"We'll have a big wedding," she said. "At the Club Solo. Thursday night."

"This is Monday," MacFarlane said.

"So what?"

"Things don't happen that fast in France. It takes time to get a license."

"We're living in sin, David. Tell that to the clerk."

MacFarlane raised his hand to the back of his neck, turned to walk away but, instead remained to examine her face each time she turned it up to him.

"Are you being serious about this?"

"Why, David, as serious as I'll ever be." More to Dan, or to the room, or to herself, she said, "Chump can be best man. Madame Sudar can be matron. You'll have to get a hold of John, David, tell him to come."

"John who?"

"John Bart Nelson."

The kitten had curled at the far end of the divan and gone to sleep.

"And you'll have to get all your New York and London people to come. They'll bring presents, make much more of a party out of it." She was leaning back in her chair, the tip of her index finger on her lower lip. "I wonder if we can get Greg up from Spain."

"Ms Tuesday, there isn't time. For the license."

She waved her hand at him. "Oh, David, you can spend money. And if things aren't just right, so what."

Still rubbing the back of his neck, MacFarlane went into the bedroom.

"We'll have it at midnight," she said to Dan. "That way we won't know whether we were married Thursday or Friday."

Through the door Dan watched MacFarlane lift a suitcase down from a closet shelf.

"I know lots of people we can invite," she said.

The clasps of the suitcase snapped open.

"What a wonderful idea, Dan; your marrying us. I know how much it means to you."

MacFarlane stopped at the door. He leaned his shoulder against the frame.

"David? Maybe you and I can go to Nassau for our honeymoon after London. Remember? While you're resting."

There was something in MacFarlane's left hand.

She turned, bringing her leg into the chair again, knee bent against its back, to look at MacFarlane in the doorway.

"You won't mind getting the marriage license, will you, David? Dan can go with you. He learned French in school."

MacFarlane said, "I think I can get the general idea across."

Walking by her, he dropped a small box in her lap.

"Why, David," she said. "A ring."

His standing at the French door blocked the sunlight from the floor.

"A diamond. How sweet!"

She put it on, herself.

"It's lovely, David. Where on earth did you get it?"

"Someplace," he said. "Amsterdam, I guess."

"It's lovely. Isn't it lovely, Dan?"

He could not see it.

"David. Come kiss me."

The patch of sunlight lit the floor again.

MacFarlane leaned over her, kissed her on puckered lips.

"Do you promise to wear it forever and ever?" he asked.

She batted her eyelids at him. "Until my finger turns green."

She laughed across the room, her legs together, holding the little, open box.

"Isn't this fun, Dan?"

22

It was the car that attracted the most attention, or the most comment, at the wedding, more than the bride or the groom, or anything else. A new, yellow Mercedes convertible, leaning nonchalantly against the curb in front of the Club Solo, front wheels turned slightly, suggestively, outward, a sculptured presence among the people on the sidewalk, the long-haired, short-haired, bearded, shaven, booted, leather-slippered, hands-in-the-back-pocketed, manicured, denim-jacketed, tailored people, friends of David, wedding guests, the car's chrome, its yellow glistening in the streetlights to burst an adman's heart. Here was something to look at, talk about without shame or shyness, David's child, symbol of David's prosperity; there with a certain, innocent past, definite future.

"Car, David. Car, car, car."

Ms Tuesday sat at the center of a line of seats facing roomward along a long table. David and Chump moved back and forth between the table and the platform. The wedding guests came by the table as they came in to say hello to Ms Tuesday, to be introduced, some of them, to each other.

"We're going to London in the morning, you know, after this thing is over. In the new car. To London, to London, to see the bean." Too dry-mouthed to fight the music, the noise, she shouted words, phrases as they occurred to her. "David's playing at the Someplace. Chump will be in the back seat, naturally."

"Sick, naturally."

Many people had come to the reception, or party, or whatever you could call an all-night bash with a wedding in the middle of it. They flew from New York and London and Rome, taxied from good apartments, hiked Paris streets from cold water lofts to wish the couple happiness. In fact, they talked about the new car, holding it swordlike over each of their own conversational groups, using it to break ice, cool heat. All the old and new jazz names were there, those who had survived, were surviving, plus the sad-eyed, twitchy-fingered folk bunch, plus a few of the newest, hottest music names, acolytes at this altar of commercial establishment, self-conscious, nervous, trying to create manners of their own, ignorant of established manners, rejecting them anyway, but shining in the significance of their inclusion, of their, too, having been able to fly to a wedding on short notice. People who had no names but were hoping that by being there, at this odd rejection of traditional society, culture, they would be creating their own names in this immediate society, culture, were most noisily there, with their guitars, new instruments, with things they had created, songs to sing, carefully, obliquely, to rouse curiosity but not to expose, to sell but not give. Recording agents, date agents, publicity agents, distributors conversationally imbalanced by their singular concern with what the public wants, had all come over from London, New York, yawning on the planes, hating this trip but doing it because this jolliness was business. The parents of the bride, of course, from Columbia Falls, Maine, could not make the trip on such short notice. Kids, sort of old kids at this point, those still being artists, musicians, writers this week, making the Paris scene as they had made the summer camp, college scenes, and with not much more involvement, the oedipal sucklings of Mother Art, slow to wean, from up the street, around the corner, the street itself, stood outside, tumbled in, stood outside again, free liquor firing in their hollow stomachs. And there were those from the right-hand fringe as well, a few, like the Baldwins of Philadelphia, those who do everything, read every book, see everything to be seen, hear everything, for conversational purposes, to bring the story home, the zoo watchers, perpetually marveling, surprised, unsure, prepared, hoping to be shocked, to have their worlds violated, in three-piece suits, inevitable small glasses of what is being drunk now in the left hand, right hand working cigarettes, lighters.

"What time will the match take place? I have no idea. Sometime after the club is closed. Where is Danny boy?" At that point there were two glasses in front of Ms Tuesday, one with ashes, a half-smoked cigarette floating in it, the other half full of Scotch. A third was being brought. "My goodness, who are all these people?"

On the platform Chump and David were working through "Deme Lo" with utter musical indifference. A group was against a side wall in two rows, one facing the other, fingering their guitars, drum sticks, harmonicas, mouthpieces, unable to be quiet, making little, jarring noises. Magazine-thin electric guitars were on the floor, propped against their legs, chair legs, crazy designs in plastic some-how reflecting light directly in this midnight place dark from indi-rect lighting.

Wedding guests took the tables the public was vacating, looking at each other, trying not to be curious: dinner jackets, denim jack-ets, one morning suit and sneakers. There were three or four pho-tographers there from the news services, ducking about, trying to find the one right combination of angles, perspective, to capture this jam by a single note. After midnight, David refrained from playing anything he had made famous, "Sorry," "Greasy Pig," "Deme Lo," refrained from playing anything at all, really, as a discouragement to the public, just phony jazz, chords, runs hardly based on a melody. Chump soared and burped through his machine irrelevantly, for once in his life devoid of pressing musical integrity. Many, seeing something private was about to happen, that they did not belong to this whole new group coming into the club, had the courtesy to leave.

John Bart Nelson arrived, looking tall and proper in his dark blue suit, white shirt and tie. He introduced Marianne, a wide-eyed Par-isian moppet who said nothing all evening. Nothing to her was of interest, worth her glance, but John. She was dressed in a flower print dress straight from the Galeries Lafayette. Madame Sudar ar-rived with a brown paper bag of peaches, which had probably been difficult to get in that season. Like most romantics, she was fully prepared to cry at the wedding, anxious in these odd surroundings she might miss the cue.

At that point, John was just finishing the twelfth, final draft of his long poem, "Pentecost," and his manner was full of the quietness, his face, the repose, of the lonely conqueror, the exhausted, the relaxed, the satisfied. Madame Sudar was describing to him in gen-tle tones, with quick, charming smiles, some affair of her own, when she was young. Marianne sat quietly, her hand in John's. Oblivious to these people at her table, Ms Tuesday blinked at the room, picked with her fingernails at the skin of a peach she had rolled from the bag. As if it were the crux of their occupation, as if they had been paid especially, bribed, the waiters freshened Ms Tuesday's drink, brought her new ones, replaced glass after glass.

And Milton Farber, having flown alone from New York, sat to one side, drinking wine, hearing the music. Milton Farber did not like flying, did not want wine and, in truth, did not like music. He liked being David's and Chump's manager.

Schatzy entered, looking most out of place in this odd society, alone, charming, eager to please, to be accepted. Older than almost anyone there, not tall, but distinguished, slim in his dinner jacket, wide-set, slapped-open eyes flared next to the gray of his temples. With erect carriage, smooth walk, he insinuated himself among those at the bar, buying drinks for, listening to, laughing with those who did not know him. The French, the Belgians, the Italians there could smell it from him, sense it, feel it, the leather-polish, gun-oil, antiseptic odor of his accent, the fact of his being now so alone, within himself, isolated, yet affable, open but correct. He brought a silver tea service for the bride, which, on such short notice, was probably the best present, too conspicuous, suspiciously indicative of significance, unfathomable.

Leaving his horn on the platform, Chump sat beside, between, behind John and Madame Sudar, obliging John to push his chair back a few inches, turn more sideways, and causing Madame Sudar to find reverie elsewhere in the room. Without prologue, Chump began to tell John about the blue window of Notre Dame, the experience of his life. Chump had decided at some time that he could talk to John, and he did so now, fully, choosing the occasion himself when he would sit, fairly straight in his chair, hand on one knee, compulsively, it seemed, and tell John everything, in long, hesitant, involuted sentences, his remarkable brown cow-eyes widening, protruding at the emission of every difficult thought, word, each slow to come, his lips utterly still, his face expressionless between phrases, between sentences. Some abhor talking to people; some just abhor talking: to Chump, talking was a grating, unstructured noise. Through John, having some of the manners, the habits, of a listener, Chump had discovered that he could talk, make sounds less than objectionable to himself and, to his mind, this meant he should talk. A dozen times a sentence, in one of Chump's long, pushing pauses, John would begin a rejoinder, only to have Chump raise his hand from his knee, palm outward like a policeman at a corner, signaling John to wait, there was something coming from another direction, and John would stop, *t*'s or *s*'s aborted on his lips, raise his eyes to Chump's face again, to wait, to time the movement of thought by the protuberance of Chump's eyes, would be only temporarily relieved to see them pop, hear the word, finally, at most, three or four words, then would wait again, until John was satisfied again that verbally Chump was exhausted, then would form new *t*'s or *s*'s, only to see the palm go up again, the eyes protrude. John followed this monologue patiently, like a trekker on a country road, believing it must lead somewhere, there must be some point, it required so much effort, continuing on the straight only because there is a curve ahead, around the curve only because there is another straight, yet all without certain or at least immediately perceptible progress, even definite direction. Like a priest beyond the screen, in the smoke, the noise, the crush, the midnight, John heard all about Chump's blue window of Notre-Dame.

Leaning over, interrupting graciously then, Ms Tuesday said, "Really, Chump, how could you let David spend so much money on a car?"

"What?"

"I bet it hasn't even got a camshaft, or whatever are those things it drives with. A universal. Does it have a horn?"

"It has a horn."

"Good, good." Her eyes, but not her lids, rose to Chump's face. "That should please you ever so much."

David stood behind her, black tie, jaunty as only a groom can be marrying someone a little younger than himself or than usual, respectable as only a man can be confronting the irregularities of his own life, the odd hours, habits, friends, at the one moment when he particularly wishes things more regular than odd. Hands on the back of Ms Tuesday's chair, his eyes, worried, fatalistic, searched momentarily in John's, for a responsibility not his own, then they became masked, in boredom, indifference.

"David." Ms Tuesday found one of his hands and put it on her shoulder, which is perhaps what the stance should have been, was meant to be. "We were just talking about your camshaft."

The fingers of her other hand streaked the condensation on her glass.

David, nervousness powering indifference, used a casual tone with an edge so thin it was barely perceptible: "Ms Tuesday, where did that tea service come from?"

"Why, David, I have no idea."

"Who gave it to us?"

"Maybe one of your New York people. A distributor. Don't they have such things stashed in closets, for emergencies?"

David's mock indifference, casualness, thresholding to fury, embarrassment, was expressed to John in a glance, and drew from him a smile, a shrug.

"I do remember someone hoped to throw in a bag," Ms Tuesday said. Like a girl, then, having messed the Pythagorean Theory: "I do hope someone remembered to throw in a bag. A tea bag."

Madame Sudar tried discussing flower arranging with Marianne, then the trick of cleaning brass with lemon juice with Chump. Two or three groups were playing, the room a garish history of music's recent past, all things together, jazz, rock, folk, new jazz, all their combinations, new this, that, in truth a great many instruments gone through genre, made personal again, brought home from the popular ear. Melodies, keys, rhythms touched perhaps with two or three others in the room, a music in itself, multi-tracked. None of them came together in one great band, the nature of the instruments forbidding it. None of the instruments was amplified: whatever instrument or group was heard depended upon whoever had the loudest passage to play, the most exuberant idea at the moment. A slim, long-haired girl, famous for her cradle voice, like Mother's, but with more certainty, reason, sat on the floor, knees crossed, leaning forward, chin in hand, listening to only one: a closed-eyed, skinny, white-faced, dank-haired boy mouthing a harmonica; single notes, in a tiresome, plodding scale. A boy and a girl, sleepy, wine bottle in her hand, stemming, sloshing from his lower back, making a curious, red tail, danced in the midst of all this noise, mixed genius, absolutely to their own rhythm. People sat at little tables, some hunched forward, concentrating, talking, stabbing ashtrays; others slumped, silent, mesmerized, eyes glazed, enveloped by, but not absorbing this continuous rehearsal-room noise. Only those with instruments were bright-eyed, moving, truly sober, alive, eager to be recognized, measured, compared, accepted, be told, assured, how they weighed in the musical scales. The Baldwins stood separate, facing each other, sipping, talking only to each other, sparingly, eyes rotating sardonically at the others, mostly at people like themselves. Schatz huddled over an American boy with studded jacket and visored cap, cut him out from the crowd at the bar, doubtlessly was telling him how he despised vodka, after six years in a Russian camp. At the bar there was only one woman. The woman, a little too old, a little too fat, a little too blonde, listening to too many men at once, laughing at all, tolerating equally nine, thirteen stages of intoxication: the football-personified, the impossible, ungainly thing that justifies men being together in the locker room, the unlikely thing that centers them. Shortly, Madame Sudar excused herself from the silent table, enquired for the powder room.

David sat the other side of Ms Tuesday, as if at a movie, watching the room, following a trite and predictable story line, waiting for the inevitable action, someone else's resolution. Slouched, his was a look of worn bemusement, that of the ignored payer, happy to provide a good time, not displeased to be excluded from it. Sitting primly, hands folded in her lap, Ms Tuesday, facially whiter than any April bride, forced on the room, herself, her diminishing ability to focus.

John said something to David, an inconsequential but turned phrase, laughed.

Ms Tuesday leaned to him, tried to smile. "That was lovely, John. Grand."

Her hand reached slowly to the flat horizontal of John's left leg, touched it, moved along it.

"How's your sex life, John?" Her tone was a grand canyon in mountains of noise, deep-shadowed. "Is it all right?"

John's eyes retreated to his hand around Marianne's, to the crease running over his knee.

"David told me last time I embarrassed you last time I asked you about your sex life. Remember last time, John? My asking about your sex life?"

"I did not," David said. "I simply said you were drunk."

"Did I embarrass you by asking you about your sex life, John? The last time?"

"Of course not."

"You see, David." She waited for John's eyes. "I didn't embarrass him at all the last time. That was just you. Why did you scold me?"

"Because you were drunk."

"There's nothing wrong with John's sex life, is there, John?"

Reacting, finally, with a cool look, a smile, John said, "That's a different question."

David said, "Tell me, John, where do you publish? I would like to read some of your work."

"I haven't published. Poetry, you know. People don't read it."

Chump said, "I don't read anything."

Loudly, coming back to the conversation, after perhaps a momentary sickness, a churn of the mess, a loss of focus, Ms Tuesday said, "Has anyone seen Baby Dan Prescott? He's running this show, you know. Supposed to marry us."

"I saw him about a week ago," John said.

A slow, concurring, significant dip of the head from her: "So did I. Isn't that a coincidence. Does he drink with you, John?"

"Yes. He drinks with me."

"Isn't that good of him. He doesn't drink with sluts. Did you know that?"

David grabbed her arm, and jerked it. "Stop it."

"Stop that, David." She raised her arm, lowered her head to examine it. "You are hurting me."

David went to the bar, walking straighter than any man in the room at that moment. After his drink was served, he spoke a moment, quietly, with the bartender.

Ms Tuesday's fingertips touched John's leg again. Above her elbow was visible a red welt.

She said, "John, I think your poetry is grand."

"Thank you."

Leaning further toward him, her hands finally clasping each other between his thighs, elbows on her knees, confidentially speaking to his bowed head, she said, "I'm terribly sorry you're black, John."

Directly, curiously, he looked at her, almost with concern.

Madame Sudar returned, talked about peaches a moment, then helped Ms Tuesday to the ladies' room. She, too, spoke quietly to the bartender.

John and Chump remained in their seats. They talked of David's car.

The Club Solo was jammed. More news photographers and reporters appeared, prudently late as always, confident in their learned conviction that news only happens after they arrive. An occasional flashed bulb was added to the chaos.

A woman reporter stood here and there in the room, trying to develop her own way of reporting the story, to establish one single perspective that would include everything in it. She would have to know all the instruments to do it, Dan Prescott, David MacFarlane,

Chump Hardy, John Bart Nelson; more than know them, empathically be them the moments they played the theme, however long, however short, their coming together, their going apart, their themes, touching in one moment in one round, yet be away from them, to listen. From Chump Hardy she got the comment, "Everything is in the key of G."

"Isn't that Doctor Schatz over there?" she asked John.

"No, it isn't."

"Then who is it?"

"Could it be the man who delivered the car?"

"The car."

Chump said, "David bought a Mercedes."

"Oh. I see."

It was then David turned from the bar, having heard something. There was a totally new expression on his face: shock, confusion, frustration, fury. He saw Ms Tuesday was not at the table.

Pushing, brushing through chatting, mesmerized groups, David grabbed Schatz's shoulder and swung him around. The gin came out of Schatz's glass in a beautiful, slow arc.

The woman reporter signaled her photographer. All the photographers, their cameras chattering like nervous monkeys, closed in.

Fists high on his hips, David hesitated a moment, curious, amazed. "You're Schatz?"

Schatz smoothed a proper face into mild surprise, amusement.

"You're Schatz."

"Doctor Schatz, Mister MacFarlane. I'm a gynecologist."

"You're a genocide."

John's voice rumbled. "Your hands, David."

"To hell with my hands. I want to strangle this pig."

Only the harmonica, up and down in tired scales, could be heard from the room. Schatz's American boy raised his glass to his mouth with both hands, wearing the same expression as when Schatz was talking to him: bored indifference.

"Have I ever done you any harm, Mister MacFarlane?"

David swung, his fist slamming into the center of Schatz's face. The room inhaled; bulbs flashed. Schatz's glass broke against the ceiling and showered on the people standing behind him. Everyone was looking down at Schatz falling back, arms out, heels off the floor, his whole body horizontal, hitting the floor with a clatter, heels, elbows, head.

"I told Ms Tuesday to keep that bastard away from me."

Schatz's face, suddenly death-white, spurted blood even before his arms gave up.

The cameras chattered. A single scream had stopped the harmonica. Schatz's boy had drained his glass and turned to the bar for a refill.

Dan Prescott was at the door, up the steps, arrested in his entrance. Black overcoat, gloves, book, somber hat on his clear, handsome, truly American boy's face, he bit his lip just once, visibly wavering. A look at John, a proper nod; Dan turned back into the shadows of the entrance, to find a place for his hat and coat, to appear again in a moment.

"David, what are you doing?" Ms Tuesday came through the crowd. The front of her hair was damp, her make-up streaked. She looked down at Schatz.

"My God, David."

"Hey, MacFarlane. Jackpot's got 'The Wedding March.' "

"Honestly, David. I'm mortified."

With his weird, inexplicable understanding, never based on facts, information, knowledge, words, Chump handed David the silver tea service. With only mild surprise, confirmation, David took it and held it over Schatz's face.

Then he dropped it.

It landed flat on Schatz's putty-white, streaming face. In that nervous, clicking silence, the tray's sliding off, its edge hitting the floor, the teapot's tipping off, bouncing on the floor, rolling to rest on its own spout, made the strangest collection of all noises that night.

"That's enough, David." John's massive hand steered David away by the shoulder, through the crowd to the men's room. Chump moved to pick Schatz up by the shoulders.

David leaned against a sink.

"Why does she do these things? John, why must she be such a bitch? I mean, why can't she be ... "

"I know."

"You do know."

John handed him a paper cup of water. David drank it in one swallow, then remained leaning against the sink, staring at the floor, as if it were brandy he had drunk and he were waiting for it to hit. John just waited, not listening to Ms Tuesday pounding on the door, saying, "David, David."

From outside, the din had risen again. "The Wedding March" was being played in jarring seven-eighths time. Chump's horn soared around it, doing with it as he pleased. Schatz apparently had been disposed of. Doubtlessly Dan Prescott had removed his coat, entered, and was standing somewhere, probably with Madame Sudar, perhaps with a social drink in his hand, finding a conversation (about the car?), being nice, suffering agonies, wanting terribly to be away.

"David, David, I want you."

23

The sky behind the lighthouse across the harbor began to lighten. Beyond the narrow strip of sand the sea was still dark but green had risen to the surface of the water inside the harbor. At each revolution the beacon seemed less strong.

There was a crumpled pack of cigarettes in his bathrobe pocket and a paper book of matches. Turning his back on the sea he lit one, watching how strong the flame of the match was in the dawn light. The melody of "Sorry" was running through his mind. The smoke from his cigarette lay horizontally across the darkness of the open balcony door.

Below him, just beyond the railing of his balcony was the beach, the waves uncurling along it almost noiselessly. Behind him, in the bed, Ms Tuesday was asleep.

"The Wedding March" had been played in seven-eighths time, Chump sweating, standing on the piano stool blowing himself bloodshot, almost everyone in the room making noise with instruments, blaring through trumpets, screaming through clarinets, beating drums, thumping on the backs of guitars, twanging, shivering electric guitars, the rest clapping hands, stomping feet, making mouth noises. A boy and girl, both in narrow pants, T-shirts, bare feet, had cleared a space at the side of the room and were dancing a wild dance, elbows, heels flying.

Ms Tuesday stepped back from the door of the men's room when they came through, her white face puffy, her eyes trying to focus on his face. John had his hand around David's elbow.

In the middle of the room Dan Prescott stood, an incongruous martini in his hand, Madame Sudar beside him. They were both looking at, listening to the room, apparently having given up all attempts at polite remarks. Two girls, very young, in bright short skirts, large, cheap, old-fashioned beads stood with Marianne just behind Dan, exciting themselves by looking at him, up and down, craning to get glimpses of his face. His collar, gray shirt front, black suit seemed one more costume in that place, one more incongruous thing in a room full of incongruities. But it was neat. It was real, and it meant something.

By the bar, where Schatz had fallen, stood an American couple, about thirty-five, holding drinks, watching. Theirs was a different kind of ugliness: a pearl-gray business suit, slicked hair; a brightly patterned cocktail dress shortened well above baggy knees. The man was the first to notice David. He nudged his wife.

The music, the din, never did stop. Chump never did put down his saxophone or stay, for a moment, still. There was no real best man. David had the wedding ring in his own pocket and when he reached for it his elbow hit John, who was standing behind him. A harmonica continued going up and down the scales, plodding; a clarinet blew cool. *That's not an A, Turkey.* Someone beat a tattoo against his guitar box, nervously, with his thumb. Ms Tuesday, the top of her head rising and falling with every sleep-like breath, swayed. David held her tightly by the arm. A woman's high voice began singing, "I Love You Truly," in several keys. Behind Ms Tuesday, Madame Sudar was crying. Flashbulbs were popping everywhere. Actually blushing, sweating, his hands shaking around his book, Dan read the vows but David never heard him. Dan's lips were moving fast. There was a skim of perspiration over his nose. Behind him, on the platform, Chump climbed onto the closed piano and waved his saxophone at somebody near the bar.

Dan snapped his book closed and looked at David, *It's all right, It's done* in Dan's eyes.

David said, "I do."

Chump, of course, Chump began playing "Auld Lang Syne."

David kissed her.

There was the ride to the Channel beginning at dawn. Ms Tuesday's head bobbed over the picnic basket in her lap. In the back seat Chump was being sick into bags David had given him, saying nothing, otherwise. David drove through black and white snow fields, black and gray towns, large wet snowflakes falling, nothing hurrying him but the need to make Dover that night. Every once in a while

Chump had to roll down the back window to throw out a bag and there would be fresh air in the car. The engine of the Mercedes tick-ticked nicely. The tires went over the slippery spots at that speed without difficulty. They did not stop to eat.

Crossing the Channel they were all sick.

Fight Pearson was waiting for them at the Someplace. A drummer friend of the owner, he had to play with them. David got angry and roared at everybody: the contract had said nothing about an obliga-tory drummer, a friend, a bed relative of the owner, or anyone else playing with them. Then he did not care. The way they sounded they needed somebody, even a nowhere drummer who was delighted to dominate the sound, find a sound he could easily dominate, enter-tain the folks with his legerdemain.

Hardy and MacFarlane opened at the Someplace last night, to the noise of somebody or other named Pearson, and if news cuts don't lie, they can't be blamed. We understand they're both due for a vacation—for one, a honeymoon. Until they've had their rest, stay home and listen to their records. Seeing them is leaving them.

"The sand feels good," she said the first morning.

The sun was incredibly hot.

"David, you're sweating like a pig." She smoothed some lotion over his chest. "Greasy pig."

Except for the area just around her suit she tanned beautifully, rapidly, her skin turning absolutely golden, evenly, matching her hair, in just a morning, an afternoon, and the next morning. Around her suit she burned. Apparently she had never worn a bikini before.

"I've been tanned a lot," she said. "David, why are you sweating so much?"

Sitting in the shade of an umbrella they had three drinks before lunch. "Isn't the sea glorious? David, let's go snorkeling this afternoon." After having three drinks on the balcony of their bunga-low together they had one more before dinner at the restaurant. "David, why didn't you really go snorkeling? I mean, you never really went in."

"My ears can't stand it."

"Oh. Poor David."

The third morning David stayed in the bungalow dressed in slacks and a loose shirt, reading a suspense novel. Ms Tuesday was lying on her towel on the beach. He was sick of the sun, of being hot, oppressed by it, of pressing himself into the sand to escape it, sweating, swallowing from a dry mouth, thirsty, headachy, dizzy all day, shivering with cold all night. Despite the lotion his nose and chest were beginning to peel. *The world was to be destroyed, burnt to a cinder, by a gadget as big as a bug.* Even reading on the divan his legs were sweating.

When he joined Ms Tuesday under the umbrella for drinks he found two men with her. Although in their thirties they both had the bodies of boys, tans they must have worked on forever, summer and winter tans, little trunks that perfectly fit their bodies, really concealing only their pubic hair.

"Did you find out who did it?" Ms Tuesday asked.

He leaned over the table and kissed her.

"Did what?"

She had not come to change for lunch.

"Killed the butler or whatever."

"It's not that kind of a novel," he said. "It's about mass annihilation." He sat down, without waiting to be introduced. The men had not risen. "The world is to be blown up, by a madman, of course."

Ms Tuesday said, "This is Philip and Jim. They picked me up on the beach this morning."

"I doubt it."

David looked through the shade at them. The dark of their hair, their eyes, their shoulder muscles all matched.

"David, you look ill. Are you all right?"

No one had brought him a drink.

"All this sun," he said. "I'm just realizing how terribly tired I am."

"You've had a nasty sunburn," she said.

"I'm really just terribly tired."

Beyond the shade of the umbrella, heat was rising on the beach in waves, distorting the blue, green sworls of the water.

"I think I'll go lie down, if you'll excuse me." Standing, he closed his eyes against the sun. "Maybe you gentlemen would do me the favor of taking Ms Tuesday to lunch."

"Of course," Jim said.

Without closing the doors, David pulled the drapes across the balcony and lay on the bed in the shade of the room. From the pillow he could smell Ms Tuesday's perfume. Outside there was enough breeze to rustle the leaves in the palm trees.

He thought of Chump in London, wanting a motorcycle now because David had a car, and of Madame Sudar, the kitten, in Paris, prowling the stairs of that house, the alleys around the house, alone. His yellow car was in a garage off Tottenham Court Road, on Goode Street. Ms Tuesday was sitting under an umbrella a quarter-mile down the beach in a pink bikini with two healthy men. Dan had looked so brave, so self-confident that morning, light brown hair, clear skin over his white collar, black suit. *I've come to ask if you two won't get married.* Behind David, during the wedding ceremony, had been John's most solid, quiet presence. *I know.*

David rolled onto his back and wiped one cheek with the back of his hand. His hands and his arms and his shoulders and his upper back were matted with fine muscle, sodden with tiredness. Over his belt hung a white belly, softened by cheap, rich food and drink, false-energy givers. His legs were always tired, simply from nervousness. The gray light of the ceiling wavered as the drapes over the door moved in the breeze.

From way down the beach he heard a child call.

Ms Tuesday was sitting on the edge of the bed.

"Are you all right, David?"

"Yes."

"What's the matter, David?"

"I'm just tired. This sun really beats me up."

"Did you sleep?"

"I guess so."

She smelled of lotion and of gin.

The drapes over the door hung straight, not moving. The hair on her forearms was very light.

"How can you drink in the sun?" he asked.

"I can drink anywhere."

He wanted his body rubbed, all of it, in a cool place, deeply massaged by strong fingers, his shoulders, his back, his legs. He wanted to vomit everything he had ever eaten or drunk until there was nothing left in him. He wanted to keep his eyes closed, lie still, sleep for a long time. He wanted to stop listening to things, for things, airplane engines, the sound of the sea, car horns, the breeze.

"Are you sure you don't need a doctor?"

"This is just a vacation," he said. "This always happens."

"What do you mean?"

"When I stop I almost die."

"You mean this has happened before?"

"It always happens. But I forget."

She said, "Do you want a drink? It's almost time."

"I hate vacations."

That night there was a second man with the taxi driver. He had a guitar.

"This here is Rupert," said Pouch.

Pouch had picked them up every night at the bungalow or in front of the hotel, taken them every morning to the stores, the straw market, early, before they went to the beach. He serviced the colony exclusively. David would pay him, thinking he would go off. Instead he would put the car in the shade of the nearest tree and stand outside, leaning against it, waiting. As soon as David would look up for a taxi he would be there with the door open.

"I want Rupert to sing the Ms Tuesday song," Pouch said.

"Would you like me to sing the song?" Rupert asked.

They were standing at the bottom of the hotel steps, after dinner, waiting to be taken to The Cat and The Moon. Other guests were on the veranda, up and down the steps.

"Sure."

Rupert had an old brown hat on the back of his head and almost no teeth. As he sang he strummed irrelevantly on the guitar.

> There goes an Inglis Missy
> Who's as pretty as kon be.
> Her eyes as pretty as the sea,
> But I see she's not for me.

"That's good, Rupert," David said. "That's fine."

Ms Tuesday said, "He's nice."

> Well now there was this Missy
> And she went across the sea.
> I could not stop her goin';
> No, she was not made for me.

Ms Tuesday said, "Oh, that's lovely, Pouch."

"I don't know," David said. "Let's go."

"Please can we stay?" Ms Tuesday asked.

"No. Let's go."

"Thank you, Rupert," Ms Tuesday said.

In the cab, Ms Tuesday said, "Did you give him some money?"

"Yes."

Rupert and Pouch were splitting it behind the car.

"That's nice. He was a nice old man. I wonder what happened to all his teeth."

"They rotted out. From singing the same phony love song to too many women."

"Oh, David. Don't you at least like Pouch?"

He said, "Taxi drivers now have apprentice thieves."

There were many people standing around under a light outside the nightclub. They had to pass through them to get tickets and go in.

A waiter gave them a table that was not in front. The front was saved for people on the cruise ships. David understood such arrangements.

"Oh, this is fun," said Ms Tuesday. "Scotch and water."

A steel band was playing. Three men in clean, sawed-off blue jeans, bare feet, open, sleeveless shirts did a contrived, athletic, leaping dance, playing bongoes. Two girls in bright West Indian costume, shortened to half-way up their thighs, just enough to swirl, twirled around, through the line of men.

"Why don't you play this kind of music, MacFarlane? Really hits you where you live."

"Doesn't it?"

Above them, a little behind them, over the main door was a rickety scaffolding holding the three dance platform floor lights. An older man in an undershirt changed the lenses from red to blue to green, according to some understanding or pattern of his own.

With him on the scaffolding platform was a gangly boy, about thirteen, fourteen, shirtless, in dirty sawed-off pants, bare feet, moving to the music, the balls of his feet touching the two bare boards at each beat, never touching one of the cables or the cracks. His eyes looking at the dancers shone from the reflected light of the lenses' frames. The muscles in his calves, ankles, anticipated every beat flawlessly. His hands were keeping a second, subsidiary rhythm, palms gently touching his thighs. All of which was far more delicate, subtle than anything the professional dancers were doing, anything in the music itself. His mouth was open, streaming air through his thin chest evenly so his concentration, his rhythm need never be broken.

"Isn't he cute." Ms Tuesday had turned around to see what David was watching. "He'd love to be out on the floor, wouldn't he?"

The sun was huge and red the instant it came over the horizon, as hot on David MacFarlane's shoulders, as burning in his face, his eyes, as it would be at midday.

Standing on his balcony over the beach in the hot, fresh sun, David thought of a melody he could write, a few notes, a phrase, a theme, and decided instantly, from its sound, its mood, to call it "Gray Day."

He backed away from her on the dance floor, with hot, sweating, swirling bodies, heels stomping around them, her bright yellow pleated skirt buoyed by the air of her movement. The music was horribly loud.

"Ms Tuesday. I can't dance!"

His feet were still on the floor, his legs soft, his left arm out to her where her fingers had slipped his, left his hand.

"Why not?"

He knew that behind the red and green and yellow lights, the boy would be watching him.

"I can't."

"Oh, David."

"It's all much too important. Rhythm. Music."

She twirled, head thrown back, her long throat hidden from him for only an instant.

"Oh, David. Let yourself go, for once in your life."

"I can't, Ms Tuesday. It's all much too important."

People, white and black, were swaying, jumping around him senselessly, their eyes on him.

"Can't you see it's all much too important?"

"Oh, David! Goddamn it!"

Pouch drove them back to the bungalow, humming to himself.

David pulled the drapes against the sunrise and took off his bath-robe in the half-light of the room.

In the bed, Ms Tuesday was facing him, looking calmly at him from across the pillow.

"Hi, Mrs MacFarlane."

"Hi."

"Mrs MacFarlane. I have to play today."

Her eyes remained absolutely still in his.

"I'll go up to the hotel and ask if I can rent their ballroom for a few hours."

There was enough light in the room for the skin over her cheek-bones to be husky red, from the sun the day before.

"Do you understand?" he said. "I have to get back to the piano."

She did not blink.

"I understand."

24

"You know anybody in London?"

"No."

"Why don't you and I go get some supper," Fight said. "There's a little place I go to. A bunch of friends."

"All right."

They met at the Regent Street corner of Piccadilly and walked down Shaftsbury Avenue, their steps slower than the steps of anyone else on the pavement, of people going home. Car engines idled in the traffic. Buses roared from their stops to go only a few feet, squeak their brakes. On Dean they walked far beyond Oxford Street.

"How come you brought that?"

"I always have the ax with me," Chump said. "I have to carry it."

"Oh."

"In case I think of something, you know?"

"Oh."

They took a table in the rear of the place, their coats beside them on pegs, and ate in silence. There was the almost continuous sound of steam from the radiators. The spaghetti was lumpy and the beer had a film of soap on it. A few old people sat at tables near the front, rustling their newspapers while they chewed.

Beside their table was an enclosed stairway, a sort of covered bridge stuck against the wall, at an upward angle, hammered together of unpainted, used wood. Pegs for coats were on a board running along the outside of the enclosure. As they ate, people came by the table, said Hello to Pearson, just that, nothing more, *Hi,*

Fight, hung their coats on pegs and started up the stairs. Saying nothing, Fight gave each of them the same low wave. Through the wood of the wall Chump listened to their boots, their sandals, their pumps going up iron grille stairs. The feet would stop at the top a moment and then there would be the sound of a metal door being pulled closed.

There were only five people eating in the restaurant, but there were more than twenty coats on the pegs.

Fight said, "Want to go up for a few minutes, Charlie?"

"Sure."

Carrying his saxophone Chump followed him into the tunnel, up the stairs against the wall to a landing. Fight pushed open the fire door and waited for Chump before pulling it closed.

The little room immediately inside the door was lit only from the big room beyond. In a pile spreading out from the corner was a great mix of clothes, pants, shirts, slips, one bra, many underpants, socks, blouses, a necktie, sweaters, a jacket, stockings, boots, and shoes lying indiscriminately together in the pile, even two beaded necklaces and a boy's wristwatch. Footprints of bare feet entering the big room were in the dust on the floor.

"You can leave your clothes there." Fight was pulling his shirt off over his head. "No one cares if you get the right ones when you leave."

The loft was bare except for thin, uncovered mattresses on the floor. Bare bulbs hung clustered at three points in the ceiling. Beyond the smoke were white walls, the windows boarded up and painted white, white ceiling.

"That's fine." Fight was rubbing his stomach.

Everyone in the room, all the young people, were nude. Their skinny white bodies, shoulders, knees, hips glistened in the harsh white smoke light. A young man with hair to his shoulder blades, a moustache, ambled past them looking straight ahead. A boy, hair slanting across his eyes, lay with his back propped against the wall, a cigarette held in his fingers over the ashtray on his stomach. A girl lay curled on the mattress, her cheek resting on the calf of his leg, her fingers fanned on his shin. Another boy sat alone in the corner, arms around his drawn-up legs, looking around. Across the room a boy and a girl made love in the standard position, their hips moving ever so slowly, no one watching them. Beside them two boys and a girl lay in a triangle, each isolated on his own mattress, each body propped on one elbow, talking quietly. Two boys sat cross-legged on a pad, knees touching, holding hands and smoking. At the far end of the room a girl showed two boys a fast dance step, her breasts bobbing. One stood, hand on his hip, left foot a little forward of the right; the other stood with his feet parallel, arms dangling at his side. Another boy and girl danced to a different rhythm at the same end of the room, bodies pressed close together, arms close to their sides, hands to each other's cheeks, their straight long hair, brown and blonde, mixing between their shoulders.

There were only the sounds of the steam heat, the quiet conversation, occasional hard breathing, a few breaths, in the room. There was the smell of grass.

The girl in the triangle pointed to Chump.

"There's a musician. You can tell. He's wearing his instrument."

One of the boys said, "Hi, Fight."

"That's fine," Fight said.

He hit Chump in the stomach, lightly, with the side of his hand.

"Do what you want. I'm going to jump into the vat."

Pearson went along the wall to the left and through another door.

Chump waited and then sat down on a pad against the wall. The saxophone was on the dust of the floor so he drew it onto the mattress with him. Between his crossed legs on the mattress were ancient stains of sweat. For a moment he fingered his toes.

Then he took up his saxophone and leaning his back against the wall began to play softly, in half-time, the melody of "Sorry."

A young man with hair on his body like dark, thick wire came through the little door and sat at the end of Chump's pad. He stared at Chump, listening to him.

"You're imitating Chump Hardy," he finally said.

Chump licked the mouthpiece.

"Who?"

"Chump Hardy."

"Oh."

"It's no good playing that way," he said. "You have to do something original."

"I guess so."

"Don't you mind doing what somebody else does?"

"No," Chump said. "I never thought of it that way."

"You've got to be different," he said. "A goddamned individual of your own. You have to express yourself, not Chump Hardy. It's the only way to come into existence. You only come into existence by expressing what is you, and no one else. Didn't you ever know that?"

"No, I guess I didn't," Chump said.

"Well, you do," he said. "You've got to be yourself."

Fight Pearson came through the door and knelt at Chump's side. There was a small plastic bottle in his hand. His skin looked wet with oil.

"Do you want one of these?"

He shook red and green capsules onto the palm of his hand.

Chump said, "All right."

He took one of each.

Fight walked across the room, rolling a little in his gait, keeping his upper legs just separated enough.

Between Chump's knees there was the round face, black hair of the boy watching him from the end of the pad.

His skin, too, on his forehead, his nose, his shoulders, seemed wet, oiled. On his lips was half a smile. His face began jumping, pulling up from his shoulders and down again, two jumps, a rest, another jump. The dark line of his eyes rose, joined the line of his hair, and his lips dropped, lit the lower perimeter of his face. There was only a slight shadow near his nose. Then, slowly, smoothly the face began rising up against no wall, the white-backed smoke behind it, the ultimate wall, seeming to slide up it with great speed but not increasing that fast in angle to himself, lifting slowly against a no-wall dropping fast. The dark eyes-hair curve at the top rounded down the sides of the circle, becoming a thinner, dark perimeter to the whole, even where the lips had lightened it at the bottom. Much time passed, a forever, before the round object had risen to a height genuinely above Chump, before the no-wall began to slow behind it, stop, hold steady.

The boy's face was a great, round window then, high in no wall, and Chump knew for a certainty that he could turn it blue by doing things with his breathing, tightening the right muscles, relaxing others. It was only a matter of time. Blue began spreading in from the edges, lightening as if watered or infused with air as it worked toward the center, became fingers that twisted around each other, wisps that swirled around each other, some evaporating from their ends, disappearing altogether. The perimeter had widened into a solid border of dark blue from which all blue for the circle was drawn. The wisps reached far enough into the circle to hit some center and explode, into globules of light blue traveling away from the center, fading, dissipating into nothing. The blue perimeter had become wider, darker. He knew he could do it. In time, much time, the fingers themselves had reached the center and began exploding against it, darting off in fragments of blue, oddly shaped, cut fragments with sharp edges and angles, and as they blasted away from the center they faded to different shades of blue, but few of these fragments disappeared. It would have to happen. Finally the perimeter had drawn close enough to the center and the fragments were staying dark enough so that they were cutting into it, blasting it from the center, shattering it in different places now three, now seven, all the blue of the perimeter moving under the surface, trying to free itself. More sharp-edged fragments attacked it, hitting it hard, with the full, undissipated speed from the center, and sections, some darker than others now, under the surface, began pushing their way free. Then one thick, dark finger of the perimeter itself, close enough to have its own blue, hit the center and there was an immediate sound wave repercussion without sound throughout the circle, all the pieces, to the furthermost, reacting, moving, sideways, backward, forward, their edges, angles, dipping, turning, regardless of their color, whether or not they had been hit. There was a wonderfully slow burst of blue, air, from the center, showering the whole circle with changes of shade, lighter, darker, affecting each fragment in its own way, making of each piece something finished.

Happily, listening to the steady drum, he watched the blue fragments move around each other, through each other, over each other, like eclipses of the sky itself. They liked each other, looked for each other, enjoyed the finding, the passing over each other, being passed over, coming out again. Dark blue, odd-angled frames were around each fragment, dark in exact relation to its internal shade. But even these could pass over, under each other, making slowly enlarging triangles, spreading parallels, disappearing in each other for one moment, thinning to the width of the wider, widening again. Against the sound of the drum all movement was smooth, without rhythm, constant.

A shaft of white light fell down the window, left of center, pulsating at first, with a slow irrelevant rhythm, becoming stronger, whiter, fading the darkest blue fragments in its path. It was inevitable. Blue played outside the edges of the stream, oblivious to it, continuing their motion precisely, only fading when one would cross the edge, perhaps passing into it, disappearing, or sliding back out again exactly as it was. The shaft had become an absolute, brilliant white.

There was the voice of the lady saying something, indistinct, a fairly long statement but too muffled, from too great a distance for anyone to make out what she was saying. She was emerging in the exact center of the window, her robe blue on one side, shimmering white in the shaft to the left, blue again the other side. He sensed the darkness of her hems. Her voice continued as she came into the window, making the same sentence, not repeating it, just not having gotten that far from its beginning.

As she emerged, her head rose above the top of the window so that Chump never did see her face, and beneath the white gown her feet were below the window. He had the impression of her straight white satin gown with more of the blue cape on her left than on her right.

She was finally there as much as she would be.

He waited for the drumbeat, then said, "What?"

"I'm asking you what it is you want of me."

"I'll tell you what I want," he said, thinking.

He decided to wait for the drumbeat again. "What color is a note?"

For the moment he was getting away with being funny.

"Which note?"

She had not noticed.

He pointed to one over her shoulder, a quarter note that was represented merely as black.

"That note. You see? That note."

She would not know and therefore his question would embarrass her.

"Are you going to ask me what color each note is?"

Instead, there were mice around her hems, gnawing at their own paws.

"Jesus," he said.

"I don't want your foolishness."

Deadly serious then, feeling the emergency, desperation, suddenness slowly in his chest cramming his neck, he said, "I am not foolish. I want to know."

"You do not want to know. You are just acting the fool."

A rat turned, showed him the stub of his foreleg.

"Oh, God. I want to know the color of any note."

There were no notes anywhere. Crusts of dried blood, unmoving.

"You don't want to know anything."

"Please," Chump said. "Mother."

The sound of the drum was making someone sob. Something was pressing down on his nose.

"You don't want to know anything."

Footprints of bare feet led into the big, white room. People sat around the walls on gray, striped islands, in ones and twos, holding hands, talking, the ones alone looking frightened out at the fog. Jesus floated by him with the eyes of a rooster, taking forever to land each time on the ball of his foot. A wristwatch lay discarded on a heap of clothes. A girl danced, her head, her legs from her knees down, in the fog, her trunk writhing slowly, her breasts rising and falling almost like weightless things. Fight sat in a dish of butter. Someone was playing the saxophone, spending forever on one note, making its tone perfect. Two boys held hands and thought, knees touching with great significance. Ms Tuesday lay on her back, knees up, legs spread, her pubic hair jungle-deep, arms raised to receive, clasp someone who was not yet there. The boy and girl who danced slowly, together, were gripped around the trunks by a hot metal band that ground their hip bones against each other. Startled, they began to flail their arms, press the heels of their hands against each other's shoulders, push away from each other from the hips up, their faces grimacing. Their bodies were soaked with oil. The hot bar that fitted through holes in the metal band pierced them then, shot through their hips from his spine to hers, locked there. Ms Tuesday had lowered her legs and brought them close together, folded her arms over her breasts, and she was dead.

Seven, eight pads had been dragged to the center of the room from their places along the walls, leaving trails in the dust. Kids sat on them in a loose circle, waiting silently, their attention riveted on something in Fight's hand. Fight was kneeling on one knee.

He inserted the bullet with his forefinger and thumb and looked across at Chump.

"Do you want to play?"

The kid nearest Chump sat with his back to him, neck invisible beyond white, sloped shoulders. The back of his head rose from the vertebrae ladder. His cheeks spread where he sat as chastely as an apron.

"All right."

The chambers were being spun while Chump settled himself between a bony girl and the fleshy boy, three, four times, making three, four clicks each time. The girl was wearing a sanitary belt.

Fight had the gun anyway so he put it to his temple and squeezed the trigger, quickly. He did it without wincing, without any expression, apparently without thinking, simply as if to get the game going. He handed it grip first to the girl.

She sat straight, pointing the barrel to her head above her ear, her arms a triangle, her other arm up as well, to the other side of her head, perhaps to block her ear. She gasped with the click, maybe an instant after it. Her navel was pulled in.

The grip was sticky with sweat.

Chump put it to the top of his head. He aimed it down between his ears, and pushed the trigger up with the ball of his thumb. He heard nothing.

He held it flat in his palm for the last boy to take it.

Sweat was dribbling from the kid's hair and his face was totally wet. A drop hung from the end of his nose. His white temple throbbed.

He wiped his hand on the mattress and took the gun from Chump's hand. A radiator cracked. In fact, he was panting, almost sobbing. His eyes protruded.

Then he closed his eyes, found the depression between his temple and his cheek bone with the barrel. His body convulsed with a tremor. He pulled the trigger.

Rolling forward, putting the gun on the mattress in front of him, he put his face in both hands on the mattress, exhaled, sloughed water from it, sagged his shoulders. Kneeling forward, the great white sack of his stomach relaxed below him.

Pearson held the gun casually between his legs.

"Would you like to have another go, Chump?"

"No. I'm going back."

"See you."

Across the room a girl lay flat on a pad as if dropped from a great height, one leg bent, fingers outstretched, chin up. Her breasts rose and fell evenly.

Chump grabbed anyone's clothes from the pile and put them on. He had just left the building when he heard the shot. He looked back, into the foggy street.

From outside no light could be seen from the loft, just dark, hollow windows. A few lights went on in buildings across the street. People were calling to each other. A window went up, the light from that window especially being reflected in the fog of the street. The black of a man's head and shoulders thrust through the window. He looked up and down the empty street, across at the dark building. A woman joined him. Their silhouettes together made a shadow show in the fog. They had difficulty getting both their heads back through the window at once.

Chump leaned against the brick corner and watched. A dark blue sedan went slowly through the street. More lights were going on.

There was a clatter and a bang and seven or eight people came out of the dark, closed restaurant and hurried away in different directions. There was the sound of a police bell coming. The woman came back to the window, her shadow looking enormous in the fog, and shouted, "Here, you! Wait!" Someone, face muffled in a coat collar, passed Chump. The woman had pulled her head in and was yelling at the man.

The police car came ringing down the street and settled gracefully against the curb in front of the restaurant. A policeman got out of the front seat, stiffly, stretched, yawned, pulled the back of his jacket down, smoothing it.

25

The clock in the old wood case ticked heavily. Doctor Murdock had not looked up from his papers.

Everything in the study was expensive, eternal. The carpet on which Dan stood was ancient oriental, faded to just the right degree of respectability. The desk was huge, solid, polished mahogany. To the right of the blotter was a folder and the week-old newspaper, opened, folded to the picture of himself standing in front of David MacFarlane, Janet, one hand under the book, holding it, the other on the book, head down, reading, someone behind him waving a saxophone. Even from this distance, upside down, Janet was obviously sloshed, her head at the angle of a horse's asleep, eyes closed, wet hair splayed on her forehead. David's fingers were holding her arm so tightly that a deep gorge, a depression in her skin, ran from the end of each. Behind Doctor Murdock was a recessed window of little panes looking out to the dead courtyard.

The casing of the study was solid walnut, carved over the fireplace. The books lining the walls were bound; some were lettered in gold. The chairs, even the light ones, were cushioned and backed with rich, red leather. Around the nine-by-twelve rug the polished floor gleamed.

There ought to be something, anything, plastic in this room.

"Well, Prescott, I suppose you're wondering what took us a week."

Doctor Murdock put his fountain pen into his desk holder and sat back in his chair. He folded his hands in front of his chest.

"The fact is, we've been trying to think what action we can take short of sending you home on the next plane."

There was nothing friendly, warm, even curious in the man's pale blue eyes. The black of his suit, white of his collar melded perfectly with his graying hair.

"The difficulty is, due to some vast error on the part of somebody, you have been ordained. We're more or less stuck with you."

His eyes went around the walls of books. "I've always believed a man should not be ordained until he is at least thirty."

Dan had not been asked to sit. There had been a trial; for a week men had sat and talked in rooms like this: he was to be sentenced.

"I believe your adviser at home is your father. Is that correct?"

"Yes, sir."

"Another unfortunate error. I am writing him a letter describing your behavior since your arrival in Paris. I shall do my utmost not to include him in my reprimand."

Dan allowed the man to see his glance to the right of the blotter. "I'm afraid the newspapers made it seem much worse than it actually was."

Doctor Murdock did not glance at it.

"We're not going by just the newspaper, and we're not talking about just that incident." *Like all men who have taken courses in how to give sermons, my father included, he knows how to ring a dramatic pause.* "It so happens I have some friends, a young couple, not much older than you, who saw you that night in the Club whatever-it-is, and they told me it was actually much worse than the newspapers made it seem. They're old parishioners of mine, from Philadelphia. They happened to recognize you, and knew you were a student here because they came across the Atlantic on the same ship as you. And apparently they've seen you several other places."

A dead leaf scurried across the courtyard, landed on the side of a mound of dirty, shaded snow.

"The Baldwins. Does the name mean anything to you?"

"No, sir."

"They mentioned your name to me the day you arrived."

He opened the folder on his desk.

"It seems two ladies with whom the Baldwins dined aboard ship had had long conversations with you and had been seriously disturbed by what you had said." He consulted a single piece of paper. "A Mrs Parkhurst and Mrs Webb. It seems you told them that if you don't believe in an afterlife, then there will be no afterlife for you."

You should have seen them dancing at the formal last night. And they're at least thirty-five.

"Do the names of these ladies mean anything to you?"

"Yes, sir."

"And you said, 'I don't care if I ever make any conversions.'"

"I didn't say that."

"Whether or not you said it is irrelevant. The fact is you terrified two Christian ladies apparently for no reason other than to show off your sophomoric knowledge."

I hate to be uncharitable, Reverend Prescott, but these people at our table, the Baldwins, are downright show-offs.

"It is not the function of an ordained minister to go about frightening little old ladies."

If it's a matter of expense, I'm sure we could make it up. Heavens, you couldn't have anybody to talk to in Tourist.

Doctor Murdock turned the sheet over.

"The Baldwins have also told me they saw you in a bar very late one night, and that you were obviously drunk. You were sitting at a table with a big Negro. Is that true?"

"Yes, sir."

"Recognizing you again, they made a point of listening to what you had to say. Apparently it was not hard for them to overhear. According to the Baldwins you were trying to explain in your stupor, to this beatnik, why you had become a minister, saying, 'Life is terrifying ... there is genuine doubt ... I know I'm trying to sell people a bill of goods.'"

Dan said, "Jack is no beatnik."

"Whatever he is. You were drunk, terribly, disgracefully drunk, and you were shouting. According to the Baldwins this big black boy had to help you through the door. And they said he had a welt on his mouth, looked as if he had recently been in a fight."

"He's not a big black boy."

"I'm sure he couldn't be a saint, Mr. Prescott. You were both drunk."

Dan said, "He just might be a saint."

Doctor Murdock closed the folder, sat back in his chair again, folded his hands again.

"We're not making a judgment of him."

"It seems you are. Jack Nelson is one of the best men I know. His being black does not automatically qualify him as anything in particular."

The cold eyes were on him. The man was not listening.

"You're not making things any better for yourself, Prescott."

All the time he had been in the room, during all the millions of measured, thudding ticks, the clock had not struck once.

"The Baldwins sure get around," Dan said.

"They're a young couple. It is to be expected that they go about more than we should. They want to see Paris. But every time they enter a dive and you're in it, you can't blame them for registering their surprise with me."

Of all the books in the room there was not one out of place, or open, anywhere.

"There is no reason why we should take the Baldwins' word over yours. Although they are parishioners, and I've known at least his parents most of my life. But when your indiscretions are portrayed in the newspaper," as he looked at it, "we have no choice but to take their word."

"What were the Baldwins doing there that night?"

"Slumming," Doctor Murdock said. "They had gone to the club after the theater to hear some jazz, for which they apparently have a taste, and to buy the obligatory drink in such places. They recognized the big Negro as a friend of yours and sensed something wild was going on, and so stayed after the closing hour. Sure enough, when the party was at its height, you showed up."

He is telling me the story, rather than my telling him.

Doctor Murdock held the folded newspaper at a distance. "Reverend Daniel Prescott, an American studying at the International Seminary, Paris!" He dropped it, folded his hands over it. "We understand there was even some sort of a brawl. Did you see the fistfight?"

The ceiling was high, a freshly painted white.

"Yes, sir."

"Both the bride and the groom were drunk, particularly the bride." He snapped two fingernails against his face. "The validity of the marriage is in question."

"I felt they had to get married, sir. They were living together. The bride is from my hometown, my father's parish."

"Mr. Prescott, you can't bring the Church into these dives. You've got to bring the people into the Church. Even if your effort was sincere, you see what happens. More than half the effort, the willingness, must be on their side, or they will disrespect everything about it. You can't just present a sacrament to them. They must have respect for it, want it, go more than halfway to get it, or they will desecrate it."

"Yes, sir. I see that."

"According to the Baldwins, those in attendance were beatniks, drunks, dope addicts, prostitutes, musicians, writers: not one single person who had respect for the sacrament."

Dan said, "Christ sat down among the thieves."

"Until you have His authority, Mr Prescott, we will ask you not to embarrass your superiors."

There was a great gasping from the clock, a grinding of gears. It struck thrice.

"The question is what to do with you. Notice of your reprimand, and the reasons for it detailed, are to be sent home. I'm afraid your reputation as a swinger in Paris will stick with you forever. Whether or not you will ever be assigned to a decent parish is greatly in question. Do you understand?"

"Yes, sir."

"There was the thought, as I say, of sending you home on the next plane. But instead we've simply decided to get you out of Paris as quickly as possible, as apparently the seamier aspects of the city go to your head. We recommend you devote yourself exclusively to the research on your paper, as we will be sending you down to the school in Provence early. We'll let you know exactly when in a few days. I should think the result of this hurried research will be to lower your mark, if not make passing impossible."

"Yes, sir."

"In the meantime, if there is any more of this, dragging the Church through the gutters of Paris, I personally will move to have you defrocked. If it's even reported to me that you've been seen in the presence of another beatnik, I will bring the strongest disciplinary action against you."

I've been standing all this time at perfect attention. What's the matter with me?

"You needn't droop like that, Prescott. You're not getting anything you don't richly deserve."

The voice dropped its tone, but the eyes became no warmer.

"You're just twenty-five, Prescott."

"Yes."

"Why aren't you married?"

Oh, my God. My Father. Why have you abandoned me?

"I don't know, sir."

"You'd better be about it, Prescott," Doctor Murdock said. "The right woman will settle you down."

In her yellow, two-piece bathing suit, her skin dark in the shade

*of the tree, she dove off the branch into the pond, her hair stream-
ing after her.*

Backing off, having to, horrified, needing the air he knew was
outside, eyes open too wide, mouth open, Dan moved backward
toward the door, backward, trying to perceive his feet behind him,
keep order, at least in his legs.

"Only Prescott: do not marry in Paris. At least you can spare us
that."

The heavy, carved walnut door to his own back, the man bent
over his desk, writing with his long fountain pen, precisely framed
by the light of the window: *there is a most Christian gentleman.*

26

Incidentally, since they began alternating with comic Sandy Barker at the New Sounds three weeks ago, David MacFarlane and Chump Hardy haven't been doing the audiences any favors. At first they sounded better than they had two weeks before at the Someplace. And there is that new song, Gray Day. But don't let them fool you. They're using you, dear minimum-payers, to rehearse for their upcoming recording date, in New York, and their subsequent concert at Royal Festival Hall. Hence, the roughness. All is for the great Mammon Wax now. Maybe their live performance in Cannes in the spring will be less than dead, if you don't mind the commute. But if you have attended them the last three weeks, you've already paid for the concert, and the record.

The lights were coming down through the smoke at him, three instead of the usual two, and everything seemed whiter, hotter. "727." "Trainman's Dust." The smoke blew in the shafts of light like high, dirty storm clouds, pushed steadily by the blowers high in the opposite walls. The table where Ms Tuesday usually sat, below the lights, to the right, so he could see her, was empty. "Number 95." "Too Long." She had gone shopping after lunch and had not returned to change for supper. Finally, at eight-thirty, he had to leave without her. *Chump, what are you doing? What am I doing?* The audience sounded disappointed, restless. There was too much talking. The way the lights were set, that third light, the ivory and even the black from the keys kept catching him, hitting him between the eyes.

He squeezed his eyes closed. He thought he was doing better.

It was during "Deme Lo" that Chump stopped playing. At first David thought Chump had had a new idea, was going to do something different, however unlikely it was at that point, and continued with the piece, waiting to hear what Chump would do. The rustle, the sudden silence, then the buzz from the audience told him otherwise and David opened his eyes.

Chump was advancing into the streams of light, holding his saxophone oddly in one hand, his right hand, as if he were going to strike the audience with it, get to a certain point and throw it at them. David stopped playing. Chump stood too far forward in the light, where it was too white, and, enveloped completely in a light-foam that reflected too directly, painfully, from his saxophone, and waited for everyone to be silent.

Then he brought the saxophone to his mouth with both hands, paused again, a Chump Hardy pause, thinking, having everyone wait, his eyes beginning to protrude with the effort. Then very softly, so softly, even David had to strain to hear, to get the tune, very slowly, so slowly the tune was barely recognizable anyway, yet precisely, he began to play "The Star Spangled Banner": straight, note after note, no variations, no slurping, no clipping, the way a boy would play it at a recital, shoulders back, feet in the V position, a very slow, dull-witted boy, holding each note five times its usual length, thinking that is the way it should be played, but lining it with a curious heartbreaking vibrato no boy could every attain.

The audience giggled nervously, nudged each other, commented. Then they saw in all that light from the closed eyes above the flashing saxophone great round tears held in Chump's lashes, sparkling there a moment, hesitating, growing, then swooping down his cheeks, as hard and glimmering as the metal of the saxophone, as soft as a baby's wet skin in the light. The audience stopped laughing.

Folding his arms over the piano, David put his head down on them and stared at his own shadow pushed sideways on the keys. He could not stop it, the shaking, first in his legs and then in his shoulders, sporadic, faster than Chump's vibrato. *And the flag was still there.* He pressed his feet to the floor to disguise, conceal his shaking, gripped his elbows with his hands, but that just made the shaking more definite, machine-like.

Chump came to the end and stopped, allowed the silence, the pause of a music box.

O, say, can you see: Of course he is starting over, doing it again.

There was a rustling from the audience, then, of legs, skirts being straightened, chairs pushed back. Through the streams of light-smoke, David saw them standing up, putting their drinks on the tables, their purses on their chairs. For the most part he could see only legs, from the hips down, skirts and trousers, standing still, shoes pointing forward, a few faces in front, flattened and white in reflected light, looking serious, concerned. In the shadow of the door at the side of the platform Sandy Barker, in his bright flowered shirt, stood looking curious, frightened, prepared to be helpful.

David pushed himself up, moved a few feet from the piano stool, stood in the hot lights more or less at attention. *Through the night.* The shaking was better that way.

When Chump ran off, David followed him. Sandy came on immediately, smiling with his mouth, his eyes searching David's, worriedly.

The audience did not applaud. They sat down.

Comes on pretty strong, for a Colonial, don't he? Next they'll be asking us to pay taxes on our tea.

Inside the washroom Chump turned around, tears still on his cheeks, and began to laugh.

"Why didn't you bring your box in? I brought my ax."

"Roll up your sleeve," David said.

David had to do it, making Chump hold the saxophone in the other hand. David looked at the inside of the arm and then into Chump's face.

"Dave. You're shaking."

"How much of this stuff have you had?"

"Not much."

"How much?"

"Only once, this stuff. Just last night. This morning. I haven't been taking it."

"Where did you get it?"

"I don't know. Some crazy house."

"Who was with you?"

"My old buddy, Fight Pearson."

"Are you out of your mind, Chump?" David was gripping Chump's arm tightly, squeezing it with his fingers, trying to cause pain. "You should know what that will do to you."

"I know what it will do to you."

"Look what it does to Fight Pearson. The guy is out of his mind."

"Old Buddy Fight."

"Do you want any more?"

"No. The lights out there just made me feel funny. I was sweating. I had beer this afternoon, too, I think."

"Because if you want any more, you had better put down that saxophone and go get it. You can't have both, Chump. You know that stuff will take the place of the music, very fast."

A drunk came into the washroom and stood against the white urinal. They waited. When he turned around, the water flushing behind him, he said, "What's the drill, laddies?"

At the door, he said, "Now don't you boys get nasty out here."

"Drunk," David said. "Chump, you know that stuff will make a great musician out of you in your mind, and you'll never really play again."

"I know."

"How can you take it then?"

"Why not?"

"Because there isn't room for it. Either you play in your mind or you play in fact. This business takes all of you."

Chump grabbed his arm away. "All of you, too."

"What do you mean by that?"

"You haven't been so good lately."

"Why do you say that?"

"Why do you think we need Fight Pearson and everybody?"

"I'm not taking dope," David said.

"Why aren't you? Why don't we both take dope and let the sounds go to hell."

"What on earth is the matter with you?"

Fumbling with his cuff button, trying to work it, saxophone under his arm, tears rolled over Chump's lower lids again, down his cheek. "Why don't we all go jump off cliffs?"

"Your vacation didn't do you much good," David said.

"Why don't we all go to Nassau and drown?"

"Come on. I'm going to take you back to the hotel."

"Why don't we all go back to the hotel and jump out the window."

"Come on."

The door was pushed open, then closed slowly, automatically, behind Martin. His evening jacket looked very black in the white tiled room.

"I'm sorry," David said.

Martin saw Chump's loose cuff.

"Is he all right?"

"He's all right. Really, it was just that light that bothered him. Where did that third light come from?"

Martin shrugged. "We thought there were going to be photographers here tonight, for color shots. *Nova*'s got a story. I would have told you, but you arrived late."

"I'm glad they didn't come." David helped Chump put his arm back through the jacket sleeve. "I'm taking him back to the hotel, Martin. The night's over, for us."

"Might as well," Martin said. "Everyone who's coming is here. We've made our money."

Martin opened the door for them.

"David, do you want me to call Milton in New York?"

"No."

"I just thought."

"No. It'll be all right."

David brought Chump to his bed, loosened his tie, unbuttoned his collar, took off his shoes, checked the windows before snapping out the lights. Closing the door, he heard Chump sniff.

Ms Tuesday had not returned to the suite downstairs.

David threw his overcoat over a chair in the living room and poured himself a drink. Nothing in the rooms had changed: Ms Tuesday had not even been there, to find him, to change. The travel clock beside the bed said quarter to twelve. He showered, brushed his teeth, finished his drink in the living room in robe and slippers.

The luminescent dial said quarter past one. All pubs would be closed.

He dressed in the same clothes, went down the bright corridor to the elevator and out into the fog.

He walked down Brook Street, through Hanover Square and up Marlborough Street. He checked a bottle club on Lexington, then crossed over on Brewer Street and checked one on Waldour. Then he took a taxi to the Edgeware Road and walked up George Street to Bryanston.

She was sitting at an unvarnished wood table with a bottle of Scotch half empty in front of her. She was the only customer. A short fat man came through the beaded curtain, watched David until the beads stopped moving, and then withdrew.

She did not see David until he had sat down.

"Oh, David. There you are. How are you, David?"

Besides being terribly bloodshot, her eyes were red-rimmed. The hair of her blonde eyebrows had stiffened at odd angles.

"Fine." He took her glass, a tumbler, really. "Mind if I have a drink?"

"Oh, don't take my glass."

"Can't you give your poor old husband a drink?"

"Yes, darling, you can have a drink. You can have anything you like."

He tasted the toothpaste again, with it.

"What's the crisis?" he asked.

"Nothing. I feel fine. I feel all cuddly," she said.

She tried to make gestures of how cuddly she felt, enfolding her arms, but the gestures did not come off. Then she sat up and looked at the table and looked at David and smiled secretively.

"I saw the doctor, you know."

"I didn't know."

"I did. That's what I did today. Shopping." With affectionate complaint: "You've really drilled me, you know."

"No. I didn't know."

Raising her chin, looking away, more distinctly, she said, "Almost as if your whole purpose is to have a baby."

Through the soles of his shoes David felt dirt, cigarette stubs, matches, dust. The table surface smelled of stale booze.

"Don't let it throw you," he said.

"Well, he should know, David. I mean, the doctor. He knows these things. I missed a period, for the first time in my life. And the tests said so."

"All right," David said.

"It hasn't thrown me, David. I'm celebrating."

"Why didn't you let me in on the celebration?"

"Why, David, you weren't here. You were in Berlin."

"I was at the New Sounds which is only the other side of Marble Arch."

"The Mubble Hatch, David, the Mubble Hatch. When in London do as the Londoners do. Put mubbles in your hatch."

He put his own match on the edge of the table, then knocked it off.

"What's the matter, Ms Tuesday? Don't you want the baby?"

"Of course I want the baby. It's your son, and I want it very much. I just don't know what to do."

"Come on," he said. "Please let's go back to the hotel. I don't like it here."

"Can I bring my bottle?"

"You can bring anything you like."

She picked the bottle up by the neck and came after him.

David had left some money on the table.

In the taxi he put his arm around her.

"Are you scared?"

She said, "I just don't know what to do."

At the hotel she stood in the bedroom door, bottle in one hand, shoe in the other.

"Why, David. You've already been in bed."

David said, "I got home early. Chump got patriotic."

"Were you alone, David? I mean, in bed?" She took a few steps forward, lurching up and down on one heel, one flat foot. "I didn't know it was possible for you to get home that early."

He showered again after she was in bed. The bottle was on the nightstand beside her at her own insistence. He brushed his teeth.

Then he stood at the window looking through the white curtain at the yellow sky over the city. Ms Tuesday was breathing evenly behind him, in the dark, in the bed.

I wonder where I could get a cigar at quarter to four in the morning. I'm a father.

Some of the cars going along the street below him had yellow fog lights. He lit a cigarette, keeping the match in his hand. *A pram, a pony cart, a house with a pool: my son.* There was a great, green rolling lawn somewhere, and it was Saturday afternoon, autumn. The kid in the sweater had not yet lost his summer's tan. He clasped his father's hands, pretending to have pinned his father's shoulder blades to the grass. His straight blonde hair slanted to his brown eyes. Everything of Ms Tuesday's challenge was in his grin. The trees around the lawn were wonderfully colorful, red and yellow.

There was the high whine of a jet from the yellow sky over the city. David smelled the steam of the radiator, felt the burning tip of the cigarette close to his fingers.

He stubbed out the cigarette and got into bed again. It was a long time before he slept. Something woke him. He lay, listening, wondering what it was. He missed the sound of Ms Tuesday's breathing beside him and put his hand over to her side of the bed. She was gone. Then he heard the clink and sat up. It was the sound of glass against glass.

She was sitting in a chair in front of the window, her form against the yellow fog. One arm was draped over an arm of the chair and her head was on her shoulder.

He got up and went to her, knelt beside her. She was sound

asleep. The bottle of Scotch was on the floor beside her, empty. The glass had dropped out of her hand and was tipped over on the floor. It was the bathroom glass. David stood the glass beside the bottle. He stayed on his knees for a moment, holding Ms Tuesday's hand.

He picked her up in his arms and brought her to the bed, laid her on it, tucked the covers around her. He went into the bathroom for a drink of water, forgetting the glass, having to come back for it. Then he got into the bed himself and stared at the gray dawn on the ceiling.

Where is Dan? Where is Dan Prescott?

27

The homburg on his head made him look slightly old, slightly silly. His one black canvas bag banging against his leg, Dan came through the station.

John said, "Hi."

"Hi. What are you doing here?"

"I thought I'd see you off. Want some coffee?"

Dan said, "I've got to get my ticket first."

"Leave your bag here. I'll wait."

His shoulders a little sloped, his steps a little too fast, nervous, Dan walked over to the end of the shortest line at the ticket counter and waited. To anyone who did not know him, he would seem perfectly erect, relaxed. He shrugged at John across the station when the line he was in proved to be slow.

A few feet away from John, beside him, stood a man holding a white and yellow balloon, on a stick. In front of him twenty or thirty schoolchildren were gathered around two nuns. Beyond them, a woman in her thirties sat on an expensive suitcase, reading sheet music.

"Sorry to take so long."

The bag did not feel that heavy to John, although the narrow handle was sharp against the palm of his hand.

"I wish I were going to Provence now," John said. "It's nice down there in early spring."

"No, you don't."

They sat at a little table in the in-station cafe. Beside them, halfway up an interior window, ran a brass bar hung with a beige curtain connected to it by big wooden loops.

"Very nice of you to come," Dan said. "I was feeling sort of lonely."

"Have to see off the Godly delegation," John said. "Hell's firemen."

"How's Marianne?"

"Come and gone. She wanted to make love to a black man. She made love to a black man." John showed the palms of his hands, the spaces between his fingers. "The pink parts of me tickled her."

He shoved a finger under his upper lip, flipped it, flashed pink gum. "Have you ever been loved for your pink parts?"

"No," Dan said. "I haven't."

"Until you have someone go ape over the soles of your feet you haven't lived. Believe me."

"How's the long poem?"

"Done. I think. Actually, it was before I took on Marianne."

"What are you doing with it?"

"It keeps dust off one part of my shelf."

John ordered a beer, and Dan, black coffee.

The waitress, a girl about seventeen, with loose black hair, was distracted by Dan. Every time she looked at him her pupils would expand. For that order, just beer, black coffee, she had to use her eraser twice.

John said, "So how do you feel about things?"

"Oh, so-so. Somewhere halfway between a spanked puppy and a court-martialed Pfc."

"You were pretty upset a couple of weeks ago," John said.

"I shouldn't have been, you know. I shouldn't have talked to you about it. I had to talk to someone."

"I know."

"I felt disappointed, of course, to have had what I thought were my quite innocent intentions misinterpreted, to have been tried, convicted, and sentenced without a hearing. But they were quite right. I shouldn't have dragged the Church through the gutters of Paris."

The girl spilled the coffee on the table.

"In fact," Dan said. "I shouldn't be sitting with you here now."

Very carefully, she was wiping around Dan's cup.

"Another bar," Dan commented.

"That's the trouble with your Church." John tasted the beer. "It keeps you separated from people, rather than with them."

"That's right," Dan said. "I can't quite accept that. You realize how closely missionaries live with the people in Latin America, Africa. The evil of those people is taken as innocent, because supposedly there is no philosophy behind it."

"Non-infectious evil," John said.

"I'm sure that what goes on in any primitive village, supported by philosophy or not, would turn the bulk of Paris' citizens gray in a week."

The girl brought another rag, lifted Dan's cup and saucer, dried the table surface again. He was not noticing.

"So you're still upset," John said.

"No. I've thought about it, when I've had the time. I haven't gotten any of the research done, you know."

"None of it?"

"None." Tasting his coffee, reacting to the heat on his tongue, he spilled a few drops on the table. "Basically, they are right, without knowing it. I professed a sincere interest in studying at the International Seminary in Paris. My application to the Board was a complete lie. I came here to find Janet."

His hand, holding the coffee cup over the saucer, was shaking, slightly.

"For the first time in my life, I lied. I cheated. I guess I really stole the money it cost to send me here."

The girl came with the rag again, lifted the saucer, dried the table surface.

"Don't be too hard on yourself."

"Well, it's true, Jack. If I had been sincere in my wanting to come to the Seminary, I never would have gotten into all this trouble. All they saw were the symptoms, the results of this dishonesty. But the dishonesty was there."

John was letting his Turkish cigarette go unsmoked in his hand.

"Other people get away with a lot more," he said.

"You don't let yourself get away with anything," Dan said. "Anything that really offends you."

The girl was leaning on the marble counter, staring at Dan.

"What do you think you'll do?" John asked.

Dan was at an angle to the table, musty drape behind his head, topcoat opened.

"I don't know. I think in a few weeks, once I get settled down there, I'll take a weekend and go somewhere, get out of these clothes. See what the world looks like now."

"Good idea."

"Then, when I get through, I thought I'd go to Spain for a while. Prolong my departure for the States to at least a year from now."

"Why?"

"To think." He opened his eyes wide, to say, *Didn't you know? I thought you knew.* "I won't be going back to anything that wonderful, you know. According to Murdock this will be my last chance to see and to know people. I'm going back to be assigned to a defunct, empty parish somewhere, where I can do no harm."

"Don't put off going back too long." John rolled his eyes, puffed his cheeks. "I say that as your spiritual adviser."

"A year. A year from now. I'm receiving a stipend now that I can't use. It should buy me some time alone, in Spain."

"Speaking of things in and out of context," John said. "There was an item in the *Tribune* yesterday about Chump Hardy. Seems he stopped a gig somewhere in London to play 'The Star Spangled Banner' for the people. He cried and they all stood up."

Dan tipped his head. "A nervous breakdown?"

"No." John straightened his lips from a smile to sip his beer. "Chump's too crazy to have a nervous breakdown. Anyone who leans that heavily on a rock can't collapse. Get upset, maybe, when the rock shakes, maybe a little nervous, but collapse? Never."

"What are you talking about, what rock?"

"His music, from A to G. Musicians lean on their repetitive alphabet the way you lean on your altar. It's all the same life-twitch." John put out the cigarette he had not smoked and lit another. "That's the trouble with Miss Twombly, you know. She's the only one of you who hasn't got something to depend upon—except you. And when she leans a little, which she has a right to do, she gets the sensation of falling, because you aren't there. At least, not when she really needs you."

John did not look at Dan's eyes. He knew them, could feel them, startled, looking for his.

"This is what you came to tell me," Dan said. "Today."

John said, "Something like that."

"What about you? Your poetry?"

"Oh, I don't lean on that. Anyone who expects anything to come from a lot of messed-up paper is really a fool." The rest of Dan's coffee looked muddy. "I practice putting no faith in it. It's good use of freedom, beats picking your nose, but I don't depend on it as the reason for my existence."

"The hell you don't."

"I don't. Therefore, I suppose, I'll never be a very good poet. At least I don't depend on it in that way for too long."

Dan poured the mud down his throat.

"More philosophy," he said. "If you remember, old buddy, after our last real seminar you had to carry me home—"

"Dribbling down my back." John said, "I'm not sure it's as much a matter of philosophy, as personalities."

"Psychology, then. Let's talk about football."

"I don't know what," John said. "I'm just against being dependent on things. People ought to need each other, be able to turn to each other. But things just get in the way."

"Anyone who places his faith in Man," Dan mused, "is bound to be disappointed."

"Religion," John said. "Art, music, poetry, dope. Television, committees, gambling, liquor. Football. They're all fine as sports, but pretty limited as interpretations of life."

"How come everybody around here is allowed to give sermons except me?"

"Because you're a chil', honey chil'. You satisfy everybody's need to have a son, rather cheaply."

"I don't see you depending on any person," said Dan. "Now that Marianne has gone back wherever she came from. Now that she's used up your pink parts."

"I will," John said. "I'm looking forward to it. Any day now."

"So this time you're trying to get a fat lip by saying I failed Janet a long time ago, by hanging onto the skirts of the Church, and then I failed my ministry by hanging onto Janet's skirts."

"You're not cut out to be a zealot," John said. "A Chump Hardy you ain't. You need people, you react to them too much."

"Chump needs MacFarlane."

"Only because MacFarlane has become a part of Chump's music, another valve on his horn. He'd be uneven for a while without that valve. In fact, he'd think the world was coming to an end. But he'd learn to play without it, again."

"You think you understand everybody, don't you, you bastard."

"What I'm saying is, bastard, there's a tremendous need for Dan Prescott, the person. For David MacFarlane, the person. For Charles Thompson Hardy." John finally took a deep drag on his cigarette, before putting it out. "But only God and the inside of his saxophone knows what sort of a person Chump really is."

"Yeah. But isn't David's music worth it?"

"Sure it is. For us. But playing on such a limited scale, David can never fulfill himself as a man. Look how his trying is screwing up both Chump and Miss Twombly. Chump is playing the American national anthem to a bunch of drunk English, and Miss Twombly is hiccuping all over the continent. Wait and see."

Dan folded his hand on the table. "Janet, Janet." His was not only a loser's face, but the face of someone who had never lost before. "Janet . . . "

John hitched his chair forward and put his elbows on the table. "Janet isn't very charming, you know." He looked into Dan's clear brown eyes. "You all have an image of her as the perfect American girl-next-door, which image she is trying to destroy as fast and as totally as she can. Are you all in love with an image, an illusion of womanhood, of America, of the world? There's a product beneath the advertisement, you know, a person beneath the image, the gorgeous, neat build, the steady eyes, clear skin, perfect teeth, honey-colored hair. Maybe she's trying to get us all to see beneath her dazzling appearance." John scraped the edge of his little finger along the edge of the table's clean surface. "I believe my black American brothers call it *gettin' down*. We all need to *get down* once in a while, to see who we are. Even sin has its purpose, Reverend." John's voice dropped. "There is an America, I hear, beneath the gleam and the glitter, the soapsuds and the sell. When we disgrace ourselves as a nation, we're just *gettin' down*, seeing who and what we naturally are."

Dan said, "Sounds like maybe you understand her."

"No. I don't. But I do believe Janet is *gettin' down*. Maybe I will understand her, maybe we all will, once she gets there. Maybe even she will."

Dan's wristwatch had a brown strap. "I've got to go. I've got four and a half minutes to find the train."

"Sure." John did not get up. "You have my address."

"Yes."

"Write me if you get any big ideas."

"I'll write you if I ever understand you," Dan said. "For now, all I can say is, you sure do talk about football funny."

He held out his hand. That foolish homburg was back on his head. "Goodbye, Jack."

"Bye, Dan. God love you."

Walking slower than he should to find a train in four minutes, his black back, hat, topcoat, trousers, shoes, black canvas bag, receded the other side of the glass door.

The waitress came for the glass, the cup, the saucer, the money. She wiped the table again.

"Is he really a priest?" she asked.

"I don't know," John said. "His wristwatch had a brown strap."

She said, "I noticed that."

28

She said, "That bike must have cost a lot of salt."

"Not much. Not much salt."

"How much did it cost?"

"I forget."

"Did you steal it?"

He said, "Yes. I stole it."

Down the hillside pasture, on the other side of the rail fence that ran along the road, the bike stood on its kickstand. Even motionless that way, posing, he could hear, feel the sound it would make. The narrow black road came down between two knolls, curved beyond the motorcycle to the left of a roof with two chimneys that rose in the near distance, on the other side of a small hill.

"You're nice to take me out like this."

She had taken off her sweater and blouse for him. It was a sunny day, but cold, perhaps not fifty degrees. Her blouse was spread on the damp ground underneath her shoulders and her heavy-knit sweater was on the ground beside her.

He rolled down her pants and penetrated her and ejaculated, once, quickly.

He sat, looking down the hill at the motorcycle. She had not moved.

"What's your name?" she asked.

"Dan Prescott," he said. "Daniel Prescott."

He sauntered down the hill, alone.

"Where are you going?"

Her little breasts hung between harlequin knees.

"America."

"When?"

"This afternoon."

He leapt over the fence and straddled the bike. He turned the key between his legs and zipped up his jacket.

"You're a weirdo!"

She had cupped her hands over her mouth.

"A weirdo! Do you hear me?"

He thrust down with his right leg and the motor roared.

Slipping it in and out of first he put the bike back on the road, wheeled it around to go the other way, the way they had come, one leg still on the ground. She ran down the hillside, blouse open, sweater streaming from her hand. He was in first gear, putt-putting up the hillside slowly before she reached the fence.

Between the two knolls, at the top of the little hill, he put the motorcycle into second gear and idled down the other side. He cut the engine in just as the bike began to slow, lose its momentum, and picked up speed, roaring well beyond the point where he could have used third, shifting finally as he crested another hill, gassing then, wildly, accelerating down the hill. He leaned toward the middle of the road in a right-hand curve, held the angle despite the yellow fender of a lorry, despite the expression on the lorry driver's face. The truck turned sharply, into its own curve, the spoked, black tire on the front right wheel suddenly having a surprising angle to the road. There was a cackle of chickens from the back of the truck.

What he loved to do in an inside curve was to run the front wheel right along the edge of the white line, if there was a white line, where it would be if there were none, lean so his shoulders, head would be on the other side of the line, pure black pavement streaming below his eyes. On an outside curve he would run his wheel along the edge of the macadam, swerving in for any potholes, cracks, the dirt, sticks, leaves, stones on the shoulder of the road streaming directly below him. He loved to crest a hill, wheels straight, with exactly that speed, that noise of the engine, that would allow his body to feel weightless that inch beyond the top, make it want to continue going up, keep that angle. His hand would revolve the accelerator counterclockwise and hold on, would pull himself down at the same time, the neck leading to the front wheel elongating for the moment as the front wheel reached for the road, stayed on it, fell to it, however weightless, the neck contracting then in its own sleeve, down and up, bouncing; then he would turn his right hand clockwise again, accelerating, looking to see how he must next turn his wheel.

The sound of the bike seemed mostly behind him on these country roads. More strongly there was the sound of the wind coming and going in his ears, depending on his speed, his angle to what wind there was, if any, in his left ear, his right ear depending on how he leaned; both ears when he was going straight ahead, causing his own wind entirely, cutting the air with his nose, chin. Before turning onto the highway he waited a moment, roaring his engine in neutral, goosing it, the sound of it pure, with no wind, the noise of the lines of traffic going by, passenger cars and sports cars, vans and trucks, other bikes, scooters unimportant next to this big noise, close, unrestrained, not engaged.

He kept to the left-most lane of the highway for the first few miles, going slowly, hearing how his engine really sounded engaged with all this other traffic, without much wind. Then he swung to the right, through the second lane of traffic, between the back of a truck and the front of a passenger car so he could hear them both, hear his own engine accelerating through them, noting only when he was in the third, right-most lane the hesitation he had caused in the passenger car's engine. Going along he swerved in and out of traffic, putting other vehicles together, combining their noises, wrapping his own noise around them, dominating them with his own acceleration, listening to them as he coasted along, idling his own engine. He found an open truck with empty fruit boxes piled carelessly on top of each other in back, a tarpaulin over them flapping, and rode within six inches of its back, his front wheel actually under the truck-deck, his neck five inches from the metal-striped threshold of the tailgate, so he could listen to the nervous chatter, rattle, of the boxes on top of all these motor, tire noises, the flap-flap of the tarpaulin.

At a traffic signal, he swerved through the cars and vans waiting in three lanes, and went on across, through the intersection, to hear the squealing of brakes first on his right side, then on his left side, closer, then behind him as cars tried to avoid each other. Through the black and gray and red-brick outskirts, passing people at the side of the road discussing their own motors, dull-eyed women pawing along the sidewalks with plastic shopping carriers, he kept his speed even, to hear the variations in the sound of his motor as it came back to him off parked cars, brick buildings, cement buildings, glass fronts, garages set back on their own cement aprons. Crossing the Marylebone Road he stopped suddenly, screeching his own rear tire, sending it in a half-circle, swish, behind him, it coming up to his right side, his standing with it angled between outstretched legs. He waved on a van at his right that had stopped, and did not have the right of way at that moment.

Dave was in the lobby, buying a paper.

"Where have you been?"

"Nowhere."

"Hurry up. We've got to leave in a half hour."

The man behind the desk was looking at Chump's goggles, tight pants, boots as if he could smell them.

"Where's the bike?"

"Beside the car. On Goodge Street. I mean, in the garage."

Getting out of the elevator on his floor, looking at the front page, Dave said, "Hurry up."

In the taxi, Ms Tuesday sat between them. Chump sat in his neck-tie and sports jacket on the right side of the back seat, saxophone case between his knees. Dave had gotten in last.

When they were passing the third or fourth sign saying they were leaving Staines, Ms Tuesday said, "I'm sorry you have to leave."

Dave said, "I'm sorry we have to leave, too. Will you take care of yourself and Oscar?"

"Yes. I'll be a good girl."

"This taxi doesn't seem to be going very fast. He must think we're going for an outing at Windsor."

The driver was the other side of a glass window.

"Maybe we are going to Windsor. Maybe all the taxi drivers in the world are revolting against the nasty things you've said about them."

"You never heard me say anything nasty about taxi drivers."

"David, you're a bore."

Standing in the airport after they had seen about their tickets and luggage, Ms Tuesday said, "Give my love to America."

"Do you want me to call your parents?"

"No. Don't bother."

"They might see in the newspaper, or on television that I was there."

"Do you want to call them?"

"Not particularly."

"Then don't. You can just be too busy."

"If the question ever comes up."

"I don't think it will ever come up," she said.

"Would you like some coffee?"

"Sure."

They went through glass doors into a dark lounge and sat at a round table. Music, long exhalations of old cats, was coming from three places behind the wall drapes.

Chump surprised them by ordering coffee for them and Coca-Cola for himself.

While they were waiting, Ms Tuesday said, "Will you write me?"

"We'll be back before a letter could get here."

"You write me, too, Chump."

Chump smiled.

"When do you go to the doctor next time?" Dave asked.

"Not for a long while. Probably not until you get back."

"Be sure and call him if anything bothers you."

"Shall I call him if the people in the next suite don't keep their television off in the morning?"

"Yes. Unless they are playing good music."

"By that you mean your music."

"Well," Dave said. "Chump is pretty good, you know."

The violins kept being interrupted by brisk voices saying Flight Number, Gate Number, Departure Time, Destination. Arriving, Mister Philip Asgood. Over the sound of the violins, the voices, there was the constant sound of jets taking off, landing.

At the departure gate, Dave said, "There's no use in your waiting. Why don't you go back."

She said, "I thought I'd go up to the observation deck."

"The observation deck. Why?"

She looked across the corridor at a clock.

"I have nothing else to do."

Beyond their own plane, steps were being wheeled up to the rear door of an Air France plane. One propeller was still revolving, slowly.

Chump sat next to the window.

Ms Tuesday was alone in the sunlight in her knee-length leather coat on the observation deck. Chump waved to her, the palm of his hand close to the window. Dave tried to get her attention by flashing his fingers up and down in the sunlight. She was looking over the plane, though, at the field beyond them.

"Nice to have you aboard, Mister MacFarlane, Mister Hardy. May I put the saxophone case away for you?"

"No," Dave said. "He holds it."

Ms Tuesday was waving at someone, behind them, not in their plane, someone crossing the field, perhaps from the other plane.

Chump drew the little curtains together.

"I think I'll listen to some music," he said.

"Okay."

29

"Beautiful," Milton said.

Chump had been playing "Both of Us: The Absolute We" phrase by phrase, flatting the note at the end of each phrase, holding the flat, laughing.

"Beautiful," Milton said.

"You're getting fat, Milton," David said.

Chump was playing it again, hitting the sharp of each last note this time. Then he began imitating Sidney Bechet, getting nothing like his vibrato by making his whole body shake, in spasms. "September Song."

"Beautiful," Milton said.

Chump leapt onto the divan beside Milton, stood on it, and began jumping up and down as if on a trampoline, playing, laughing, trying to make the sound shake by shaking the saxophone, himself, the divan, Milton.

The phone was ringing.

Milton had his arm up to protect his bald fringe.

"Beautiful," Milton said.

"David? Is that you?"

A Fifth Avenue bus roared eleven floors below them.

"Ellie?"

Chump roared from the sofa, "Hi, Ellie!"

"I saw in *The News* you were in New York."

"Are you in New York?"

There was a knock on the door.

"I have been for two years."

"I missed you."

Milton was pulling himself up to get the door.

"Hey, buddy. I see you got married."

David said, "Yes. Ms Tuesday stayed in London."

Chump jumped off the divan and shouted, "Hi, Ellie!" into the receiver.

"I can't hear you, Ellie. Can we have supper together?"

"Hi, Chump," she said. "I'm free as of seven tonight."

The bellboy said, "The people in the next suite are complaining about the noise."

"Oh, go to hell," Milton said. He gave the kid a dollar. "The boys are just having some fun."

"Look, Ellie. At seven-thirty. At the Fjord."

"Are you playing tonight?"

"We're not playing at all. Just making a record. Do you know where it is?"

Milton threw a divan pillow at Chump and hit David.

"I know where it is."

Chump slammed the bathroom door behind him.

"I'll see you then. Seven-thirty."

"Seven forty-five," she said.

"Old Man River" was being played in the empty bathtub.

"Hey, Ellie," David said. "I'm a father! A father-to-be."

She had hung up.

Milton was standing, suitcase open, white shirt stretched across his stomach, hands on hips.

"You're getting fat, Milton."

"That's because I haven't had to worry about you two," he said.

On the way to the Fjord the taxi stopped at a red light on East 47th Street. Among the cars, on the pavement, a little boy was curled up, about nine years old, his haunches looking awfully small in blue jeans, the dirty sneakers awfully still. While they waited for the light a priest bent over the boy and made a gesture with his right hand. Then a brown blanket was placed over the little boy. The light changed and the taxi moved.

Ellie was sitting on a velvet divan in the foyer. In her lap, folded over her arm, was a sable wrap.

David said, "You're beautiful."

Her short veil brushed against his cheek.

Holding his fingers under the wrap, squeezing gently, she said, "David. David. David. So good to see you again."

After he had given his coat to the check girl he stood beside Ellie in the doorway. Her dress was dark and well cut.

"Ellie, you're beautiful."

"I blossomed in my late twenties," she said. "It must be my English blood."

Sitting at the table he looked at her again.

"I can't get over it," he said. "What are you doing?"

"I'm retained by a holding corporation, if you'd believe it," she said. "They give me forty-five thousand dollars a year and a ninety-thousand-dollar cooperative, furnished."

"What for? What do you do?"

"I entertain," she said. "In the holding corporation, I'm what the customers hold."

"That's great," he said. "Wonderful. How did you get that?"

"Through a meat packer in Chicago. A gentleman who wanted to get rid of me."

"I remember. John Harrison. Is this holding corporation in the meat business?"

"Machine tools, oddly enough. Don't try to get the connection. It's all very hi-fi."

Automatically, he had ordered martinis.

"So sin pays," he said.

"I even pay taxes. What do you think of that?"

"Lord," he said. "You're respectable."

They nodded their glasses at each other.

"How do your new customers compare with your old ones?" he asked.

"Their underpants are cleaner," she said. "But their desires aren't."

The silver choker at her throat highlighted the smoothness of her skin, the length of her neck.

"There are fewer of them," she said. "That's the important thing."

She had learned to use make-up, beautifully. Her mouth, her nose, her eyes were all clear-lined, accented, but without the slightest appearance of cosmetics.

"I had to do something when Harry's closed," she said.

"Harry's closed?"

"Didn't you know? About two and a half years ago."

"How did that happen?"

"Oddly enough, you and your idiot-savant friend made Harry so famous as a discoverer of young talent that he was flooded by every kid with a horn in this country."

"No."

"The place changed completely. Remember? You never went back. Harry listened to them all, all day, every day. They listened to each other, taking up table space and buying nothing all night. No one else came."

In the room to his right people circled slowly around a buffet. Two empty green plates had been left on top of each other in the center of their table.

"The rugs wore thin. Harry began buying his meat and liquor off the lake barges, you know?"

"Yes."

"Finally, the inspectors closed him, after three warnings. Harry's gone back to being a butcher."

"Poor Harry."

"And I got my hooks into a saddle tramp with eastern interests and became a nuisance."

"Beautiful," David said. "Ellie makes good."

"Don't laugh," she said. "I learned a lot during those days."

"And from appearances, I'd guess that corporation never made a better investment."

She smiled under her short veil.

"I go on their booze account," she said. "How is Chump? Does he still get the shaving soap all over him?"

"He's fine." David roughed his ear, to make the airplane bubbles go away. "He's got a motorcycle, and so far he's frightened half of London with it."

"He's such a delightful nut."

She had barely sipped her martini.

They took their plates around the buffet and returned to the table. On her plate was a little roast beef, a little chicken, a little lobster.

"David? You're married."

"Yes."

Her sable was strung across the back of her chair.

"Does that mean we can't?"

"No," he said. "Of course not."

Her apartment was on Park Avenue, in a new building up the block from the Regency Hotel.

She waved her hand at the lavender floor-to-ceiling drapes along one wall. Their folds were lit indirectly.

"The terrace is through there," she said.

There was a baby grand piano standing in its own carpeted well. On one wall was an original by Dubuffet.

She dropped her wrap on a silk chair and pushed a button on a tape console. Immediately, without warming up, there was himself, Chump, playing "Don't," not from the beginning, from about halfway through.

She put her arms around his neck, kissed him. *I have been in this room, my music, a part of everything that has ever happened in it, this room, this apartment* . . . There was a smell of lavender from her, lighter than he had ever smelled it, with fresh air in it.

He pressed the wide, plastic, blonde button that said OFF.

"I'm sick of myself," he said.

Without her veil her forehead was wonderfully rich, smooth below her waved hair.

"I have nothing else," she said.

She stepped into the piano well.

"You never can do anything when there is music, can you?" she said. "It so distracts you."

She took the prettily wrapped package off the piano and brought it to him.

"I have a present for you."

It was a book.

"*The Hawk's Done Gone*, by Mildred Hawn. Wherever did you get this?"

"I ordered it from Vanderbilt Press."

"I don't remember ever mentioning it to you."

"I've been saving it for you."

"Terribly unfashionable, I'm afraid."

He dropped the wrappings into the silk chair, put the book on the mantel, where he would see it.

"That's the way you are, David."

She loosened his tie, undid his collar button and slipped the top of his jacket off his shoulders without unbuttoning it.

"No, no," he cried. "I'm a virgin."

"Don't be afraid, little boy."

His arms were behind his back.

"But, lady, I ain't never made love before."

"Don't be scared."

She pulled his tie from his collar, dropped it to the floor.

He wriggled his arms.

"No, no!"

"It ought to happen to every boy, sometime."

"Lady, lady. Please let me go home. I won't never whistle at you in the street again."

"Take it easy, little boy. It's going to happen."

"Maybe I can't. I'm scared."

"Don't be scared. Nothing bad will happen."

She put her cheek against his bare chest, kissed him.

"Please lady, please," David said. "You're getting me all excited."

"Don't you like that?"

"No. I want to go home. I'm scared."

She looked solemnly into his eyes.

"Don't be scared. Just do what I tell you."

"What do I have to do?"

She snapped the button on his coat.

"I'll show you."

From the bed he could see along the lavender drapes in the living room, the light streaks on their folds.

She said, "It's good, making love to someone you haven't made love to in a long time."

David said, "It's good to be home."

"David?" Her light shoulders were sunken into the soft, powder-blue pillow. "How is she in bed? I mean, Ms Tuesday."

"Fine."

"No, I mean really."

"Doing an exercise in gym class."

She put herself under his arm on the pillow.

"I'm so glad to see you," she said. "To love you."

She stroked his fingers on her breast.

"The important thing is she is the mother of my child," he said. "Maybe my son."

David kissed her forehead, rubbed his jaw over her hairline. She had not taken it as news.

"I wonder what he'll look like," she said.

"His mother is handsome."

"She is?" Her eyes asked him if he was serious. "I saw her picture in *The Daily News*. At the wedding."

"She was drunk," David said.

"Oh."

"She really is good looking. Very natural."

"And will he be a genius?"

"I hope not. Just a good, happy, healthy kid."

How small his haunches were; how used those sneakers; they had covered him completely with the blanket.

"No silver horn in his mouth, uh?"

"I hope he becomes a bank clerk. Keeps sacred the hours from nine to five."

Her right hand moved from his stomach to his thigh.

"You probably do," she said.

"Handsome boys always become salesmen," he said. "Have you ever noticed?"

He felt the exhalation from her nostrils in the hair on his chest. Between pale yellow sheets her legs were neat, trim.

"I bet he is a handsome, happy kid," she said. "I hope he has his father's hands, anyway."

"He'll probably be blonde," he said. "From Ms Tuesday. At least at first. I hope he has her eyes. I'll want him to play every game there is, be good at everything that isn't important, not care too much about such things as math, history. He's got to be able to dance. And he'll lie a little, with straight eyes, about where he was last night, the night before."

"That's wonderful."

"And he'll look at his tired old Daddy and say, 'What's bothering you? How come you think life is such a big sweat?' "

"And you'll say, 'Shut up and eat your trust fund.' " Her fingers were gently tweaking his hair. "David, what's his name?"

Oscar. "I don't know."

"Call him Peter."

"Why Peter?"

She rolled over, half onto his stomach. One leg was inside his.

"And if it's a girl, call her Vagina."

"You wretch."

"They go together."

A siren screamed down Park Avenue, again.

Later, she said, "You're tired, David."

He was sitting on the edge of the bed, before going into the bathroom.

"I don't like the idea of this record," he said. "Neither one of us is up to it. If it were my first, I wouldn't make it."

She said, "It'll sell a million."

30

Dan brought his satchel into the men's room of the train fifteen minutes before it was due to arrive and, standing on one leg, then the other, bouncing off the walls, trying to hold himself up, keep his clothes off the floor, let them touch nothing, he changed. The only other clothes he had were a faded pair of blue jeans, a cotton blue checked shirt and brown loafers. He had no socks but black ones so he wore none. He put his black shoes and socks into the bottom of the satchel and folded his trousers, his shirt, his jacket over them. Beside his collar, on top, went a book he had been assigned Friday to have read by Monday, *Economics of the Church*.

He did not return to his seat but went through the doors quickly, into the coach ahead, and stood, waiting, by the forward door while the train slowed.

A woman with fat ankles looked him up and down over the Paris edition of Friday's *New York Herald Tribune*, his shabby little black canvas satchel, his bare feet braced, set apart, in loafers, his bare ankles, his faded blue jeans. Her eyes followed each arm to his hands, stuck in the back pockets of his jeans. His sleeves were rolled up, tightly, and the top three buttons of his shirt were open. She narrowed her eyes to stare at him full in the face.

He smiled.

He was the first off the train, down the steps, through the station, whistling "Summertime," swinging his satchel. Outside the station he stood a moment in the sunlight, everything pastel around him, and turned his face up to the sun, felt it on his forehead, cheek-bones, his throat, his arms, the V on his chest, his lips, even felt it through the cotton shirt. The hand that held the satchel pulsed. A taxi driver looked away when Dan brought his head down and looked at him.

Halfway down a side street to the harbor he found a *pension*, with a dark, cool, stone interior.

"*Madame?*"

She came through the dining room, wiping her hands on a white, filmy apron. She was slim, in her forties.

DANIEL NELSON. STUDENT. 16 RUE S. JEROME, PARIS. U.S., was how he registered.

The stairway was wide and white, with a turn in it, and a firm, black wrought-iron bannister. His room was perfectly square, with a high bed, a cardboard commode, a bureau-washstand, a rug, a rocking chair. He heard girls' voices. There were wire hangers but he dropped the satchel into the bottom of the commode unopened, and pushed the cardboard door shut. There was no mirror in the room. Down the hill, through his open window, over the roofs of other buildings, was the harbor.

An old man was sculling his dory across slowly in the sunlight. Immediately to the left of Dan's window was the ledge of the flat roof of the *pension*'s ell.

Leaving his room, he turned right and then right again toward the sunlight-filled arch he had noticed, instead of going left, toward the stairs. He went up two or three steps, hands in his back pockets and into the sunlight through the arch.

Two girls were lying on towels on the roof, sunshades on their eyes, cream on their noses, men's folded handkerchiefs diamonded on their pubic hair.

Hearing him, one took off her eyeshades. She raised herself to one elbow, her hips still flat on the roof. The other did not move.

"What do you know, Clarice," she said. "A boy."

"Not a boy, George!" Clarice rolled her head, two inches, put her nearer cheek to the sun. "A boy-boy?"

"A boy-boy."

Dan had never seen bodies so tan. He did not know human flesh could become so mahogany.

"Too bad."

Under his watchband his wrist was wet.

Dan said, "Hi."

Clarice sat up, using only her stomach muscles. She took off her shades.

She said, "Hi."

George said, "Hi."

Dan said, "Hi."

The low parapet around the roof was off-white stucco. The deck was colored squares set in cement. Nowhere on the roof, on the parapet, the deck, in the corners, were there other clothes, robes, bathing suits. Over the parapet was the Mediterranean.

"This isn't private," Clarice said. "I mean, you're staying at the *pension*."

"Sit down," said George.

"Take your pants off," said Clarice.

George lifted herself onto her stomach. She flipped the handkerchief onto the towel. Clarice's legs were raised a little, open at the knees. The calves were relaxed. Her legs were remarkably muscular.

"I bet he's got underpants on," George said.

"Is that why he won't take his pants off?"

"He's probably ashamed of having underpants on."

"He's got no socks on," Clarice said.

Dan pulled his shirt out of his trousers, pulled it off and sat down. He flipped his shoes off with his toes.

"What's your name?"

"Dan Prescott."

"I'm Georgia. This is Clarice."

The roof burned the back of his heels and the palms of his hands.

Georgia put her cheek flat on her forearm, to face Clarice.

"I'll bet this boy-boy thinks we care whether he takes his pants off or not."

"Maybe he cares," Clarice said.

"Where are you from?" Dan asked.

"Philadelphia." Georgia put her chin on the back of her hands. "Clarice is from London."

"Philadelphia," Dan said. "Do you know the Baldwins?"

"No-I-don't-know-the-Baldwins," she said. "Screw the Baldwins."

Clarice laughed. She was lying down again, eyeshades in place.

Georgia picked up her handkerchief. The weight of her shoulders was on her elbows. She blew her nose.

"Sun always makes my nose run," she said.

The underside of Clarice's breasts were hardly tanned at all. Georgia's breasts, from that angle, were completely tanned.

"What are you doing here?" Dan asked. "I mean, in Sete."

"We're go-go-dancers," Georgia said. "Topless, you know? In G-strings."

Clarice said, "Ye-ye."

Georgia said, "Like who cares."

The roof-patio was terribly hot.

"Do you ever go out?" Dan asked.

"Out?"

Georgia's cheekbone was on the heel of one hand. The handkerchief was crumpled in the other.

"You know. Like with boys."

"Boy-boys?" Georgia asked.

Her legs were waving behind her, from the knees up, crossing and uncrossing in the air, shin striking calf, calf rubbing skin. Both calves flashed golden in the sunlight.

"You know what I mean," Dan said.

"What do you mean, boy-boy?"

Dan sat up. He crossed his legs. The outside of his ankles burned.

"I don't know what I mean."

Georgia was squinting through the sun at the center of his chest, where there was hair.

"What do you want, boy-boy?"

There was one straw on the roof, a strange piece of hay, lying crosswise to a crack. *How did that get here?*

"I don't know what I want," he said.

Georgia put her head down again, on her forearms, to look at Clarice.

"How come every boy-boy we see wants the same thing, Clarice?"

"I don't know, George."

"You'd think they'd learn after a while."

Dan ran the end of the straw along the crack. The sun was so bright he seemed to be seeing the tiles, the crack, the straw, in the negative.

Clarice said, "Flick off, Boy-boy."

Naked, he lay face down on his bed in the cool of his room. Occasionally, infrequently he heard the girls' voices through the window, a few words, a question, a sentence, a sentence, then a long pause. There was a film of sweat on the side of his nose. Beside him on the bed were his blue jeans, flung, legs at a crazy angle, his underpants, flat. Beside the bed, on the floor, was his satchel, open but still full.

In a while he heard them leaving the roof, talking more, but lazily. In his mind's eye, he saw them come through the arch, down the steps into the shade of the hall, trailing their towels on the floor behind them. In each other hand would be a white handkerchief, crumpled.

He turned his face toward the wall.

31

While the group from West Germany was playing, David telephoned the Hotel Bedford twice, asking for his own room number, 812.

Chump said, "Is she there?"

"No."

The desk clerk in the London hotel had given David the telegram he had sent from New York telling her the flight number and time of arrival and suggesting she not bother to meet them. The clerk handed David the key, the telegram, and said nothing. The cosmetics in the bathroom were left as he had last seen them. A pair of panties she had washed out the morning they had left were still draped over the shower rail. Except for the things the maid would have done, nothing in the suite had been disturbed all week.

The concert at Royal Festival Hall was important. It had taken a lot of planning, arranging and rearranging of schedules, contracts. The audience would be large, reasonably sober, critical, and of most importance, with record-buying habits. David and Chump were to play only those ten songs they had just recorded. David could not miss an important concert because he was out looking for his wife.

He showered and shaved, keeping one ear cocked for the telephone or the door. He waited until the last possible moment, sitting in the dark, smoking a cigarette and looking at the door. *Ms Tuesday knows I had to return today, for the concert.*

"I wonder where she is," Chump said. He looked away from David, toward the shaft of light in the stage entrance.

First a quintet from America played, then a group from West

Germany, then David MacFarlane and Chump Hardy. After the inter-
mission they played again, in the same order, and again David called
the Hotel Bedford. The audience demanded the encores from Mac-
Farlane and Hardy, four of them, applauding and cheering the old
tunes, "Greasy Pig," "Deme Lo," "Lech," "Sorry" far more than they
had the new ones, "Gray Day," "Whistlin'."

The taxi was slowed by the crowd they had drawn. Then he plod-
ded through the after-midnight hotel lobby, through the cigar smoke
into the elevator, said good night, see ya, to Chump on the sixth
floor, went down the hotel corridor to his own door, feeling all the
strain in his ears, the strain of the earphones tight against his head
in New York, Milton saying, *Beautiful, beautiful,* of the electronic,
impersonal voice from the control booth, seemingly originating
from inside his own head, saying, relentlessly, *Do it over, Take it
from just after the release,* the sound of his own music so much
around him, so overwhelming he hated it, physically, the strain of
the airplane, the sound of Royal Festival Hall, the piano not itself
amplified, microphones picking up both him and Chump, sending
their sound out into that huge hall, dark world, from which it never
returned, the applause so loud, so multitudinous that behind the
lights it was positively frightening, no matter how much he had
heard it, frightening each time, starting below them, in the front
rows, sweeping up the sloped floor to the back, up the walls into,
from the balconies. In the center of his head, between his ears,
behind his eyes, at the back of his nose, in the center of his stomach,
he was sick of sound.

He snapped the lights on in the living room. Ms Tuesday was
standing just away from the window. She looked at him. The window was closed. Her pupils dilated in the sudden light.

Her face was white and drawn and her eyes looked frightened.
Her hair looked as if it had not been combed for days. She was
wearing the same dark brown dress she had been wearing when
they left, now with spots on it. She had only one shoe on, the heel of
that one making her stand crookedly.

"Oh, David. I've been vomiting."

"Did you call the doctor?"

"No."

"I'll call the doctor."

He waited for the desk clerk to answer. He had not yet taken off
his coat and hat.

"Oh, David, don't call the doctor. You mustn't."

"Why not?"

He put down the receiver, just hearing the desk clerk answer.

He took off his coat and hat and placed them over a chair.

The fear in her face was frightening. He took a step toward her, but she shrank away, clumsily, staggering on her one shoe heel.

He persisted, while she examined his eyes, her temples throbbed, her faced drained even more. He took her by the shoulders with both hands.

"Don't be afraid," he said.

"I got rid of the baby, David."

Her face, then, her face went from fear to the momentary courage, brashness of the bald statement, to more immediate fright, then horror. Then all that, squeezed, like a sponge, became compressed in all the lines of her face, centering in her nose, eyes, mouth.

"I got rid of the baby."

She cried and then laughed, trying not to bring her hands to her face. At first, David was curious to know the depths of her shock, her grief, her hysteria. Shaking her by the shoulders did no good. Eyes wide open, staring at David, she began to shriek. She seemed to be without need of breath. David slapped her across the face with his open hand, knocking her out of his own grip onto the divan. All the horrid noise in the world had been in the shriek, and he had hit at it.

She sat, half falling off the divan, fingertips touching her cheek, numbly. She looked up at him. Suddenly her face was expressionless.

"My God," he said.

She was breathing hard.

"Who helped you? Who did it?"

"Schatzy," she said.

"Why?"

"David, I tried to be here before you got back and tell you it was a miscarriage, but I couldn't do it. I drank."

"Why?"

"I'm afraid he gave me a terrible scraping, David."

"Why, why, why? Why did you do it, Ms Tuesday? Do you know why you did it?"

She said, "No."

"Is it completely gone? How do you know it worked?"

"It was surgical, David," she said. "It worked. It's gone."

He left her as she was, half off the divan.

David undressed in the bathroom, leaving his clothes in a heap on the rug, and stood in the shower, letting the warm water stream on him. *Were there four, or five encores? I'm glad I left "Deme Lo" to the last. That's the one people want to hear most, because that is the one they heard first, learned to like first. It goes way back with them, takes them back to another time, any other time, another place. They will come to feel the same way about "Gray Day," "Purple Skin," someday, when they are far enough away from first hearing it to say, I remember. I first heard that at Royal Festival Hall. I first heard that in the record department at Macy's. Jenny was with me. Christ, they are both falling apart, Ms Tuesday, Chump. Oh-o say, can you see? No, I can't see. Other women have babies. Of course I have no idea how we sounded. Having the piano itself greatly amplified helps me hear myself. It does indeed. Gives me a fantastic sense of power. That huge piano, unamplified, in that huge hall: I felt like I was blowing up a truck tire with a leaky hand pump. The goosed-up boxes really spoil you. In one place, small places, the pianos are goosed-up and you don't feel you're reaching the audience because of the liquor and the smoke and the talk. In big places, with big pianos, unamplified, you can sense the audience listening, like a million tigers, eyes glowing in the dark, about to leap, and you're not sure you're reaching the audience then, either, because there is such a big, big space to fill. I began to bang in "Homeward Bound," until I realized it. Christ, I had no chance to test that piano, work out on it; before a concert, yet! Stupid Milton. He could have gotten us to London a day early, instead of taping that fucking program. I said something funny; what did I say? Oh, yeah, I called Garner the Earl. Not very funny. Duke Ellington. If only I could have had an hour and a half on that piano this morning, not enough to get tired, just enough to see what sound would do in that empty hall, instead of sitting on that fucking airplane. Trying a piano in an empty hall throws you off, too. Belgrade. That was a beautiful piano. I enjoyed it so much I played too much trying it out and muffed the concert. I wanted to hear how everything sounded, all the pieces, all the ones I care anything about, on that piano. In Belgrade I gave a concert for myself. I have written things I don't care about now.* His bathrobe, the white terry cloth one, was still on the back of the bathroom door. He popped two aspirins into his mouth without water.

He came out of the bathroom in his robe. Ms Tuesday was still on the sofa. He looked around for the bottle he knew would be there. *Ms Tuesday tried to be drunk, but she couldn't make it. She was too scared.* He poured himself a whiskey and soda. *It was not a very good concert. You know that? It was not a very good concert.*

She said, "Will you give me a drink?"

"Sure."

He poured her a drink and brought it over to her.

"David," she said. "If you want me to get out, I will. I'll get out tonight, if you want."

"No," he said. "Don't be silly."

He drank half the whiskey-soda in one swallow.

"I couldn't blame you if you wanted me to do that. You've been very generous, with the joint checking account and this lovely suite and all. If you wanted me to do that," she said.

"No."

"Are you terribly disappointed?"

He sat down on the divan beside her. He had finished his drink in one more swallow.

"Does it hurt terribly badly?"

"Yes," she said.

"It's lucky he didn't kill you."

"He performs twenty, thirty a day. It was my own fault," she said. "I drank afterward, worrying about you. I made myself sick."

They were sitting on the divan, side by side, talking, discussing, having a chat. Ms Tuesday was looking into her drink, watching the liquid move in her glass as she moved her wrist.

"How much money did you give him?"

"None. He wouldn't take any. He did it as a friend."

David said, "Some friend."

"I'll be all right. I suppose I feel good considering everything."

"What an inane thing to do."

"I know, David. I don't understand it. I was so terribly scared. I called Schatzy in Paris and told him exactly when you were leaving for New York. He told me not to worry."

"You mean you had it all arranged? Before we left?"

"Yes. He came over for it. To do it here. In another hotel."

"What were you scared about? Other women have babies."

Quietly, she said, "Obviously."

At the bathroom door he turned around. "Do you want me to get a decent doctor to check you over?"

"No," she said. "I'll be all right. Schatzy is a good doctor, really."

"Yeah. Great."

He left his robe on the pile of clothes and stepped into the shower again, making the water warmer this time. *It is the back muscles, the neck muscles. It's not right to blame the piano. I'm lousy; Chump is lousy. Ms. Tuesday is lousy. I suppose Madame Sudar is lost by now, one more Parisian alley cat. Those phrases in "London Bridges": God, I was off. Oh! I was off. And for so long. I thought I'd never get back. I almost had to stop. Who knew it? Who heard me? God. There was one other place, where was it; oh, yeah, in "Tales of a Beach." I was a little quicker then. Frankly, I was on the wrong phrase altogether. I had to jump. Poor Chump, I had to jump. Blue notes all over the place. My heart was uneven. Do you know that? Do you know your heart is uneven? Christ, you can't even trust your pulse, at any speed. They applauded anyway. At those prices, they had better get the exercise. The more they applaud, the better time they think they have. So they applaud more. That West German group was good. They have all the excitement, now, the freshness. They're really inventing something new, based on us, ahead of us, me, already. I should have listened. I am getting to the point where I will have to learn more. What I need is routine, any kind of routine, to get the pulse steady, the big eardrum metronome. Shit, I was bad. I've got to go back to paying attention. I can't stand being bad, the mistakes, the errors. Chump said, What about you? You haven't been so good lately. Why don't we all go jump off cliffs? Christ. I even messed up the release of "Gray Day," cut it. We did it so many times for the record, that stretch over and over, I got confused. How did Chump stay with me at all? Why would she kill her own child? Tomorrow night. I've got to be better tomorrow night. Saturday night concert. How can I be?* He dried himself slowly.

He put on his robe again and went back to the living room.

"David, do you want me to go?"

"No."

She was sitting in the same position, legs straight to the floor, ankles crossed, fingers picking each other in her lap. Her drink was marking the end table.

"Never mind," he said. "Only one more concert in London, tomorrow night, and then we go down to Cannes."

"I don't want to go down to Cannes."

"Sure you do." He was pouring himself another drink. "You like the sun. They'll be having the film festival there, and that will interest you. You're sick, you know. You can't treat yourself this way without being sick."

"Oh, David, I am sick."

She was crying, working her mouth, biting her lips, trying to hold it, something, in, her eyes vague-gray behind the tears.

"Oh, David. There was no baby."

"What?"

"I don't think there ever was a baby."

"What are you talking about?"

"I was only five or six weeks, David. Seven."

"You said. Your period. What about the tests?"

"Tests aren't always right, David. Not at five or six weeks."

"What makes you think there was no baby? What did Schatz say?"

"He didn't say anything. He just looked funny. He wouldn't tell me."

"Didn't you feel anything, see anything?"

"David, I was out cold. He just looked at me funny. He said he wouldn't tell me. I don't think there ever was a baby."

"Jesus Christ."

I was in bed with Ellie, talking about my son . . .

"In other words," he said. "You had a D. and C."

"David, there was no baby."

He found himself facing the curtain of the window, dimly aware of the lights, glazed, inspecific, uncertain, of the city beyond. He was taking this drink more slowly. Ms Tuesday was on the divan behind him, crying into her hands.

"That's all right," he said.

Then he was sitting on the divan and her face was buried in his lap, in the terry cloth robe. He stroked her hair.

"We're young yet," he said. "We have plenty of time, Ms Tuesday."

"Call me that again," she said.

"Ms Tuesday?"

"Yes. Call me that again."

"Ms Tuesday, Ms Tuesday, Ms Tuesday," he said. *Shall I tell her about Ellie, how we talked in bed?*

"I like to be called Ms Tuesday."

32

There was a roar behind them.

"Oh, my God. Where did he come from?"

"Chump? Is it Chump?" She twisted around to look through the car's rear window.

"Yes."

In the rear view mirror the black motorcycle was just cutting in front of the car behind them, swaying to keep balance, so sharp was the turn. Black leather shoulders, sleeves, blonde hair, circular goggles showed above and behind the glinting handlebars. The car behind braked in surprise, nosed toward the side of the road. Three days before, Chump had roared off the quais at Calais without them, heading for Cannes by himself, and they had not seen him since. Now, in the villages above Cannes, he had apparently waited for them, seen them wend their sedate way along the road after lunch, had left whatever he was doing, girl, jam session, fight, God knows, to give chase. *No, Chump.* He was accelerating on the narrow road to pass, weaving, unbelievably trying to time his passing the Mercedes at the same time as an oncoming truck, ducking behind the Mercedes' fender then swinging out, to go between them.

Ms Tuesday screamed, "Chump!"

David believed if he had not swung in, given Chump that extra inch, he would not have made it. The truck did not swerve.

Chump had to cut in so close in front of David his big rear wheel was actually skipping on the dry tar. Again, he was swaying, for balance.

"He doesn't even have his helmet on," David said.

"Does he always drive that way?"

"He couldn't."

Chump had gone around a curve and the sound of the engine faded curiously fast.

David said, "He's a damned fool."

Around the curve they could look down the ribbon of road falling down, through a valley. Chump was nowhere in sight.

He was to their right, on a dirt road, behind a hedge, waiting for them.

"Oh, no. David?"

The engine fell into first and without much acceleration, he was riding along beside them, on the right, at the edge of the road. Ms Tuesday's window was closed. The skin of Chump's jaw looked blue, drawn back. His eyes were narrow, nearly closed.

David waved his hand. "Go away!"

With a little spurt of power Chump darted ahead of them, swinging immediately in front of the car, this time forcing David to swerve outward, toward oncoming traffic, a Jaguar sedan. Chump then went ahead a little way, into the left lane, slowed, made David pass him on the inside, fell behind David, then proceeded to pass him on the right again. Cars behind them had slowed in a line, were honking.

"How can he be so stupid!"

That time when Chump was directly in front of the Mercedes, he tried to shift, do some glorious, unlikely, racing shift, which did not work, and for a fraction of a second his rear wheel froze, locked, screamed on the tar, smoked blue. Chump's shoulders swerved in the air, as if lassoed. David braked, his own tires going *eerk*, swung the wheel, which only meant he would have hit, run over Chump at a different angle. Then Chump, ingloriously in his old gear, straightened up, spurted ahead again as if kicked on the rear fender.

David pulled off the road, onto the grass, put the car in neutral, and rolled his window down the rest of the way. He waved on the curious, angry, frightened drivers behind him, to pass, which they did, tentatively.

David and Ms Tuesday waited.

In a moment Chump came down the opposite lane slowly, like a bowling ball, looking for them. He saw them, U-turned, skidding. The rear wheel bounced sideways on the tar, causing more horns to blow.

He said, "Hi."

He landed the heel of his hand against the canvas roof, then relaxed his arm, fell in, pushed out, in, out.

"Shut that thing off," David said.

"What? I can't hear you."

The saxophone was in the back seat.

Ms Tuesday said, "Hi, Chump."

"Hi."

David yelled, "Chump, you're going to kill both of us, driving that way. You go on ahead. Leave us alone. We'll see you in Cannes."

"I was in Cannes two days ago," Chump said.

"Get away from us. You'll just kill all of us."

"All right," Chump said.

Chump pushed out from the roof and kicked with his feet. The back tire shot so much sand at the car David ducked. Chump swerved onto the road without much speed, in front of a car, making it brake, honk, then he roared up the road.

"My God." David waited for the traffic to pass before rolling the Mercedes back into lane. "He was in Cannes two days ago. He must have gone like hell all night. And that's considering all the times he must have gotten lost."

They had driven fairly constantly at a regular pace, rising early, breakfasting lightly, coffee and croissant, an egg for Ms Tuesday, stopping only for an hour's lunch while the car was being serviced, then riding through the afternoon, from north more or less to south more or less, a little east, seeing the world flash by through the car windows, city, town, country, town, city, each city getting smaller, lighter, less crowded, less hurried, each town quieter, more separated. The gray and brown of early spring in the north gradually changed to the green and yellow of the south. They had not talked much. The inns they had stayed in had been the most charming and quaint David could find, the oldest, draftiest. They had not made love, due to David's cold, her "condition." She had sat quietly beside him on the ride, pale and apparently contrite, hands folded in her lap, on her pocketbook, looking through the window for daffodils and jonquils in the dooryards. Frequently, especially before they would stop somewhere, for lunch, for the night, but not just then, sometimes just riding along, she would do something he had never seen her do before: take a little silver compact she had bought in London out of her purse, stare into it, at each part of her face separately, fragmenting it into eyes, nose, mouth, wipe her make-up with a tissue, then touch it up, apply more, pressing her lips against each other, batting her eyes, inspecting her nose from four angles.

Coming down the hills they had caught glimpses of the Mediterranean.

"We're just a few minutes to Cannes," David said.

Coming around a long curve they saw cars parked oddly on the other side of the road, run onto the grass, abandoned. There were cars parked on this side of the road, too, drawn up on the grass in a neater, apparently less hurried, order. There was one police car parked in the road itself, its top light rotating, its radio crackling. It had come from the other direction. A white-helmeted policeman was in the middle of the road directing traffic.

David said, "Oh, no."

There was a group of people in the field, down to the right.

He backed up and parked his car at the end of the line on the right side of the road and turned the motor off. Ms Tuesday said nothing.

David walked along the line of cars, finally going between them, to the field. The grass was in its spring-green lushness, and the ground beneath its thickness was sodden. Nowhere, on the road, off the road, in the field, the grass, was there any sign of the motorcycle.

The people were chattering at each other excitedly in French, explaining to each other what had happened, asking the details, insisting on this point or another. One man, short, skinny and bald, in a workshirt, was shaking his head and apparently denying responsibility, eager to pounce verbally on anyone who implied the contrary.

Chump was lying face up on the grass, staring quietly at the sky as if he had just awakened. There was a clot of blood on the grass, a few drops, a bump over his right ear, hair and blood mixed as if exploded from the inside. There was blood drying below each nostril.

A Frenchman in workpants and rolled-up sleeves was leaning over him, screaming some question over and over, loudly, trying to correct ignorance with volume. Chump was not even looking at him.

There was the happy, ice-cream-truck bell-ringing of the ambulance.

Chump's eyes moved, finally. He saw David. His eyes hesitated, moved away, began to protrude.

David leaned down, hands on knees, to hear him, over the shouting, the ambulance bell, the excited conversation.

"Dave."

"What."

"Dave. Take care of my horn."

David stood up. *What would these people say, do, if I belted him, smashed him right in his mouth, right in his bloody nostrils?* "You IDIOT!"

Chump swallowed. He returned his gaze to the sky.

David went back to the road.

Two men were taking the stretcher out of the ambulance.

"Is this a private ambulance?"

The elder demurred to the younger, for language.

"Yes, sir."

"Will you take him to the British-American hospital outside Nice, please?" David took a few steps to his own car before turning. "He may not look it, but he has plenty of money. And I'll be along later."

"Yes, sir."

Ms Tuesday had not changed her position in the car or her expression, even slightly. Through her window could be seen a lush green bush, with yellow sunlight in it.

David started the car.

"How's Chump?"

"He has a bump on his head."

Trying to get by the ambulance, the police car, David was stopped by the policeman. He looked through David's window.

"Pardon me, Monsieur, Madame. Were you witness to this accident?"

David said, "No."

"Merci, Monsieur."

The boulevard between the hotels and the beach was crowded, Rolls Royces and Cadillacs, Citroens and Chevrolets, heavy old men, deeply tanned, in loose clothes, light-skinned girls with cloth stretched tightly across their derrieres. Moving slowly in the traffic, in the sunlight, with the top up, the car became insufferably hot. Over to their right, on the beach, people were sending a bright, striped beach ball high into the air, again and again.

"I'll drop you at the hotel. You can get settled in. I'll go directly along to the hospital."

"All right."

The bellmen took things out of the unlocked trunk so fast David did not even have to get out.

Alone, he speeded up east of Cannes, went along the cliffs over the sparkling sea. He realized what a long way he had sent the ambulance.

The nice lady in a gray suit, in an office just off the foyer, thanked him sincerely for the information Chump had not been able to give her. ,

"I'm afraid he was rather stupid when he came in. We weren't sure who he was. The ambulance driver just said an American kid."

"He's about twenty-six," David said.

"We have so many of these motorcycle accidents a week," she said. "He wasn't wearing a helmet, was he?"

"No, Ma'm."

"You should always wear your helmet."

David waited in a square, cool room, dark in comparison with the sunlight streaming through the French doors that looked onto the terrace, over the sea. The furniture was pleasant, the rug a faded oriental. After driving he wanted to stand; tired, he wanted to sit. He wandered around the empty room, angered by the single copy of *National Geographic* on the side table.

He was standing when a husky, forty-five-year-old man, bald fringe, steel-rimmed glasses entered. His white tunic, pants, shoes looked crass in the decor.

"Mister MacFarlane, I presume. I'm Doctor Gluckstein."

The man's hand was damp.

"My news is not good. He has a serious concussion, Mister Mac-Farlane, and two broken legs. He's also exhausted."

"That's certainly possible."

"But I also suspect he's full of it."

"Full of what?"

Magnified brown eyes seemed to grow through the lenses: "Dope, Mister MacFarlane. Drugs."

"Oh."

"He's a musician, isn't he?"

David said nothing.

"God knows what he's got in him," Doctor Gluckstein said. "I can't figure it out."

David said, "With him you can't tell."

"I suggest you leave him here with us, for a week or ten days. In a private room. Give him a chance to catch up with himself."

"He's supposed to play tonight. In Cannes."

"Well, he can't do that." Hands on hips, the doctor was ready, with his wide chest, shoulders, short, stocky build to withstand an assault: "And are you all right?"

"Fine. Just a cold. Do you have something you could give me for it?"

"No." His glasses, eyes, turned away from the light of the windows. "I don't."

                              *   *   *

The desk clerk seemed embarrassed, confused. He gave David his key, said Room 715 and something in French about baggage.

"My wife brought it up," David said.

His baggage stood just inside the door, alone. The suite was quiet. "Ms Tuesday?"

No windows had been opened. Her luggage was nowhere. There was nothing in the closets, in the bureau; nothing in the bathroom. The bedspread was smooth. There was nothing of Ms Tuesday's anywhere in the suite, no evidence she had been there, ever.

David started a call through to Milton in New York, then began to unpack. As he waited for the phone to ring, listened for Ms Tuesday's noises, the suite crackled with silence. He stopped to open the windows, let the noise of the traffic, the beach across the boulevard in. The phone rang.

He told Milton about Chump, just that. Milton said, *Beautiful.* David asked Milton to call the people here in Cannes, explain: Chump was in an accident and would be in the hospital a week or ten days. David did not want to have to answer questions. *Beautiful.*

"You might lose some weight, Milton."

Then David called the airlines in Cannes, each one, separately, and asked if a reservation had been made in the name of Mrs David MacFarlane, going anywhere. None had. He finished unpacking. He realized her passport was still in the name Janet Twombly and called all the airlines again. No reservations in that name, either. *Trains, buses, and a million private cars. Boats.*

First he ordered a bottle of Scotch and a bucket of ice. He sipped three drinks by himself, letting the room grow dark, waiting for the phone to ring. At about ten, he ordered a sandwich and a bottle of milk.

Around midnight, the phone rang.

"Hello, David. How are you?"

She sounded unusually vague.

"Where are you?"

A pause. "I'm in New York. I'm in Greenwich Village."

"You are not. This isn't a transatlantic call. The operator was female."

"Well, I'm someplace," she said.

"Where?"

"I don't know. Someplace. In New York. I'm in New York, David. There's an American sailor here who says I'm in New York."

"Are you in London?"

"No. I'm in New York."

There was the sound of glasses and laughter and chatting. Sense-lessly, he blocked his other ear to hear better.

"Listen, Ms Tuesday. Where are you?"

"I'm sorry I left you, David, but it wouldn't have worked. I was only being unfair to you. And all the other things, you know?"

"What other things?"

She was breathing slowly.

"The things you're supposed to say," she said. "I'm saying the things you're supposed to say at a time like this."

"Listen, Ms Tuesday, where are you?"

"I've got to hang up now, David. Somebody needs the phone." Then she said, "You drink lots of milk, David. Maybe you'll have a baby of your own."

David slammed the receiver down.

The phone rang again.

A man's voice began talking quietly, rapidly, in French, *Allo, allo*: something about a motorcycle.

"Oh, go to hell."

He called the hotel operator to ask where the long-distance call had originated, and she said Cannes. Her English was fake: good for numbers only. David kept her talking until she said something about London.

He called the airport and made a reservation for himself, to Lon-don. Then he called the hospital to leave the message for Chump that he was going to London to look for Ms Tuesday. He didn't care if Chump understood.

The phone rang again.

Ms Tuesday said, "I'm sorry I said that about the milk, David."

"Listen," he said. "Ms Tuesday, tell me where you are."

"I'm in France. I'm in Paris." The background noises had not changed. "Yes. I was just outside and the store across the street says *Patisserie*."

"That could be anywhere," David said.

"The place is full of Americans, David."

"What place?"

He heard her ask somebody the name of the place.

"The bartender doesn't know, David. Why did I call you? Oh, yes. I'm sorry I said that about the milk and the baby."

"Listen, Ms Tuesday. I'm coming to find you. Go to my hotel wher-ever you are, and check in."

"Hotel? What about a hotel?"

"I said—"

"Oh, David, hello? Somebody spilled something on me. I've got to hang up. Give my love to Chump."

It was then David took his fantastic trip, alluded to in many magazine articles, newspaper stories (WHERE IS MACFARLANE?—THE WORLD: AROUND AND AROUND IN TEN DAYS—WHERE MAC-FARLANE REALLY WENT [a monastery] WHAT HE DID [prayed]). The reporters came to the hotel to ask about Chump, were told something about Ms Tuesday: such is news during a film festival.

David re-read *The Hawk's Done Gone* and *Tales of the East Tennessee Granny Woman* entirely on planes, in airports, trains, *The Pit of Death* from Cannes to London (by way of Gibraltar and Madrid), *Darkness Coming Deep* from London to Paris, *Barshia's Horse He Made, It Flew* from Paris to Rome, *The Spring Is Trusty* from Rome to New York. In London he checked the Hotel Bedford, asked if anyone had seen her around the Someplace, the New Sounds, went through Mayfair, Soho, Westminster, Paddington pubs and, after they closed, through the Mayfair, Soho, Westminster, Paddington bottle clubs. He checked both names at every hotel he could think of, from high class to low. He wandered and taxied through the streets at night. *What am I doing?* In Paris he talked with Madame Sudar, who cried ("Well, I have kept the cat, Monsieur. You see his coat?"), with John Bart Nelson ("I see. I'll call you in Cannes, David. She's hard to find."), checked the hotels, the cafes (*You always know where to find me.*), the streets. In London, he saw a shabby, bearded old man with his nose, fingertips pressed against a lit store window, staring at a mannequin. In Paris, he saw the remains on the sidewalk of a girl who had jumped from a window. In Rome he followed the same system. In New York, just guessing, prowling the village, he did essentially the same. Tired of planes he took the train to Boston, reading *Apple Tree*, plus *Newsweek*, *The New Jerusalem* on the way back. The only place he thought of going but did not go was Columbia Falls, Maine. Taking one thousand milligrams of vitamin C a day he flew back to London, reading *Mclungeon-Colored*, thinking *What am I doing? Where is Dan Prescott?* remembering the noisy places she liked so much, the discotheques to which he would never bring her, suffering, with a cold, their noise now, the pubs again, the bottle clubs, the hotels. He also checked the hospitals. He thought of Schatz but did not know how to contact him. In Paris he did not see Madame Sudar or John again, embarrassed, *What on earth am I doing?* but he sat a while in the Luxembourg remembering he had always meant to take a walk with her there, perhaps with a child. To Rome, *Wild Sallet*, his ears paining him terribly, throbbing, sick of the taste and action of chewing gum. Then, incredibly enough, *What on earth am I doing?* to New York again, *God Almighty and the Government*, Boston, *Square Bread*, London, *The Hawk's Done Gone* again, Cannes, *Pa Went A-Courting*.

"There has been a call every day for you, Mister MacFarlane. From Paris. At precisely six." The clock over the desk clerk's head said five-fifteen. "The gentleman said he had no number to leave, but would keep trying until he had you. New York has also called, and left messages for you to call back. A Mister Milton Farber. There was one call from Brussels, which was transferred to New York."

"Thank you."

David took a shower, using the warm water spray to loosen, drain his sinuses, especially over, behind his ears, feeling phlegm slide down his throat.

He was in his robe, waiting, when the phone rang.

"Hello?"

"David? This is John Bart Nelson."

"Hello, John. How are you?"

"I've been calling Cannes every day, David, because I knew you had to go back there."

"Right."

"David, Janet is here."

"She is? Where did you find her?"

"She was in a schoolyard, David, up the street from my apartment, sitting on a swing."

"Where is she now, John?"

"She's with me, David."

"Is she all right?"

"David, she's been living with me for a week now."

David said, "I see."

"She's perfectly all right, David. She said she was looking for me."

"Is she all right?"

"David, I thought you'd want to know, at least where she is."

"I see."

"She's all right, David. She's living with me."

"Thanks for telling me, John."

"How's Chump?"

"He's fine. I'm going to the hospital to pick him up tomorrow morning."

"Are you coming to Paris, David?"

"No, John. Not immediately. We're due in Brussels."

"Okay, David."

"Thanks for telling me, John."

"Right, David. Bye."

In bed that night, David re-read again, here and there, from *The Hawk's Done Gone*.

At ten o'clock in the morning David brought his car around to the back door of the hospital. Chump was waiting on aluminum crutches with a nurse.

"I want to drive," he said.

"You can't drive with broken legs."

Only one leg, his right, was in a cast. Over his left ear his hair had been shaved, and there was a patch. His face looked rested.

The nurse said, "Keep your leg straight."

They were trying to fit the leg into the car. Chump was reaching for his saxophone in the back seat.

The nurse closed the door and stood at the window.

"Goodbye," Chump said to the nurse. "Thank you."

David rolled the car around the corner of the building, down the short drive to the road. He waited for the traffic to clear.

"How was life without your sax?"

"Tastes funny," Chump said.

"Aren't you going to play it?"

"No. Not until we get to the hotel," Chump said. "It will be better there. It was hard without it."

"I know."

"In the hospital, I mean. Even when I had the headache. It was hard without it, you know?"

Only a few cars went by.

They drove along the road, going down the hill to Nice on their way to Cannes, seeing the bright blue of the sea below them.

"I met a man in the hospital," Chump said. "A Mister Hersey. He promised to take me out in his sloop when I got better."

"I don't think we'll have time," David said. "There's Brussels and then the June Music Festival in Rome."

There were the sails of three or four boats out on the sea.

David drove around the first square in Nice and found his way out to the *Promenade des Anglais*.

"Where's Ms Tuesday?"

"She's in Paris. Living with John Bart Nelson."

"Are they going to get married?"

"They might as well."

On the right they were passing many marble buildings shining in the sun. On the left the sea was low, flat beside them.

Chump was looking through David's window.

"I wonder what a sailor's life would be like."

"I have no idea."

"Have you ever wanted to be a sailor, Dave?"

"No. I've never wanted to be a sailor."

33

There was snow, pushed into heaps at the ends of the runways, plowed into gulleys along their sides, banked against the chain-linked fence. Dan had wanted to see snow.

In the airport he checked his baggage, confirmed his reservation to New York and then found the gift shop. He bought a large, fluffy, blue dog, with a pink ribbon, black button eyes, which played the "Marseillaise" after its tail had been turned. *Lucy, Lucy: I'm going to meet Lucy.* He never could remember if it was blue for a girl or pink; after an instant's reflection he realized he did not care. *I'm going to meet Lucy.*

He ran through the airport with the dog under his arm like a football, his necktie flapping, and then had to wait ten minutes in the cold for the airport bus. *Lucy is French. Just think of that. She was born in Paris.* The man next to him in the bus left him little room. He was fat, had a great, black, skirted overcoat on, and was carrying, handling, three paper bags, finding places for them, putting them down, picking them up, settling them, resettling them. One had plums in it. He was blowing his nose continuously, looking sideways at Dan behind the handkerchief, rolling on his haunches as if purposely to make Dan uncomfortable, make his old, fat, germy resentment known. In just his brown tweed sports coat, slacks, Dan was shivering. A wet, heavy sky hung over Paris. *Look at the oil derrick! What an oil derrick. What's the Eiffel Tower doing in Paris?* There was a girl walking along the sidewalk in plastic, see-through boots. Over-sized lapels blossomed around her head. At least a foot and a half of hair was piled on top of her head. Dan laughed. The man rolled against him.

Dan was fast enough, despite the man's slowness in letting him out of the seat, to grab the first taxi in the line. He sat in the back seat with the fluffy dog between his legs. Going around the Arc de Triomphe the dog let out a few notes of the "Marseillaise" and the taxi driver looked at Dan through the rear view mirror. Dan watched the human race on the sidewalks, in the cars, trucks.

At first he thought he was being brought to the wrong place. The taxi had entered a district of old Paris mansions turned into apartments but still obviously expensive. They had great stone facades, gleaming windows, wide, swept sidewalks, trees spaced along them. The taxi slowed and the driver was looking for the number.

The taxi stopped against the curb and the driver pointed to the number on a black, iron-grilled door, backed with glass, 93. Dan sat forward. He pulled the letter out of his inside coat pocket and checked the address with the driver.

"Yes, Monsieur. Number 93. This road. There."

By the time Dan had gotten out with his blue dog, paid the driver through the window, and turned around, the door of the building had been opened. A man dressed formally, sixty, slight and balding, stood in the door, waiting.

"Is this where the Nelsons live? The John Nelsons?"

The taxi behind him drove off.

"Yes, Monsieur."

The man bowed his head, just slightly. He stood aside.

The foyer floor was black and white marble squares. On the off-white walls were enormous mirrors. Red cushioned chairs stood against the walls, between the mirrors.

There was an open elevator cage on one side. Dan stood in it while the man closed both front doors.

"Yes, Monsieur."

The man closed the gate, handled the old, shining brass controls with white-gloved hands.

There was a baby carriage outside the door. Dan heard the ring. The man continued to stand behind him, in the elevator.

"Dan!"

Janet let go of the knob, put both arms around his neck. Her cheek against his, she kissed him. She was in a housedress.

"Dan, my love! It's so good to see you."

Behind him the elevator door closed; the machinery hummed.

"Hi, Janet. I came to see Lucille."

He held the dog out to her.

She took his arm, drew him in, closed the door.

"We got your note saying you would try to stop. We've been so looking forward to it."

There was a foyer, with a brown-framed mirror, a table, a light under it, straight chairs either side. The corridor ran to the right and the left. Across from him was an open double door leading to the living room. The brown curve of a baby grand piano could be seen under a window.

"How do you explain all this?" he asked.

"Didn't you know? John is rich. He inherited from an old uncle."

Jack was in the double door, in a loose, gray, crew-necked sweater, fingering a pipe, grinning.

"A little money," he said. "Hi, Dan."

Dan handed him the dog but Jack evaded it, somehow, with his pipe, his box of matches. They shook hands instead.

"How tan you are, Dan," Janet said. "I've never seen you so tan. Why, you're absolutely negroid."

Jack chuckled. He cupped the back of Dan's neck with his hand and shoved him toward the living room.

There were windows along the length and width of the room, softly curtained with white, draped in burgundy.

"And your hair is so light," she said. "You're a beautiful sight to see at the tail-end of winter."

"I've come to see Lucille."

He still had the dog in his hands.

"You can't. She's asleep. And believe me, you learn to take advantage of those few moments she's asleep, even after just a few weeks. What time does your plane leave?"

"Not until three this afternoon."

"Good. Then you can have lunch with us. I've prepared some bouillabaisse."

Dan said to Jack, "Thanks for writing me. I really celebrated Lucy's birth."

"Jan insisted."

Dan held the dog toward them and twisted its tail. "It's the best I could do, without paying customs."

Janet said, "You're our best man, Dan."

Jack said, "Sit down."

There was a wide, deep fireplace. On a beige, patterned rug a light, richly upholstered divan faced two chairs over a coffee table.

"I'll get some sherry," Janet said.

Jack sat on the divan, across from him.

"You've been gone a long time," he said. "Even longer than you expected."

"I know. I'm in real trouble. I was supposed to return in the fall and here it is the end of March."

Beyond Jack, beyond the curved side of the piano, through wide doors, Janet was at the buffet in the dining room.

"I didn't know you played that."

"What?"

"The piano."

"I whack at it," Jack said.

He was looking at Dan's white shirt, tie, sports jacket, not commenting.

"What were you doing all that time in Spain, Dan?"

Jack's sweater looked full on him. Probably he weighed no more, but his body had softened.

"Thinking."

"What did you decide?"

"That I need to do more thinking."

Janet came in with a tray. A sherry decanter was on it, and three glasses. Dan found himself standing up. The dog was leaning against his chair.

She slid the tray onto the coffee table. She sat beside Jack on the divan and began to pour.

"Blissful moments of peace," she said. "Luce is still asleep."

"Luce is now a month old?"

"Five weeks," Jack said. "And very bright. Just the other day she said Goo."

Dan laughed. He crossed his legs and opened his jacket.

"Tell me, you two. How did you do all this so fast? I mean, divorce, remarriage."

"Oh, we weren't really married," Janet said. She was pouring carefully, not getting a drop on the silver tray. "David and I. Despite your best efforts."

"You weren't married?"

"No." She handed him his glass of sherry, inspecting the bottom of it for drips. Jack reached for his own. "There was something wrong with the ceremony. It didn't take."

"What was wrong?"

"Oh, John noticed some little wrinkle that got us out of it."

"What was wrong, Jack?"

Jack opened his mouth to speak, hesitated.

She said, "It was David's fault, not yours." She had drawn her legs onto the divan, under her dress. "He got the wrong kind of license. A dog license. Something like that."

Dan said, "You never were married."

"Too bad you missed the second go-round," Janet said.

Dan dropped his free hand. "I could never go through that again. I never would."

"It wasn't like that," she said. "Tell me, have you heard anything of David? Out there in the big world of airplanes and recorded music?"

"I saw him in November," Dan said. "He and Chump were playing in Barcelona and I went down to see them. He treated me to a lavish lunch the next day at La Venta. He seemed awfully glad to see me, for some reason."

"David is really very generous," she said.

Jack was sitting back, ignoring his sherry on the end table. He lit his pipe.

"They were just on their way back to New York from Australia. They had played in New Delhi, Bombay, Athens—I don't know where else. He talked a blue streak."

"How did he seem?" she asked.

"A little heavy. He seemed tired to me, but then again he always has."

Janet was using make-up, white powder on her face, lipstick, not much. Her hair was dark, straight. Her face was thin. There was a bulge around her middle. Her legs seemed a little thick in nylons. *Janet has become a young matron.*

"You know," Dan said. "David has become a lay priest—whatever that means."

Jack said, "What's that?"

Janet said, "My God."

Dan said, "Precisely."

Her eyes had popped.

"David never was one for doing things halfway. If he could avoid it," she said. From a room down the corridor a baby mewed. "Let her wake up a little. David had better be careful of the next person he marries."

"My, my," Jack said.

Dan said, "David didn't mention anybody."

She put her sherry glass, still more than half full, back on the tray.

"I didn't see much of Chump," Dan said. "He seemed all right, on the platform."

The baby, Lucille, was crying.

Janet sat on the edge of the divan, back straight, hands on knees.

"I shall go and powder and diaper and cuddle. And then bring the princess out."

She was looking at Dan. She looked at Jack. Neither said anything.

At the door, she said, "Do you know she's got red hair, Dan?"

"Really?"

"For the moment. She was born with red hair. The ladies in the hospital were quite surprised."

"Your uncle had red hair," he said. "Your Uncle Jim."

"So he did."

The sound of the cry increased as a door opened.

"Well," Dan said. "What are you doing with your great, and totally undeserved wealth? Besides spending it."

"Writing a play. Trying to write a play." Jack seemed completely relaxed in the corner of the divan, filling the space up with his pipe, his sweater, his stretched-out legs. "What else is an unearned income for? I mean, who else can afford to write a play but someone with an unearned income?"

"And you still don't believe a man should be dependent on an idea, right? Art, religion, football ... ?"

"A man should never be entirely dependent upon his own neurosis. Life is much too comprehensive to be totally sublimated."

"Will you be coming back to the States?"

"Do you think we should?"

"I don't know," Dan said. "Americans are so prejudiced against poets."

"I don't think soon," Jack said. "Sometime." His loafers were clean but not brightly polished. "I'm not sure we're ready for that yet. There's Lucille to consider. Why throw her into a boiling stew?" He sat forward, showing the roll of his stomach beneath the sweater. "One has enough problems, just being a human being."

Dan said, "I'm glad Janet had the sense to marry you."

"It took guts."

Over the fireplace was a modern painting with thin black and red angular lines. In front of it an old mantel clock ticked.

Jack was smiling at him.

"Shall we go in and see what all this is about?"

Dan grabbed up the blue, pink-ribboned dog.

"Let's."